A VEIL OF TRUTH AND TRICKERY

ANALEIGH FORD

A VEIL OF TRUTH AND Trickery

Analeigh Ford

A Veil of Truth and Trickery by Analeigh Ford

For permissions contact:

analeighfordauthor@gmail.com

For all those who never stop seeking.

I know I never will.

LAND OF AVARATH

OF

AVARATH

AVARATH
SEA

CHAPTER ONE

THERE WAS A CURSE OVER THIS WORLD.

That curse was me.

I came out of the womb colored like starlight—skin blue and hair spun from sun-bleached bones. I was fae-marked in that instant, damned forever to live beneath the sideways glances and whispered words that all said the same thing.

Cursed, was their whisper. *Cursed*, was in their eyes.

The incarnation of the fae shone through me, and for that I would never be allowed to rest.

Long after my skin flooded with more human color, my hair remained a brand of my affliction. That affliction led those most superstitious to believe me a changeling, a creature of the fae realm itself. Those less so simply believed me unlucky. Most of the villagers fell somewhere in between, a place where they didn't quite try to burn me at the stake but still crossed the street when passing, just to be sure.

One thing remained constant.

Wherever I went, I was unlikely to be trusted. Even less likely to be accepted.

And I couldn't blame them. Not really.

Not when the fae that marked me were known for their trickery, for the games they played with humans and the treachery that was sure to follow. It didn't matter that the fae had barely been seen in decades, that in some places their kind hadn't been sighted in as long as a century.

They'd made their mark in the time that they were here. That latest mark, it seemed, was me.

In all the years that followed the unfortunate circumstances of my birth, I'd yet to discover a curse over me, but I supposed there was still time left. Most curses lifted on the day of one's twenty-first birthday, and mine was fast approaching. The closer the day grew, the more whispers and stares I drew in my direction. The whole village was waiting, watching on with bated breath as the moment of truth drew near.

Me, more than any… but not for the reason they might've imagined.

For them, they waited to see if they were finally free from the fear of my curse.

But me … I secretly *hoped* for the curse.

I'd have hated to learn after all the years I'd been treated as an outcast for it all to have been for nothing.

"Delph, if you don't get that bottle out soon Raful's going to have your head, you know that."

It still took me a moment to snap out of my stupor, my hands stuck working an endless circle of polish into the already streak-free silver platter laid in front of me on the buffet. At the rate I was going, I was a bit surprised I hadn't polished a hole straight through it.

As it was, I shuddered a bit at the flash of my own reflection when I went to set it back up on the shelf where it belonged—

one of the last tokens of the wealth once amassed by the Otto estate. An estate long since fallen into ruin.

Ruined or not, the estate had given me work when no one else would… and despite the dwindling staff over the years, had continued to employ me against the advice of the other voices in the village. I'd lost track of the number of times I'd overheard the same questions. I'd taken to tuning out any words that followed a surreptitious glance in my direction, since it always turned out to be the same question.

Why keep a fae-marked girl so close?

"What is it with you, today, Delph?" Ascilla's voice cut through my thoughts again, the hand reaching out to knock some sense into me only stopped because Leofwin, the lord's valet, materialized in the narrow cellar between us.

"Tsk, tsk, Ascilla," he hummed, mock disapproval in his voice. "Is that any way to behave this close to Midsommar? Let Raful catch sight of that, and little Delph's slow table service will be the least of your worries."

Ascilla's eyes rolled back toward the beams crossing the low ceiling overhead, their dark wood marred by centuries of hooks dug into them for hanging meat and herbs to be dried.

"Hey, Leofwin," I said, whirling to deal Ascilla's intended blow to the back of *his* head instead. "I can fight my own battles. Maybe worry about your own damn business for once."

I may have misjudged my own strength, however, because he pitched forward far enough to have to catch himself. Of course, the thing he found to catch himself on was me—his hand wrapping around my ankle while the rest of him nearly disappeared beneath the tangle of my skirts.

"And here I was thinking you're all bark and no bite," he said, one hand clamping onto the edge of the buffet to start the clamber back up onto his feet.

I had no opportunity to respond to him, not when his other hand had ventured so dangerously far up the back of my skirts that I could feel his fingers teasing my bare thigh above the top of my stockings.

I was grateful for the dim light of the storeroom, otherwise there'd be no hiding the stark contrast of red against white as blood rushed to my cheeks. This wasn't the first time Leofwin's hand had found its way to parts of me it had no right to... if only in the strictest sense. Parts of me had found their way to parts of him as well in the last year of my service here at the estate. There was a mutual understanding between us, a secret that was spoken more in sighs and soft moans than it was with any actual words.

It was better that way—especially when most of the words that dropped from Leofwin's lips made me want to murder him more than it made me want to take him to my bed.

Still, I swore and fumbled with the wine bottle now in my hands, nearly dropping it as Leofwin's hand slipped just a little higher.

"You're the one who should be watching out," Ascilla said, the disapproval thick in her voice. "You're not as subtle as you think you are, you know."

"Yeah, well, I won't have to be subtle soon. After today we'll be lost in Midsommar with the rest of the village. And I'll be happily lost elsewhere."

Even the dark couldn't conceal the raging red in my cheeks now. "Not a chance. I won't be there. Not when Lord Otto needs me."

"Oh, and that's such a good thing? He might not be so afraid of a little fae mark soon."

Not once Midsommar's passed, and I've aged out of any chance of a curse.

It was no secret that the current lord of the estate had a weakness for two things—wine too old for his coffers and women too young for his own good. The wine I could handle. The women, well, I had no fear of that. Lord Otto's wayward hands had never made their way over to me. I'd come to look forward to the holidays where the rest of the staff left the estate to the two of us, when the lack of wandering eyes and wagging tongues meant the lord and I spent most of our evenings sitting by the fire together. He never spoke of the marks that branded me, and I, in turn, never stopped filling his cup.

This quiet companionship couldn't last forever, I knew. Lord Otto would marry another woman too young for him, one that didn't like the look of the fae-marked girl she spotted in the hallways, or he'd eventually run out of things to pawn and would have to let go of the already meager staff. I just didn't like to think of what I'd do when that day came.

I certainly didn't like to think that it might come sooner, rather than later.

A hollow feeling welled up in me but wasn't allowed to settle, not when Leofwin's hand made a less than subtle dart further up my skirts, making me shriek as I tried to bat him away.

"You little—"

"What's going on in here?"

This time, the voice joining us in the already cramped cellar made all three of us snap to attention.

Raful, the head of the lord's estate, stood in the doorway looking on, his own disapproval putting Ascilla's to shame. I'd never seen Leofwin straighten up so quickly.

"Nothing, sir," he said, hastily moving a step away from me.

Raful's eyes only narrowed further, but he wasn't here for Leofwin. He was here for me.

He snapped his fingers together and pointed at the bottle in my hands. "That won't do for today. Lord Otto has a visitor."

I glanced down at the bottle. "This is what he always serves guests."

"Don't argue with me, girl," Raful snarled. The corner of his mouth turned down, not unlike that of a disgruntled frog. It would've been funnier if it wasn't accompanied by the crackle of a leather riding crop stretching between the two hands tucked behind his back.

All three of us—Ascilla, Leofwin, and myself—flinched a little at the sound. There was only one man who'd dare lay a hand on me in this house, and it was him. Even Otto was more afraid of Raful than he was of me.

"This is no ordinary visitor," Raful said, his eyes still searching me in the way they did when he was trying to decide whether or not a beating was necessary. It usually was. "You'll serve the top shelf."

My eyes flickered up to the shelf in question, and despite the crackle of leather, I wasn't able to stop myself.

"Are you sure? There's only one bottle left. Otto—"

"Lord Otto." Raful's reminder carried as much of a snap as the memory of leather on my skin. I felt, rather than saw, Ascilla and Leofwin slink back a half step as the butler stepped down from the door to close the space between us. My own eyes had fallen to the floor, where they settled on a particularly interesting crack in the boards. "Unless you've forgotten, that's who you serve here in this estate. A *Lord*. The rest of the world might be falling to pieces around us, but that title still means something."

He drew himself up beside me, a man impressive only in his height. For someone made seemingly entirely out of sinew and bone, he'd left enough bruises on my back to make my skin smart when he so much as stood this close to me.

"You of all people shouldn't need reminding," he said, his breath stinking as he drew near to my ear. "If it were up to me, you'd have been removed from this estate years ago. If it were up to me, you'd never have been allowed to step foot in here in the first place."

"Well then," I said, wishing in that moment that I could bite off my own tongue and be done with it, "I guess I'm lucky it isn't up to you."

I'd seen Raful's face darken before, but never like it did now.

I could practically already feel the welts beginning to form on my back. I knew what was coming. Raful's hand lifted, and I braced myself against the blow that was sure to come. And it did.

Two blows stung the space between my shoulder blades, carefully placed below the back neckline of my gown so that Lord Otto wouldn't see. I gritted my teeth, willing myself not to let out so much as a single syllable. I wouldn't give Raful the satisfaction.

My silence only bought me a third blow, this one less carefully placed. I felt the shift in Raful before the leather crop hit my skin, too high this time—no fabric to soften the sear of pain that erupted across the surface of my skin.

I bit my tongue to keep from crying out, the taste of iron in my mouth bitter as bile.

Raful's face was flushed when he straightened back up, a wicked glint in his eye. He made no secret of the fact that he enjoyed our abuse. He lifted one hand to wipe the froth from his lips before jutting his chin back toward the last remaining bottle still perched on the top shelf.

"Bring it to the west sitting room, and then go straight to your quarters and stay there. Lord Otto has strict orders that his guest is not to be disturbed by the staff. Besides, you're in no condition to be seen, anyway."

Gums red with blood and a long red welt across the top of my shoulders, he means.

Of course, Raful never intended for me to serve the lord. He came here looking for his own twisted satisfaction, and as usual, he'd found it.

"I'll have a word with Lord Otto. You've grown far too comfortable here. I always warned him you would. Now, hurry to it. You've already kept the lord waiting long enough."

I stretched on the tips of my toes to reach the bottle, but my fingers didn't so much as graze the bottom of the shelf. Out of the corner of my eye, I saw Leofwin twitch toward me, as if to help, but one glare from Raful left him shrinking back.

"Surely you have work left to do before the estate closes for the holiday. Unless you'd like to be left here with Delph."

There was only the briefest hesitation before Leofwin stepped back, nodding once. "Whatever you say, Raful."

Neither Ascilla nor Leofwin could meet my eye as they left. The moment we were alone, Raful was suddenly at my side. Under the guise of reaching for the bottle above my head, he pressed his body against mine until my stomach was pinned against the wooden furniture. His chest pressed into my back, the buttons of his uniformed dragging across the fresh welts on my skin.

Breath hitched excitedly in his chest when I couldn't hold back a wince of pain. His hot breath, stinking of stolen wine and rotting fruit, drew too close to the back of my ear.

"Only days now until Otto realizes you're nothing special," he said, not bothering to keep his voice low. "You think he'll protect you then? I'll have you out of this great house and back on the streets where you belong. Mark my words."

His free hand clamped onto my shoulder, thumb placed carefully so as to dig into the freshly made welt there. Hot tears sprung to my eyes against my bidding, and with it rose my maddening temper.

"Say what you like, Raful," I snarled back, finally managing to tear myself free of him. "But this isn't a great house. Not anymore. It hasn't been for a long time—and it has a lot more to do with cowards like you then it does me."

I pried the bottle from his hands and stormed off before he could deal me another blow. I knew it was a foolish response, one that I'd pay for later.

I didn't care. I'd never been good at holding my tongue.

I forgot in my blind rage which sitting room I was supposed to be delivering the bottle to. I knew the moment I opened the door that I'd picked the wrong one, because suddenly, my concern over the butler's retaliation seemed the very least of my worries.

Not when the first fae sighted in decades was standing right in front of me.

CHAPTER TWO

He didn't look how fae were supposed to look.

He didn't have hair like starlight or skin so pale the veins peeked out in crisscrossing lines of blue beneath the surface.

But somehow I knew, the minute I laid eyes on him, exactly what he was.

He stood at the edge of an armchair by the fire, his body frozen as if he'd heard me coming and leapt to his feet the moment before I burst through the door. His chest rose and fell with breath, the softest breeze from the summer air nudging the lone strand of coppery hair that had fallen over his forehead.

It shimmered in the dim light, each soft strand lit from its own light within.

That was where his softness ended.

His eyes were stony, glaring at me with a severity that made me want to shrink inside my own skin. His gaze bored into me, seeing something inside of me that I didn't want to be seen. The line of his jaw could cut as surely as a knife, as surely as the downturned corners of his mouth would slice me with a curse spoken from those drawn lips.

He towered over me, easily seven feet tall, with broad shoulders and arms that could squeeze the life out of a human without trying. He was no willowy creature of fairytale. He was massive, looming, and oh so very real.

It was more than that, though. More than his overwhelming physical presence. It was a feeling. An aura.

A danger.

A glamour.

The man, the *creature*, standing in front of me was more vicious than any wild beast I might encounter. More dangerous still than any fiend in a storybook.

Power emanated from him like the heat from a flame. It simultaneously drew me in and sent me stumbling backward, mind reeling.

"I… I'm not supposed to be here," I stammered, my eyes not daring to look away from him.

It was the wrong sitting room. Part of me was sure I knew that all along, that I must have been drawn here, to the fae. That was their nature, after all.

Tricksters.

It wasn't trickery I was afraid of, however, in that moment. The fae in front of me didn't look like he was going to try to back me into some poorly worded deal. No. He looked more like he was going to pick me up and pull me apart like some kind of helpless rag doll.

"I wouldn't be so sure of that."

I was unable to look away from him, his own eyes roving over me with a keen sort of interest that made the hair stand up on the back of my neck. I was looking at him for the first time, but the way he looked at me…

It was the familiarity sparking in his eyes that left me unsettled. More than that, it was the way his gaze lingered on my black eyes, my pale skin, the shining white of my hair. He didn't shrink away from me the way Lord Otto's other visitors did.

Moments hung between us, a silence that held weight. It would have hung there forever, until I aged into dust and he remained a shining beacon of unadulterated youth, if I hadn't broken it. Though I broke our gaze first.

My first mistake.

"I have to go," I muttered, eyes dropping to stare at the floorboards. I started to turn before he could answer, my instincts kicking in at long last as each fiber of my being screamed for me to get away from this predator as fast as I could.

Not fast enough, apparently.

"Those marks on your skin… what are they?"

The question caught me so off guard that it made me pause despite myself. Hot embarrassment burned in my cheeks as my hand slithered up to gingerly touch the mark still smarting at the top of my back. I risked one glance over my shoulder at him again, hoping to catch some glimpse of what he meant by asking that sort of thing. I regretted it immediately.

There was a new question in his eyes, and it wasn't kind. It was feral. Wild. The knuckles of his hand had turned white at the strength of his grip on the back of the armchair. Those eyes stared at me like a predator.

He's sizing me up, I realized, but for what purpose… I had no idea.

I shook my head. "I think you know the answer to that already," I said, ever so quietly.

The fae opened his mouth to respond, but before he could, I heard a creak in the doorway leading to the hall and his eyes finally lifted from me to rest on Lord Otto himself as he appeared, flustered and red-faced, beneath it.

The lord's eyes flickered between us, the wine already

running through his veins making his movements a bit too slow, his emotions a bit too visible.

"Ah, well, I see you've met Caldamir, then," he said, speech slurring. He tried to force a welcoming look on his face as he stepped forward, one hand reaching to take the bottle still grasped between my fingers. The other rose up to catch my shoulder. It was all I could do not to flinch back at his touch, as well meaning as it was. "Best run along now. There's work to be done."

That could only mean one thing when it involved a fae.

There were deals to be made.

I knew I should leave, get out while I could. But I glanced once more between the old fool and the likely even older trickster, and I paused.

"Are you… are you sure?"

For one moment, Lord Otto's face sobered. The grip on my shoulder tightened, and he fixed me with a harder stare than I'd ever seen on his ruddy features before.

"Leave us," he said. "And have Ascilla take you home."

"But Midsommar …"

His voice dropped this time, taking on a tone that had become all too familiar in the last years since he took me into his household. "Would it really kill you to do as you're told for once?" he asked, the words making a slight lump rise in the back of my throat. "For once, Delphine, do this for me."

I'd never seen him so serious. There was fear in his eyes, a fear I'd never expected to see there. Fear for me.

I had no choice but to do as I was told.

I nodded once, and slipped away before either of them could respond. Before the fae could trap me with honeyed words.

Or, at the very least, any more than he already had.

Already in just this short meeting, Caldamir had undone

every idea I had about the fae. The way he looked. The way he talked. The way he *felt*, his very presence different from what I'd been taught to fear my whole life.

I realized in that moment that I'd been lying to myself all this time. The way my heartbeat deafened any other sound, any other thought, revealed the truth.

I'd only wished for a curse because I'd truly believed there wasn't one. Now, faced with an actual fae, the suddenly very real possibility of a curse sent my feet tripping over themselves in a building panic.

The fae were no longer just warnings whispered in old texts and fairytales.

Fae. A fae was here.

And he'd seen me.

More than that, he'd seen what I was… and recognized it.

"WHAT'S WRONG WITH YOU? You look like you've seen a ghost."

It was surprisingly easy to catch up with Ascilla and Leofwin on their way out of the estate. The gates were still open and the hallways bustling with the last of the preparations to close the estate for the coming days as Midsommar dawned. It was a traditional precaution against the fae who'd once made a habit of visiting terror on Alderia on this holiday in particular.

Fae, like the one that now sat as a guest in Lord Otto's drawing room.

I didn't answer Ascilla right away. My mind was too preoccupied as I hoisted the hastily gathered bundle of clothing up over my shoulder and glanced over it, my eyes seeking out the window to the East study—and finding it. I swore for a moment that I saw a face in the glass, a near-gaunt face looking out from the top panes, but it disappeared just as quickly.

If only the pit in my stomach would do the same.

"Shit, Delph …" Suddenly Ascilla's footsteps ground to a halt, forcing myself and a half dozen other servants to have to narrowly avoid being run over by a hand-pulled cart just as we stepped out of the main gate. "Did something happen? Seriously. You don't look well."

I batted away her hand with my own, shaking my head as I forced my thoughts ahead and away from everything I'd just left behind.

"It… it's nothing," I said with one last shake. *But it wasn't nothing.* That fae Caldamir wasn't the only problem I'd left on the other side of that gate. There'd be more than one debt to pay when I came back to the estate.

Raful wasn't the kind to forget slights, however small. I had a lashing in wait for me when I came back.

If there was any estate left to come back to.

Who knew what the fae was here to do—make a new deal or collect on an old one? Either way didn't bode well for the ruined lord. There was nothing left for him to give. And making a new deal, well, that was always a bad idea. Surely he wasn't such a fool as to agree to one now?

If the lord did make a deal with the fae, I didn't know if any of the staff would agree to come back and work for him. I wasn't even sure if I would.

I'd had trouble enough from the fae without ever actually having dealt with one.

"What? Did Otto finally decide he'd waited long enough?"

This time the high-pitched question came from my own personal harpy, my stepbrother's betrothed, Lavinia. She appeared from Leofwin's other side, her face pinched up a bit as she took me in with a critical eye. "It was only a matter of time. You know his wandering eye… and hands."

"Lord Otto wouldn't do that," Leofwin interrupted, his eyes cutting over to me for a moment before quickly darting away. Not, of course, before I saw the jealousy narrowing them. "Besides, Delph wouldn't let him."

It was a strange thing to hear him say, given that he'd insinuated the same thing less than an hour before.

"Oh, I don't know," Lavinia said, her hand raising up to brush a lock of hair off her shoulder. "From what I've heard, your precious *Delphine* is all too happy to give it away for free."

"At least I don't have a price," I snarl back. "You're not the only one spreading rumors, you know that, right? Or did you not tell Draigh that your father squandered your dowry? I wonder if he'd be so keen to wed you if he knew."

Lavinia's face stayed focused forward, but her shoulders tensed.

"Come on," Ascilla whispered, her elbow jabbing into my side. "Do you really want to start this now? Can't we have three days' peace away from the estate without having to drag Lavinia, of all people, into it?"

We fell back a step, letting a gap form between us and the others. The trees here leading up to the estate had already started to grow wilder as the walled-in buildings shrunk behind us.

"Easy for you to say," I said, glancing one last time back at the estate, now in the distance. As I looked on, the gate finally closed, where they wouldn't open again until after the festival. I wondered if that would change this year. Would Otto spend his entire holiday locked inside with the fae? Though, I supposed if the fae was still there, he probably had his own means of getting in and out that didn't involve the lord having to re-open the estate. "You don't have to practically live with her."

Ascilla let out the smallest of sighs. "I suppose you're right."

When my gaze once again turned to the road ahead, I fell back one more step. "Ascilla …" I started, glancing between Leofwin, Lavinia, and the few other members of staff who'd finally fallen out of earshot. "There's something I need to tell you."

She didn't hear me, however.

Not when the handcart just in front of the rest of our group suddenly lurched to a halt.

Two women on horseback had appeared up ahead, their mare melting out of the forest like a specter of the night.

I knew who they were immediately. More importantly, I knew what they were here for.

Who they were here for.

Whether they knew it or not, they were here for me.

CHAPTER THREE

The moment Ascilla saw the women on horseback, she moved to block me from view.

For once, I followed her lead, swearing under my breath as my hands fumbled at the cloak I'd used to tie up the few things I'd had the time to bring with me from the estate. A cloak hood would be useful right now, something to hide the silvery strands of hair that had started tumbling over my shoulders in the summer heat.

I didn't need to see the emblem stitched into the saddlebags at the horse's side to know who these women were. Still, the shape of the flame-engulfed circle was enough to make a pit form in my stomach.

I'd dealt with their kind before.

I knew them all too well. These were self-called truth-bringers, though what they truly brought was fear. *As if our world, our kingdom, needed any more of it.*

"Traveling home for the festivities?" the woman holding the reins called out from her place atop the horse, her voice carrying the unmistakable tone of disapproval.

"Just let us pass," Leofwin said, stepping forward as he hoisted his own bag a bit higher up over his shoulder. "We've no quarrel with you."

He stopped for a second, glancing sideways at the grumbling cart-bearer and Lavinia at his side.

This first woman, younger than her companion, though with the same hair streaked gray far too early, let her gaze come to rest on Leofwin. "We've not come to quarrel. Just to bring news."

Even Lavinia sucked on the inside of her cheeks, her eyes flickering forward up the path anxiously. We were still at least an hour's walk from the village, and darkness would be falling soon if we didn't hurry. There weren't exactly bandits in these parts, but drunk and belligerent festivalgoers wandered off from the village were almost as bad.

Especially when the rest of us were still violently sober.

"The end of this kingdom is nigh. You must repent. End your bargains with the fae and their old ways, or else be caught up in it."

It was the same message they'd been speaking for the last twenty-one years. The same message they'd been speaking long before that.

It was always the end of the world. It was always just around the bend, waiting, like a bad bedtime story, to snatch you up and carry you away.

I almost pitied the young girl holding the reins. *Almost.*

Ascilla shifted her weight again, concealing me behind her a bit more. Her hands wrapped back, nudging me slightly toward the shade of the trees closer to the edge of the path where we stood.

"Unless you have some *actual* news to bring, then let us pass," Leofwin said again. Beside him, I could tell the cart-bearer was considering running straight into the truth-bringer's horse if that meant we'd get moving sooner.

"You can't ignore the end of all things. You have to face it head on as we have. The fae set into motion things we can only begin to understand. Just because you can't see them before you doesn't mean their poison won't one day drain you too."

When Leofwin's face didn't change, the young woman's attention flickered over to Lavinia instead. "It'd be such a shame to see a pretty young thing like you waste away, just because you're too vain to listen."

The rest of our party flinched at the words, knowing the woman's mistake well before Lavinia's mouth spewed her own venom.

"Just let us go, hag," Lavinia snapped, eyes flashing. She reached back and grabbed Leofwin by the collar, a motion that made something hot and angry flash up inside me for a moment. He didn't flinch back from her touch. Didn't bat her away. He just let himself be led several steps forward, halfway around the truth-bringers horse before the woman holding the reins spoke again.

But not to her.

They'd finally spotted me.

"Stop, you there. Fae girl."

I froze, as did the rest of my party. Leofwin's eyes flickered back to meet mine as the younger woman urged the horse forward through the middle of our party. He had to step back to let her pass.

He made no move to stop her, not even when she drew the mare so close that the horse's hot breath blew short strands of hair back from my face. He just stood there, collar still being tugged by Lavinia, as the cart-bearer started rumbling forward.

Then all of them did.

No use waiting for the fae-marked girl.

"You." It was the old crone's voice that cracked as she looked over me across the shoulder of her companion. The sight of me, my black eyes and contrasting hair so obvious even now in the fading light, somehow filled her with the strength to straighten in her saddle. One crooked hand raised from her side to point into my face, her own twisting up with each word that followed next.

"You will be our undoing. You cursed kind. You fae-marked abomination."

Words like that might have drawn a reaction from someone else, but I was used to them.

"I'd heard there was a marked girl around here, but that was years ago. I'd assumed the village would have already put you out of your misery."

I did twinge a bit at those words. For one moment, the old woman's eyes flickered first to Ascilla, and then to the retreating backs of Lavinia, Leofwin, and the others.

"Did no one ever test her? See if she was a changeling? You know how it's done?"

Her eyes turned back to me then, and there wasn't a single ounce of kindness in them. All I saw in its place was hate. For me.

She leaned forward, spit flying from her cracked lips as she made sure to pronounce each word with cruel purpose. "You hang them outside in the dark, overnight. Even the creatures won't touch a changeling. If the babe lives, then it's one of the fae, and can be dealt with before it grows to curse all that touch it."

A bitter laugh bubbled from Ascilla's mouth. "Or more likely the human baby is picked apart by wild animals, or simply dies from the cold."

"Better that than to allow a single changeling amongst us," the old woman spat back without a second's hesitation. "You know, they say the fae blood bleeds blue. I wonder …" One hand reached for the side of her bag, where I spotted the silver hilt of a long knife peeking from between the flaps of leather. "If I were to cut you… what color would you bleed?"

The horse drew closer, forcing both Ascilla and I to stumble back or have our feet crushed beneath its powerful hooves.

Up ahead, I caught sight of Leofwin pausing for just a second. He glanced back at us, concern furrowing his brows as the old woman's hand wrapped around the knife's hilt.

But then he glanced back at the others, at the way Lavinia's eyes narrowed in disapproval, and he turned back. He left us.

He left me.

The brief flash of jealousy I'd felt earlier was nothing compared to the hot anger I felt at the sight of his back turned to me now. I'd told him I could fight my own battles, but this wasn't what I meant. He knew that. He knew what he was doing when he walked away.

Bile rose in the back of my throat as Ascilla and I were left to these two women, one of whom had started to draw a wicked blade between us.

For a second, I thought she was going to slash me with the rusted blade, but in the moment before she did, her eyes lifted up to the old estate barely visible in the background, and something she saw there made her pause. Her eyes grew wide and her lips parted. The horse breathed out a hot snort, its head bowing low enough to force both women to hold tight or risk being thrown as it pawed the leaf-strewn ground.

By the time Ascilla and I glanced back, not so much as the usual light shone in the estate windows, but whatever it was the women had seen still left its mark. The blade returned to its sheath, however hesitantly, and the two of them shared a pale-faced look. A whisper passed between them, so quiet I couldn't make out more than the flicker of fear mirrored on each of their faces.

They glanced at me one last time before the younger girl tugged hard on her mare's reins and they turned to disappear off the path in the same direction they had come.

"Wretched old bitch," Ascilla grumbled.

"Yeah …" I agreed, casting one last look over my shoulder at the fading estate. "Wretched."

But it wasn't the old crone's words that left me seething as we quickened our footsteps to catch up to the rest of our party. That I could handle. That I was used to.

It was Leofwin's betrayal that stung the most.

Though soon his would feel like nothing, not compared to the one that came next.

CHAPTER FOUR

THE FACES OF THE RIDER AND HER COMPANION LINGERED IN MY MIND long after they'd disappeared. I was used to disdain from strangers, threats even, but this was something else entirely. Though Ascilla made faltering attempts to try to convince me that they wouldn't have actually *used* that knife on me, I don't think she really believed that herself.

She'd seen the look on their faces too.

If it weren't for whatever they'd seen over our shoulders... I had no doubt that I'd already be nursing far more than hurt feelings. Just as I had no doubt about what it was they saw.

I'd seen it too, after all.

Which was why I couldn't hurry my footsteps fast enough, trying to put as much distance between myself and the estate as possible.

The sight of the village—more of a run-down collection of cottages than it was an actual village—wasn't as relieving as it should've been. Not at least, for me. The rest of our party let out a collective sigh at the first glimpse of the familiar, dilapidated gates. The village walls had been built in a time when the truth-

bringers had convinced much of Alderia of some kind of imma-
nent fae attack. No fae attack came, not in the millennium since
they first arrived, and eventually the truth-bringers were seen
for what they were.

But not all their fears had faded so. I was living proof of that.

For Ascilla and the rest of them, they were home. They could
finally put the short, far-too-eventful trek behind us.

For me, however, it was only the beginning.

The stares and sneers of the villagers upon spotting me were
nothing compared to the look I got from my stepmother, Nerys,
the moment she glimpsed me from the window of our family's
cottage. Her lips formed my name like a curse, prompting a
flurry of movement behind her in the house. By the time she
appeared in the doorway, face reddening with each passing
moment, she wasn't alone.

My stepsister, Ixora, appeared at her side, her face peering
like a pale moon from the shadow over her shoulder. She was a
mirror of my stepmother, her face pinched up so tight it'd be
comical if it didn't mean I'd soon find my name on the tip of the
sharp tongue hidden between those pursed lips.

"Not going to lie, I don't envy you right now," Ascilla
muttered at my side, her footsteps slowing to a shuddering halt
that kicked up the dry summer dust. "Sometimes I forget why
you usually stay at the estate."

"Yeah well," I said, hoisting up my bag higher on my shoulder. "I don't."

"You sure you don't want to come along?"

I sucked the inside of my cheek, glancing back over at the
retreating backs of the rest of our party headed in the opposite
direction. Lyre music and raised voices carried over to us, the
early throws of the Midsommar festival already well
under way.

I shook my head, even as I locked eyes with the two women still glaring at me in disbelief from the doorway.

"Go on ahead without me," I said, pushing open the gate to the small garden separating our cottage from the worn village road. "Better to face this head on."

"You so sure about that?"

No sooner had Ascilla left my side to join Leofwin and the others than another stepped up to fill her place. A pit formed in my stomach as I recognized the voice of Draigh.

His hand snaked through my arm before I had time to whirl and face him, his fingers tightening around me until I'd have to make a show of pulling away. That hand held me in place so I was forced to watch as the expressions on Ixora and Nerys' faces changed. I'd never seen faces go from despise to delight so quickly.

"Ah see, that's what people are *supposed* to look like when you show up unexpectedly," Draigh whispered into my ear.

Draigh's hand made no move to let go of me, even as he twisted his own face into a friendly mask and used his free hand to wave to his mother and sister. By the time it had dropped back down to his side, the other had begun to leave a bruise on my upper arm.

I tried to jerk my arm free, but he wouldn't budge.

Draigh's face tilted down to look at me, and this time I had no choice but to look up into his face. His lips curled up in a cruel smile.

"What, not happy to see a hero returned home from the front?"

"I'd hardly call you a hero," I snapped back. "You're not even a proper soldier. For you to be a soldier, there has to be a war. How long's it been since Alderia saw so much as a skirmish? A thousand years? Two?"

Draigh bared his teeth at me, hand tightening further. "You don't know what you're talking about."

I wasn't given the chance to respond, however, not when Nerys and Ixora had finally reached our side.

"You weren't supposed to be here," Nerys hurled at me like an insult. "I would've liked a bit of warning next time."

"Draigh!" Ixora took the alternate route and ignored me altogether in favor of her brother, elbowing me out of the way and into the bushes. I didn't mind though, not when it afforded me a glimpse of the small boy lingering at the top of the steps.

While Ixora and my stepmother took turns shooting me dirty looks and fawning over Draigh, I ducked around their skirts to sweep my half-brother Sol up in as tight a hug as he'd allow me. At first, he squirmed between my arms, trying to disentangle himself until he finally realized it was a futile fight.

Once he gave in, he wrapped his arms around my waist and squeezed me back, just for a second. His round face was smeared with dirt when I finally let go enough to hold him at arm's length, but no amount of dirt could hide the rosy glow of his full cheeks.

"At least I can tell they're feeding you well," I said, laughing as I reached up to try and wipe some of the smudges from his skin. He let out a feral kind of growl and this time did successfully manage to wriggle free of me.

He didn't run away, though. He just beamed up at me for a second before remembering to screw up his face in an angry pout.

"You were gone too long this time," he said, blinking up at me.

I let out another laugh, but this one was choked—because he wasn't wrong.

"I have to work. You know that."

"It isn't fair," he said, folding his arms across his chest. The sleeves of his shirt tugged up almost to the elbow with the motion, and for the first time, I realized just how much he'd grown. Soon, he'd no longer be a boy at all.

"Yeah, well," I said, reaching over to tousle the dark hair he'd inherited from our father, "life isn't fair. At least you don't look like you were fished out of a lake too late."

"I don't think 'fished out of a lake' is exactly what the townspeople call it."

My father's small smile greeting me when I looked up over Sol's head. He didn't exactly reach for me, didn't pull me into an embrace like I might have once wished for, but the fact that his was a face that didn't screw up in some form of disappointment at my unexpected appearance was enough. For me, it was enough.

"At least one person here's happy to see me."

"I'm happy to see you!" Sol cried out, but I fixed him with a look.

"You're just hoping I brought sweets."

"No ..." he said, hands swinging around to clasp behind his back as he shifted his weight between both feet. "Momma says I'm too old for sweets now."

I arched an eyebrow up at him. "Too old for sweets? I didn't know there was such a thing."

One of my hands disappeared into my pocket, only to return a moment later with an outstretched palm of wax-wrapped candies. They'd been bartered from the cook for my own private Midsommar celebration, but they were put to much better use in Sol's hands the moment he greedily forgot my stepmother's words. He snatched them up before she could try to order him otherwise. He didn't get them stuffed into his own pockets fast enough, however, and soon he and Nerys were racing around the front of the yard—she trying to steal the sugared honey drops from his hands, and he trying to eat them all before she inevitably caught him.

"He's grown so much," I said, shaking my head as my father and I stifled laughter. "I can't have been gone only a year. Please tell me you're not letting that witch turn him into another one of her minions. The last thing this village needs is another Draigh."

Another slight smile twitched up at the corner of my father's mouth. "I think Nerys' first husband had more to do with that."

"Well, he did produce *that* thing," I said, nodding toward Draigh at the end of the garden path. Lavinia had finally spotted her beloved and latched onto his arm like the bloodsucking creature she was, trying to tug him toward the festival already. Even Ixora seemed a little annoyed by her presence.

It might've been the only thing my stepsister and I ever agreed on.

Perhaps the biggest sign that I'd been gone too long was when Sol successfully managed to evade Nerys by leaping into the branches of a tree and climbing out of reach. He dropped at least half the remaining candy in the process, but it didn't matter. By the time my stepmother had gathered them from the ground, Sol could be heard happily munching on the rest well up out of reach in the thick branches of the tree.

"Glad to see he's at least giving her hell."

Nerys had paused to catch her breath down below. Her shoulders rose and fell with exaggerated motions, her usually perfect hair falling onto a face now damp with sweat. It was always like this with her. She was so put together. So perfect. Until I got involved.

Turned out I wasn't the only one thinking the same thing.

"You know, if you'd wanted to come home for your birthday this year, you could have just said."

My father's words hit me like lead in the gut.

"Did I have to, though?" I asked, after a long pause. I looked up at him through my lashes, unable to stop the sigh that whistled out from between my lips. "I didn't think I needed to ask to come home."

"Not ask… just… sent a warning," my father said, flinching a little at the sound of his own words. "You know how she gets."

"Oh, I do."

This time, he didn't let my slight go unnoticed.

"I know you don't like Nerys, but it's not entirely her fault you know. She didn't ask to have to deal with you."

"To have to deal with me?"

I'd suddenly found myself stepping back, heart thumping. "If you really feel that way, then I don't have to come back at all, you know." My breaths hitched a bit, that aching pit in my stomach that had been forming all day solidifying further with each word. "After tomorrow, I could find my own way. I'd never have to darken your doorstep again."

"Oh, wouldn't that be a treat?"

Nerys had finally gotten close enough to overhear, and of course she was quick to agree. "But we both know there's no getting rid of you. Curse or not, we're stuck with you. Now don't just stand there doing nothing. Get inside with Ixora and help with supper. Did you learn nothing in the last years of service to the lord?"

"The lord?" Sol's voice piped up from where he'd settled into the nook of the tree. A small wax paper wrapper drifted down from the branches overhead the moment before his small face appeared between its leaves. "Lord Otto?"

I couldn't help but grin up at him. His face had a way of doing that to people, even to me.

"Sure, what about him?" I called back.

His hand jabbed out over his shoulder toward the road. "Isn't that his carriage?"

The smile on my face faltered.

Just as he said, a carriage had appeared at the gates leading into the village. But that wasn't what drew villagers away from the festivities so that they spilled out into the streets to look.

It was who rode alongside him.

I knew, even before the carriage rumbled to a halt outside our own gate, that the worst had come at last.

Because Lord Otto was here, and he wasn't alone. He'd brought the fae.

CHAPTER FIVE

I'D THOUGHT CALDAMIR WAS TALL BEFORE, WHEN HE LOOMED ABOVE me in the dark of the study. Out here astride a fae horse, a creature so magnificent in its own right that it put human horses to shame, he was positively massive. He rode head and shoulders above the top of the carriage, his face fixed stoically forward as if he didn't see the faces of the humans peering up at him from either side of the road.

Further up, the music of the Midsommar festival had ground to a halt. Word had spread fast, and for good reason.

A fae was here. And more than that, he was here in broad daylight—or what was left of it. Fae didn't just ride horses through the middle of town. Not now. Not in hundreds of years. Maybe not ever.

"But that can't be …" Ixora whispered, ignoring her mother's tugging at her hand as she stared in horror at the gorgeous creature looking on as Lord Otto appeared, red-faced as ever, in the open carriage doors. She tore her eyes away from him for only a second to scrutinize me. "You look nothing like him."

"Maybe," I said, through teeth gritted so hard I'd already

started to get a headache, "it's because I'm not fae-marked at all. Like I've been trying to tell everyone my whole life."

"Doesn't mean you're not cursed," she snapped back. "After all, why else would he be here?"

That, there, I couldn't argue with.

Why *else* would he be here?

I saw the looks of recognition on other faces as they realized what Ixora had. He wasn't the fae from their storybooks—those human-looking creatures with white hair and black eyes, their skin so pale the very paper the images were inked onto appeared almost translucent—but he was fae.

Unmistakably so.

"What've you done?" Nerys whispered, her face going pale as she finally managed to usher Ixora and Draigh into the house. Lavinia followed despite at first trying to slip away, only to find Draigh was now holding onto *her*.

Sol, however, Nerys was having more trouble with. He wouldn't budge from his spot perched up in the tree branches. She eventually gave up when Lord Otto's feet finally kicked up dust from where he landed, choosing instead to throw the remaining candy she'd gathered up to Sol with whispered threats to follow the bribe to stay in place.

I, meanwhile, glanced over my shoulder toward the door Ixora was quickly wedging behind her.

"Shouldn't I hide too?" I asked, hesitantly.

My father took a moment to answer, and when he did, it was him I turned slowly toward instead of the door. "Why would you?"

The way he said it, so resigned and without remorse, made me want to vomit. He stared forward, eyes locked on Caldamir as he and Lord Otto followed the curving garden path up to stand before us.

How my father made me feel in that moment was nothing compared to what rose up in me when I saw the way Lord Otto wouldn't look at me when we'd finally risen from greeting him. The horses pawed the ground in the street, shaking their manes as their eyes rolled in their sockets as if they were trying to keep the fae's horse in sight.

The fae's horse, in turn, snorted and lifted back its lips to reveal long, pointed fangs. I don't know if the horses saw with their blinders, but they stirred and jostled together as if they had.

Lord Otto's eyes reminded me of the horses', the way the whites of them flashed in the encroaching dark as he avoided looking me in the eye. As if I didn't already have an idea of why the fae was here.

Fae might come marching through the middle of streets on horseback instead of slipping through the trees of the forest like a shadow, but they still only came for one thing. They came to make a deal.

Or to collect on one.

There was an awkward moment where Lord Otto and his guest stood before us, no one speaking. It took me that moment to understand why, that it was because no one stood beside the Lord to introduce him. With all but the butler away for the festival, that duty would have fallen to Raful… but he was conspicuously absent.

Outside the gate, the villagers continued to step ever closer, one shuffling footstep at a time, to get a better look at this fae.

To see what he'd come for.

As if we didn't already know.

Finally, the lord did manage to speak, but it wasn't an introduction. It was an apology.

"I'm so sorry, Delph." His watery, red, eyes met mine, and with those few words he crushed my heart to dust.

"Please, Lord Otto, tell me you didn't," I said, throat barely croaking out the words.

The lord's hands reached out to clasp mine, but I drew back. He looked like he'd been slapped.

Annoyance crossed the fae, Caldamir's, face before he spoke, his voice sounding almost as bored as it did powerful.

"No need to look so disappointed," he said. "This is your own doing. Now, if it's all the same to you, I'd rather not stand here until Midsommar has already come and passed."

All this fae had to do was speak above a whisper and the villagers once creeping closer paused. Not one of them dared to step foot inside the garden gate. For all their years harassing me, they see a real fae and suddenly they're not so anxious to come pick a fight.

I should've been focused on the fae, on fearing and hating him, but instead... it was *them* that sprang to mind. *The cowards.*

My disgust with them was second only, I learned a moment later, to that I felt for my stepmother. Nerys had spotted the villagers too. With each flicker between the crowd and the fae, her nails dug a little deeper into my father's arm at her side.

"I completely agree. No need to stand out here on the stoop for the whole village to gawk at," she said, with a nervous laugh. "Should we take this inside?"

She tried to make a gracious gesture toward the door, but it fell flat when Caldamir tilted his head back to look over the outside of the cottage and he made no attempt to hide the way his face twisted up in distaste.

"No need for that. I'd rather not waste any more time—I already have what I came for."

"And that is?" I asked, breathless.

"You."

I'd known the answer, of course, but that didn't stop it from causing my heart to still.

"You see, girl," he continued, "the lord here and I made a deal. He's no longer able to fulfill his end of the bargain, so in exchange, he's offered me you."

The already splintered world shattered around me. It left me speechless, drowning as if suddenly pulled beneath the surface of water I hadn't realized I was barely treading.

When I didn't reply, Caldamir leaned ever so slightly closer, his brows knitting together slightly.

"That means I'm taking you to faerie."

I wasn't given the chance to respond this time either, not before my stepmother did for me.

"Then do it already." Nerys moved slightly, shielding her body behind my father's shoulder. "You didn't have to come here and make a spectacle of it."

Of course, that was what she was worried about.

Her stepdaughter was about to be kidnapped to the fae realm, and all she was worried about was how it'd look to the rest of the village. She might've been ready to be done with me, to throw me to the wolves she'd always been looking out for, but I was not.

I wasn't the only one annoyed by her response, however.

"I'd hardly call this a spectacle," Caldamir said. "The girl's been called fae-marked, has she not? From what I've been told, this is hardly unexpected."

He straightened up slightly, eyes scanning over my parents now with the same disdain he'd shown for our cottage earlier. "From where I'm looking at it, I'm doing you all a favor." He turned to look at me again. "You, the most of all."

"Doing me a favor?" I squared my shoulders and pretended my knees didn't want to collapse beneath me at any given moment. If this was the curse, then maybe there still was a way to get out of it. That was the way of the fae, was it not? Their deals were wordy, specific, ambiguous. If I didn't want to be spirited away so close to the birthday that was supposed to free me, then I was going to have to fight for it.

"What right do you have over me?" I asked. "I'm not livestock to be bargained with."

Caldamir tilted his head, considering me. "Are you not, though?" The slightest look of amusement, or some sort of annoyance close to it, flickered across his features. For a second, his dark eyes seemed to alight a bit, as if lit from some tiny spark within. "The lord, he owns all who work his lands… no?"

I gritted my teeth together, but he still understood the meaning of my words when they were forced between them.

"Only by technicality."

"Well, that's it then." Caldamir straightened back up—as if he should be able to straighten up at all, given his height. His eyes took on a disinterested look, as if he was already planning how he'd cook me for supper as soon as he'd gotten me out of Alderia. "A bargain was made, and it has to be fulfilled."

"But it isn't my bargain," I pressed. "And why does it have to be me? Can't you just choose someone else?"

"Why would I do that when fate already so graciously chose for me?"

Caldamir's hand reached out to me then, and I froze, unable to shrink back from him. But he didn't touch me, he instead twisted a finger around one of my silver locks, the look on his face almost mesmerized by it.

"I've never heard of a fae-marked before," Caldamir said, finally drawing his hand back. "But I'd be a fool not to recognize fae work when I see it."

He leaned down to me then, his eyes settling on me so close I could see the markings in his iris. From further back, I'd thought they were dark like mine—pools of black that would threaten to suck me into them. But they weren't. They were dark, sure, but flecked with gold the same color as his hair. I'd thought I'd imagined their glow before, but once again, the color from within seemed to burn a little brighter as he looked the rest of me over. "You'll soon learn that none of us are true masters of our own fate. Our lives were decided for us long before we were born. Human or fae, that's where we're the same."

"We're all victims to fate," Caldamir said, finally straightening up. "I'm as bound to the magic of the deal as you are. But you're right. There is an alternative. There always is, with these deals. You can choose not to come with me. I'll only take a willing victim."

Before hope could so much as spark within me, Lord Otto crushed that, too.

"If you don't do this, then we lose everything," he burst out, fear making his words stumble over one another. "Not just the estate. The lands. The fields. The village."

He shook his head.

"It's either you, or all of them."

I stared at him in growing horror. "All of them …?"

"Your village, in its entirety, will be enslaved to the kingdom of the Woodland Fae," Caldamir said, calmly.

Murmurs erupted through the crowd pressed closest to the garden gate. They shared terrified looks, some of them, others just glanced at me with renewed hatred.

Out of the corner of my eye, I saw my father draw Nerys in a bit closer. At least he was trying to keep the slight flicker of hope off of his face. My stepmother, on the other hand, made no effort to hide the emotions crossing her own.

Not that I'd need to ask her where she stood on the matter.

Not that I'd have to ask any of them. I knew that if this decision were up to anyone else in the village, they'd give me up in a heartbeat. To them, I was fae-marked, after all.

To them, this was what I was born for.

And maybe they were right.

"If you're trying to find a way to justify your own selfishness, then know that at least if the whole village gets enslaved they'll just be enslaved here," Caldamir said, stopping for a second as a slight shiver wracked his body, as if the idea of so many humans crossing over into faerie was unthinkable. "Think of it this way. I've seen the way the humans here treat you. You're less-than to them. You're not considered fae yet you're not human to them, either. This way, at least, you get to be remembered as a hero."

I've never laughed so hard at anything in my life.

All the rest of the faces around me looked on in horror, their eyes wide as they glanced between myself and the fae to see how he'd react as I doubled over, one hand pressed to my midsection as I tried to gather myself together to find words again.

"You really think you can trick me so easily?" I asked, finally. "First you offer me a choice that isn't really a choice, and then you try to make me grateful for it?"

Finally, the last of the humor dripped from my tongue, melted away from the heat now rising in my face flushed with rage. "At least have the decency to be honest with me … if that's possible for your kind."

"Fine then," Caldamir said, any remaining trace of kindness disappearing from his face. He straightened up again, once again somehow surprising me with his overwhelming height. It was easy to forget in moments, exactly what he was. He had this way of subtly shifting his weight and posture to fit in with us. To disarm us.

Though there was no attempt to disarm me when he spoke

next. The same subtle shift had seeped into his voice. It'd taken on a more direct tone. Sharp. Cutting.

"I didn't have to ask for you. Lord Otto didn't hesitate to give you up, and neither would any one of the villagers here," he said, towering over me as the words rolled over us with terrifying candor. "In the few hours that I've been here, your own peoples' disdain for you is disgustingly obvious. They'll be glad to see you gone. If I were you, I'd choose the village and let all of them rot right alongside you. But you humans never seem to choose that option. When faced with an impossible choice, you always choose to sacrifice yourselves. So, unless you want to surprise me—and trust me, I would be surprised—then you might as well accept your fate."

His breath came out all at once then, as if it was a relief even to him not to have to glamour his own words. "So, what will it be? We're all slaves to the old magic, eventually. The sooner you learn it, the better."

I could feel the entire village holding its breath.

No one spoke up for me. Not Ascilla, not Leofwin—their faces peering back from the front of the crowd they'd pressed their way through. Not even my own father.

But it wasn't their faces I sought out, wasn't their fear or terror that caused me to make up my mind. It was the only face among them who didn't understand, the one with rosy cheeks and sugared syrup glistening on his chin, that peered down at me from above.

It was the only person here who wouldn't *want* me to choose faerie that made me choose it.

I chose it for Sol.

CHAPTER SIX

THERE WAS NO TIME FOR GOODBYES, BUT IN A WAY, I WAS GRATEFUL.

I wasn't sure I'd have the strength to look Sol in the eyes and tell him where I was going. That this time, when I left, there'd be no coming back.

I expected Caldamir to grab me and whisk us away through some kind of magical spell, but instead, he just led me to his horse where he stood for a moment by the steed's side. It took me another moment to realize why we'd paused. He'd offered out his hand, the white of his palm the brightest thing in the long-faded twilight.

I hesitated a moment too long before taking it, apparently.

Frustration creased his brows, and he suddenly dropped his hand and used them both to lift me up from the ground to place me up on the horse in one swift motion. I was startled for a second, even more so when he didn't climb up behind me. Instead, he took the great mare's reins and started leading her away on foot. *Leading us away.*

The crowd parted before us with each step, leaving a wide berth through which we passed. No one followed us. No one tried to stop us. They just looked on in silence, unmoving, as we followed the path back out of the village.

Even when I passed by the faces I recognized, not one of them so much as offered a word of remorse. Not Leofwin, who stepped to the side like a stranger. Not even Ascilla, the one friend I'd had in the entire world. It was her face that cut deeper than Sol's. Her face the one that stayed, haunting me, in the forefront of my mind.

Because Sol didn't understand.

Sol's face, when I peered back at it one last time in the treetops, was just confused.

All the rest of them, friend or stranger, *did* understand and they still showed the same thing.

Relief.

At the end of it all, Caldamir was right. Not his honeyed lies, not his empty promise that I'd be viewed as some kind of hero.

No.

It was what he said when he'd finally stopped lying.

They were glad to be rid of me.

After all that they'd done to me, I should've been equally glad to be rid of them.

They'd treated me as a pariah from the moment I was born. They'd spent their whole lives waiting—no, hoping—that something like this would happen to me.

Then, at least, all their hate would be justified.

I hoped they were happy now. They, at least, had gotten what they wanted.

I had too, in a way.

But the cool night air that filled the void of the village behind us brought me none of my own relief. One day to Midsommar.

One day to my twenty-first birthday.

I'd gotten so close. *So close.*

I never should've hoped for a curse. I never would have, not if I really believed in it, not if I'd known what that truly meant. I shouldn't have been surprised. The fae were known for kidnapping.

I was just the latest in a long line of victims.

"It'll be better for you if you just accept it."

Caldamir didn't turn to look up at me when he said it, just kept walking with one hand on the mare's reins. We'd been walking like this for some time, enough for the very last of the blue sky above the trees to fade to black. If it weren't for the moon above our heads, waxing large and silvery white, we'd have long since been cast in blinding darkness.

"Are you able to read my mind, too?"

Caldamir glanced back at me suddenly, and it took me a moment in the darkness to realize he was trying to tell if I was serious or not.

When he looked away, he shook his head for a moment as if to clear it. "No, human. I can't read your mind any better than you can read mine. If you want to keep your thoughts private, though, you might want to work on keeping them off your face."

Caldamir said nothing for a long time after that. The silence of the forest was pressing. Even the frogs ceased to croak and the insects quieted their rhythmic chirps as we passed closer to the river that wound through the forests bordering the traitorous Lord Otto's estate. Not a single creature rustled through the grass as we passed. It was as if the whole world held its breath in the fae's presence.

I, among them.

Only Caldamir seemed content in the quiet. In fact, each moment it dragged on he seemed to grow more confident, comfortable, even.

Maybe a little *too* comfortable.

Each of those same silent steps was carrying me toward some terrible, unknown fate.

The night might have been dark to me, but I worked on composing my face. If I was going to survive, let alone have a chance to escape this fate, then I had to be better about hiding my thoughts. I had to find out more.

I had to find out as much as I could, starting with this 'deal' that had gotten me into this position in the first place.

"You keep talking about this deal like it's not your fault," I said, finally, ignoring how strange my voice sounded in the darkness.

"Because," he said, "it's not my deal. I'm just the one who's come to collect."

"So, you're some kind of glorified delivery boy?"

Caldamir peeked at me, just for a second, out of the corner of his eye. "Call it what you like."

"Then why do you care so much?" I asked. "What do you get out of this?"

"It's better not to question the workings of the fae," was Caldamir's irritating excuse for an answer. "The deal is done. Best to accept that."

Acceptance. That's what I'd been doing all my life.

I was tired of it. After all, what good had it done me?

Kidnapped by a fae, that's what.

This time, when Caldamir returned to his silent trek leading us forward, I cast my gaze back over my shoulder. I wondered, briefly, as I glanced back toward the shadowy road behind us, what would happen if I ran now. If it weren't for Sol, I'd let Caldamir condemn them all now anyway—the whole village. Let them face the same fate they were all too ready to consign me to.

"There's a bridge up ahead that will take us away from here.

Don't even think about running away now. Simply taking you won't fulfill the details of the bargain."

That was twice. Twice he'd claimed not to know my thoughts but had guessed them anyway.

"Besides," he added. "I don't have time to go off chasing you again. We're already short enough on it already."

"What's the rush? If you're in such a hurry, why travel like this? Why not just use magic?"

The road ran alongside the river still, but it was set far enough back into the trees that I could barely make out the glimmer of its dark water through the branches. In the winter, when the trees dropped their leaves and the thick undergrowth had gone barren, it would be easy to make out.

This road led toward the next village, but it was at least a half-day's ride … if one of the riders didn't walk alongside the horse instead of in its saddle. But it didn't matter. We could ride for a thousand days and never reach the fae lands.

It was a fact that, given our current situation, I felt the need to remind Caldamir.

"You can't just cross a bridge into faerie," I said, watching the back of his head. "Otherwise humans would just be stumbling into it all the time."

And the fae into our realm.

"Who said anything about crossing the bridge?"

He kept looking ahead, but the muscles in his neck tensed up a bit. "If you're going to survive long on the other side, then there are some rules about magic and the fae realm that you're going to need to learn."

The sound of the river had started to grow louder. It wasn't just coming from one side of the road anymore. It was distant, but the noise swelled with each step.

I couldn't see the bridge yet, but I knew we were drawing close.

"First, always assume that danger is nearby."

Something moved in the forest, rustling the leaves and making me squirm in my saddle. More than that—I practically leapt out of it, and might actually have, had Caldamir not suddenly moved to my side to steady me. Both our eyes scanned the forest floor until we spotted the culprit.

It was nothing more than a rat, its own figure frozen in fear as it looked back. Whatever spell Caldamir's presence had cast on the rodent wasn't strong enough to stop an owl from suddenly swooping down between the trees to make a silent meal of it.

"Second," Caldamir said, his hand pulling the reins to start our trek toward where the bridge had suddenly made a moonlit appearance up ahead, "remember that nothing—and I mean nothing—is as it seems."

Just a few more steps, and we were already at the edge of the bridge. We moved too quickly for humans, too quickly for a man and horse even when each was practically a behemoth in their own right. If it weren't so dark, I would have noticed before.

But here, on the bridge, all I could pay attention to was the sudden thrumming sound that filled the air. It started quietly, a nudging at the back of my mind. It grew until it drowned out the very roaring of the river itself.

Caldamir stepped close to tighten the straps on his mare.

"And third …" Here he paused, his hands still gripping the tightened straps of the saddle beneath me. "Just as fae are rare here, humans are rare where we're headed. You won't be feared, but you will be hunted."

"Hunted? What for?"

Caldamir turned to me then, before tightening the straps one last time.

"For your blood, of course."

I had no chance to respond, not when that rushing sound grew to drown out his voice. My own thoughts. It grew until I wanted to scream, but I had no choice.

Not when I was fixated on him.

He took the bundle of my things wrapped up in my cloak and tossed them to the side. "You'll have no need of that now, not where we're going," he said.

His hands reached to take hold of his mare's bridle, one hand on either side of the creature's powerful jaw. His head bent until his forehead nearly touched hers, both their eyes closed as if in some silent prayer.

It started with a breeze, a wind that whipped at the fabric of his breeches and the ends of his shirt. His hair blew away from his face, and the mare's mane into my eyes as this wind began to tug at me too. My own hair pulled free and swirled around me in a blinding, stinging halo.

That thing that resonated within me seemed to spread until it met with the roar of the air outside me. I reached up one hand to shield my face from my own hair, but in that moment, everything suddenly stilled.

By the time my hand returned to my side, I knew what had happened.

We'd crossed.

Not from one side of the bridge to the other—but instead, from one world to the next.

The mare whinnied beneath me, but Caldamir's hands stroked down the middle of her face until she settled back down. Then he looked up at me, that fire once again alight in his eyes.

"Welcome," he said, "to Avarath. The land of the fae."

CHAPTER SEVEN

By the time I'd exhaled by first breath, I was already becoming keenly aware of just how much *more* Avarath was.

Though it was nighttime here as well, the darkness wasn't the same. It was filled with light, not just from the twinkling stars up above that seemed to hang lower in the sky, but from the forest itself. Everything was alive in a way it wasn't just moments before. The trees—massive and ancient—were dotted with moss and mushrooms that gave off a glowing light of their own. Small insects blinked in and out of existence all around us. The very rivulets of sap that pooled between the grooved bark seemed to glitter darkly.

And where the forest on the other side had fallen into silence, the forest here instead seemed to come alive in Caldamir's presence. The very grass beneath our feet bowed in some unfelt breeze, their blades moving in a kind of excitement.

In the place of the bridge was a small footpath leading over a bubbling brook. It was no river, but somehow it was even more impressive. The water moved more carefully here, as if some force other than gravity pulled it through the crevices in the ground. It trickled because it chose to, just as the rest of the forest grew for the same reason.

With some greater purpose.

If I was starstruck by Avarath, I couldn't be blamed. But it also didn't last long.

Where Caldamir paused to take a deep breath, his lungs filling with air he drank in with the same hunger as downing a fine wine, I found myself choking. The breaths here were heavy, far too dense for my lungs. It weighed down on me, pulling me lower in the saddle as my head grew suddenly light. The edges of my vision swam, my grip on the saddle loosened, and I surely would have fallen to the ground entirely if it weren't for the sudden rumble from between my legs.

"Deep breaths, girl," the voice spoke, coming from somewhere beneath me. "Even we horses struggle with the transition sometimes."

The words nearly startled me out of the saddle again.

"We …"

"Ah yes, good advice, Rynn," Caldamir said, his eyes opening as he turned to give his mare another affectionate pat. "I forget sometimes how frail humans are."

Both fae, man and beast, looked up at me through the corners of their eyes. I, meanwhile, just continued to choke—half from the thickness of the air, half from the shock of discovering the horse's ability to speak. Not that it should surprise me. Nothing here should. Of *course* it wasn't an ordinary horse, one look at it should've been enough to warn me of that.

I must have looked a fright, because that rumble started up again from beneath me, this time from the unmistakable shake of laughter. The sound was foreign, a kind of wheezing whinny that under any other circumstances I might have found utterly terrifying.

At that moment, however, I was far too preoccupied with trying not to pass out.

I might have, had I not caught the glimmer of mirth mirrored in Caldamir's eyes. He tried to look away from me, to hide the sly smile that had started to tug at the corner of his lips, but he was too late.

Rage bubbled up in me and forced a breath so deep that I was finally able to feel the rush of air settle into my belly enough to rekindle my fire.

"Shut the fuck up."

I've never seen a man's face drop so quickly.

I swung one leg over the saddle, and without thinking, dropped from the massive horse down to the mossy footpath below.

I immediately regretted it.

The fall alone was enough to turn an ankle, to say nothing of what came after. The moment my feet hit the ground the whole world tilted around me. I thought that it was the air here that was strange, but I was wrong. Everything about this place was wrong.

The forest around me reeled. The water started to trickle toward me, vines turned their leaves as if to inspect me, and the air thickened, choking me again. Or maybe that was just me, a side effect of the way the world felt wrong.

It felt upside down, or more accurately… like I was upside down in it.

I'd have fallen, collapsed in a useless heap on the forest path if it weren't for the way Caldamir caught me almost immediately and placed me straight back on his horse. Rynn acquiesced by shifting her weight beneath me while I regained my balance. My head still pounded once I'd finally sat back up, but I no longer felt like I was going to fall straight through the ground to the center of this world.

It was still a moment later, long after I was no longer in danger of tumbling off the mare's back, that his hands let go of me. They left a heated imprint in their place as he stepped back and cleared his throat.

"Fae realms can be difficult for humans. It could take you some time to adjust."

"How much time are we talking?" I asked, each word struggling to escape my lungs and make it past my lips.

"A while."

The mare shot Caldamir a look then, but I couldn't read it. All I knew was that there was something more that the fae wasn't telling me.

"Fine then," I grumbled, reaching forward to grasp the horn of the saddle to steady myself again. "Keep your secrets. Just… just tell me one thing."

"And what is that?"

"Am I ever going to leave Avarath?"

I knew the answer before it came. I didn't need to be able to read the intricacies of a talking horse to know what it meant when she wouldn't look me in the eye.

Caldamir took the mare's reins in his hands and gave her the gentle tug signaling the return to our journey. "No, Delphine," he said, feet trudging forward once again. "No human ever leaves Avarath alive."

I'd supposed as much. None of the old stories—however fickle they'd started to turn out to be—made mention of any humans returning from the land of the fae once they'd been spirited away.

I should've been focused on that, been caught up in mourning the fact that my old life was well and truly dead. But, instead, I was fixated on something else.

Delphine.

It was the first time I'd heard the sound of my own name on his lips, and just the thought of it brought a small shiver to my spine… and I hated him for it. No man, human or fae, should have that kind of power over me. The power to simply utter my name and make my mouth go dry.

It had to be some kind of spell, some glamour, that did it. That didn't make me hate it any less, nor did it change the fact that I longed more than anything to hear him use it again. Next time, I swore I'd see the shape his lips made when he said it.

Right before I hit him squarely in that sharp-as-anything jaw.

Not that it'd actually do anything.

I didn't know much about Avarath, about fae, about anything here, really… but that I knew. I knew that compared to the fae, I was barely more than one of the gnats that buzzed around us in the forest.

I also knew that curse be damned—if I wasn't going to leave this place alive, then the very least I could do is make sure I didn't die here in peace. I'd make Caldamir and all the rest of the fae here rue the day they'd made the deal that brought me to this place.

If Avarath itself didn't kill me first.

We travelled through the night until I wasn't able to sit upright in the saddle anymore. Still, it was the third time I nearly slipped off Rynn's back before he we stopped—and then only at the horse's insistence.

"Surely, we can rest for a bit."

"She won't make it through the night in this forest. We'll just have to tie her to the saddle so she won't fall off," Caldamir said in response.

"Like hell you will," I barked out, my voice croaking from the sleepless night. I pointed my finger at his hands already reaching toward thick twine in the shadows of his bag. "If you dare put a rope on me, I'll … I'll hang myself with it."

He cocked his head to the side, lips parted in surprise.

I straightened up despite my aching muscles and nodded once, hoping my face looked more resolved than I actually felt. "Yes, that's exactly what I'll do. Lot of good that would do you and your little deal wouldn't it. You need me to make it to this forest court of yours alive, yes?"

Caldamir's jaw worked, his hand rubbing the twine so tight between his fingers that it started to unravel. But after a moment, he just nodded.

"Fine then. But don't blame me when you fall off her and don't wake back up."

I swallowed hard. "You could keep us both awake by telling me the details of the deal that brought me here," I said. "I think I deserve to know that, at least."

Caldamir eyed me suspiciously. "So, you can try to find a way out of it? It's a bit late for that."

"Oh," I said, leaning forward to press one hand to the mare's neck. "I think it's never too late for that." Rynn made a small sound of pleasure as I picked a gnat from between her shoulder blades.

"Leave them be," Caldamir said, flicking the twine still clamped between his fingers to wave my hand away. "They're some of the last magical creatures left. Can't afford to kill them anymore."

"Some of the last ones left?"

"Actually ..." His eyes took on a glazed look for a moment. He ignored my question and suddenly started swatting the mare all over. When his hand reappeared between us, it was splattered with more of the small insects. Blood and broken insect parts splattered the palm he held out to me.

"What am I supposed to do with that?"

Rather than answer me directly, he instead demonstrated. He pressed one nostril shut with one finger and dipped the other to his palm and snorted up the remains of the gnats. A heady noise issued from the back of his throat as he stood back up to his full height.

The brightness had returned to his eyes, if with a slightly maniacal gleam this time. He held his eyes a little too wide and seemed to keep forgetting to blink regularly.

"No way," I said, shimmying in my seat as if trying to prove I was no longer in danger of slipping from the saddle. "I'm not snorting faerie bugs."

"They're harmless," Caldamir said with a shake of his head. "In small doses."

I screwed up my nose again. "Not happening."

Caldamir nodded for a moment, then looked down at the string in his hands and started slowly, methodically, unraveling it again.

My heartbeat quickened as I imagined his hands binding mine. I could practically already feel the rope cutting into the flesh of my thighs, my stomach, my waist as he wound it around me. Around and around until I wouldn't be able to move, until I was even more at his mercy than I already was.

The thought should have terrified me, but what terrified me more was the heat that bloomed within me. I was no stranger to the feeling that tightened the muscles between my thighs, but I was also not enough of an idiot to imagine indulging in it.

It was one thing to lose myself in Leofwin, a servant boy who threatened little more than temporary heartbreak—another entirely to imagine getting entangled with a high fae far more likely to break *me.*

So, rather than face these thoughts, these feelings, I reached up and caught the first gnat I could get my hands on and pressed it between my lips.

I'd never tasted something so bitter. It took every ounce of self-control not to spit it back up and dry heave out the rest of my stomach's contents. Even Caldamir wrinkled his nose up at the sight, his eyebrows raising in slight surprise when I finally forced myself to swallow.

"That's one way to do it, I suppose," Caldamir said, shrugging once. He gave me an unreadable once-over before conspicuously replacing the twine and giving Rynn a soft tap that told her to start plodding forward again.

Eating the bug, as vile as it was, had two benefits. I did get a small rush through the front of my brain, something that awakened me enough to hold myself straight once again in the saddle. Better still, was that the overwhelming urge to vomit had replaced any of that inexplicable heat that had, just for a moment, made my mind and body wander toward the ultimate betrayal.

The kind that would have been my own undoing.

These fae were my enemies.

I had to remember that … and it was a lot easier to do when I could blame Caldamir for the ensuing hours of nausea.

Just when I thought I wouldn't be able to stay astride the mare for a moment longer, dawn arrived. With it came a glimmer through the forest. Something shimmered from between the trees, something tall and sturdy, but still alive. It wasn't until the path turned a corner that I was able to see what it was.

A great wall had been erected in the midst of the forest, built from the very trees that surrounded it. They'd grown together, interlocked and interwoven into a long, winding mesh of branches and roots that stretched out of sight in either direction. The wall thinned as it grew up into the treetops, but where the trunks left gaps, huge swaths of otherworldly vines grew down in their place. It left only the tiniest glimpses of what lay on the other side.

This was a far cry from the wall built around the village back at home. It made our sorry excuse for a defense against the fae look laughable in comparison. We'd built a mere pile of sticks to keep out the most powerful force our world had ever seen.

Here, that same force had gone into much more trouble to protect themselves.

But what the fae wanted to keep out … I didn't want to imagine.

The branches of the walls began to churn as we drew near, their interwoven branches and roots rippling like the surface of a great pool of water until a doorway opened before us. Light spilled through the gap, casting us in a golden shimmer as sunlight finally broke through the tops of the trees beyond.

The silhouette of a fae appeared in the gap, and in that instant, something inside me froze. The fae descended from the open door, and for one moment, I wasn't sure I hadn't fallen into some kind of magic-induced slumber … because the creature standing before me looked like something straight out of a dream.

He was smaller than Caldamir, but that wasn't saying much. His slender body was powerful in its own right, more lithe and narrow—but no less dangerous. His hair, long and rosy hued, cascaded over his shoulders in the softest waves. Full lips parted in an effortlessly sultry smile to reveal perfect, pearly teeth.

On his head was a crown, not that he needed one.

If this man, this fae, wasn't born a prince … the whole world would have long since bent the knee. He was the most beautiful thing I'd ever laid eyes on.

And from the way he looked at us, he knew it, too.

"Welcome, travelers, to my Woodland Court."

CHAPTER EIGHT

I STARED IN DUMBFOUNDED SILENCE AS THE FAE PRINCE approached, the corner of his lips turning up a bit more with each step. He had a sort of softness to him up close, an almost feminine grace that only made it more impossible to look away from him, let alone form a single, coherent thought.

He held out one hand in a welcoming gesture, his palm turned upward as the other crossed his chest to rest over his heart—if fae had hearts.

"Good as always to see you, Caldamir. Better yet since you've brought my prize."

My prize. His gaze turned from Caldamir to me when he said it, startlingly green eyes flickering over me, taking me in. He passed judgment on me in an instant, and something shifted within him… I just didn't know what.

Caldamir made a deep sound in the back of his throat, drawing this fae's eyes away from mine.

"No need for the dramatic greeting, Nyx."

As if in agreement, the mare beneath me let out a loud snort. Caldamir and she exchanged glances ever so briefly, and I wondered what unspoken conversation passed between them. In the silence that'd fallen in the last hours of our journey, I'd already started to forget the creature could actually speak.

Between the three of us, I was probably, for all current intents and purposes, the dumbest creature here.

I wasn't the only one who noticed the look, and for one second a hint of something like annoyance flashed across this new fae's face, like he didn't appreciate being left out of the joke.

"Oh, but we so rarely have guests," Nyx said, keeping his stare on Caldamir level, even as his lip jutted out in a pout. "And even less often royal ones. Give me this, at least."

Caldamir made another one of his grunts, but he didn't disagree.

"Royal ones?" I asked.

Nyx's face lit up, that smile broadening as he looked between my confused face and Caldamir's unmoving one. He looked delighted to be on the inside of the joke this time.

"What? Did Caldamir not tell you he's a prince as well?"

So much for being little more than a delivery boy.

My throat, already parched, somehow grew even drier. "Caldamir didn't tell me anything."

Nyx nodded at that, eying his friend with a small shrug. "Ah well, at least one thing in Avarath hasn't changed. No one can say the Mountain Court doesn't stand steady and unchanging as ever."

This new bit of information begged the question—what kind of deal had been made that prompted a prince of the fae realm to come and collect? No fae are spotted in Alderia in decades, and the first one that is … is a prince?

"I'd be amiss if I kept you out here waiting any longer." The fae before us made the subtlest of bows before rising up with a small flourish of his hands. "Please come, taste the delights of my court. It's still Midsommar, is it not?"

A simple tilt of his upturned palm made the sunlight pool in its center, almost like it was filled with golden honey. Only, when he tilted his hand back, it *was*.

Nyx saw my eyes widen at the sight, and this time, his delight bubbled over into a musical laugh.

"Ah yes," he said, lifting up his palm so that the thick, golden substance started to dribble down the inside of his wrist. "The glamour still lives in the Woodland Court. At least for today."

He lifted his wrist up to his lips and licked the honey from his skin in one long, slow swath stretching from his inner arm and up to the tips of his fingers. His lips glistened, wet with the sugary substance, when he parted them again, eyes returning to mine.

I nearly melted beneath his gaze, and would have, if it weren't for the voice of a newcomer that cut out above the silence.

"We can all stand around licking honey from your palms, or maybe not, because there are more important things to be done."

It still took me a minute to realize where this next voice came from, because I was only just discovering that we weren't alone —Caldamir, Nyx, Rynn, and I. More fae, several dozen of them, had spilled out through the same doorway Nyx appeared in.

They were dressed similarly to their prince, all in an array of earthy hues and textures that looked like they'd been plucked from nature itself—all shimmering, waxy greens and earth tones in thick woven cloth. Their skin had a bronzed tint, as if they'd spent just one too many days lounging in the same sunlight that had tinted their hair with shimmering gold, giving them a perpetually backlit glow.

The voice, however, came from the only fae present who *didn't* look like all the rest.

His skin was more than bronzed, and his hair dark and coarse, so thick it could rival the mare's beneath me. His eyes were lighter than either Nyx or Caldamir's, a blue so bright they couldn't be more different from the pools of black embedded in my own skull.

The eyes that were part of the reason I was so hated, and had yet to see on a single other actual fae.

But then, nothing about the fae was anything like what I'd been told.

Nyx's expression didn't waver, even as he turned back to face the only fae present who wasn't completely enraptured by his display. "I can't imagine anything more important than indulging in life's pleasures. Why else would we be blessed with such long lives? Surely it's not all meant to be suffering."

He turned back to me briefly, eyelids fluttering shut for a moment. "No offense meant to present company, of course."

It should have felt like a slight, but the slightest attention from this fae just made my heart skip another beat. I'd been prepared for the fae to have some kind of glamour, but Nyx … he was just too much. Even Caldamir had fallen under his spell for a moment.

A spell that he cleared away with a deep rumbling from the back of his throat at the sight of this newest fae.

"Armene is right," Caldamir said, hands tugging on Rynn's reins so that she started forward again, causing the other two fae to step back half a step. It also had the added benefit of shaking me from my Nyx-induced trance. "There's not much time left. Unless you want your *prize* to die before the deal is fulfilled, then by all means … keep making more palm honey."

Instead of getting angry, Nyx just cocked his head to the side.

A genuine look of confusion tugged at the inner corner of his brows.

"What's the rush? There's plenty of time to rest before the end of the night."

Caldamir moved a step closer to Nyx, but his hand never let go of Rynn's reins. "The rush," he said, "is that this human is about to collapse, but she can't touch down until she's cured."

"Human?" Nyx's eyes suddenly grew wide. "You know, I entirely forgot for a moment. But can you really blame me? You've got to admit, the resemblance … it's uncanny."

"I was about to say the same thing." The newcomer, Armene, was watching me a little too carefully as he spoke. He moved closer, his footsteps carrying him in a slow semi-circle as he took me in. "A little too uncanny, if you ask me. You say she's human?"

"Please, Nyx, Armene," Caldamir growled, actually *growled*. He kept his voice low, but I saw the other fae leaning closer to try to overhear his next words. "We'll discuss this later."

"But if she really is—" Nyx started, only for Caldamir to silence him with a look, followed by a well-meant clap on the shoulder as he tugged Rynn back into motion.

"Just don't forget tonight. Armene and I will handle the rest."

I half expected Nyx to argue with that, with being told yet again what to do in his own kingdom, but instead the only thing he seemed interested in were the flecks of dirt left on his shoulder after Caldamir touched him.

"Don't worry," Armene, the dark-haired fae, said to me from where he'd appeared on my other side, "Caldamir and I won't let him smother you." He stood close to the mare's side as we passed between the other gathered fae of the Woodland Court. "Or any of the rest of them."

It was clear who he meant when he said it. The other fae of

the court were watching me as intently as I'd watched Nyx when he first appeared. For some, it was a look of wonder or curiosity.

But for most, it was hunger.

"Wait."

We were nearly through the gate when Nyx's voice carried over to us. He was still staring down at his palm, his gaze fixated on what he found there.

"Did you … did you kill these creatures?"

Both Caldamir and Armene exchanged a glance, but it was the tightening of Caldamir's hand on the reins that made fear start to rise in my stomach.

"They were just gnats," he said, carefully.

"Just gnats?"

I might've been imagining it, but for a moment it seemed like the forest grew a shade darker around us. The vines swaying overhead came to a halt, their stillness almost as unsettling as the way the roots beneath Rynn's feet started to subtly shake.

Nyx's face remained smooth and unchanging, but his hand balled into a fist until I could imagine hearing the bones start to crack. "You of all people should know better, Caldamir," he said, the musical lilt of his voice a pitch too sharp. "Everything inside these woods belongs to me. It's not up to you to decide what lives or dies."

"Is that really up to any of us? Last I checked, a few gnats were the least of our worries."

The second time, there was no denying the darkening of the forest.

The fae in the court grew restless, their eyes darting through the branches of the trees. It wasn't fear, though, it was a kind of nervous energy—an excitement.

It was magic, the fae's glamour. I could feel it.

And from the sound of Caldamir's sigh, so it seemed, could

he. He held out the reins he'd so carefully guarded through the night.

"Armene, take her to the pool. You know what to do."

Armene took a half step back, his eyes trained on the reins like they were snakes instead.

"Unless, of course, you want to deal with Nyx ..." Caldamir added.

Armene took the reins but made sure not to spare a glare at Caldamir before he headed back toward the Woodland Fae, hands still balled at his sides. The ground beneath us had begun to shake more, the roots and branches that made up the entrance curling up at the tangible excitement building in the air around us.

An excitement that I wasn't going to see unfold, it seemed.

As soon as the court's attention had turned to Nyx and Caldamir, Armene pulled the mare's reins and ushered us the rest of the way through the forest gate. I watched over my shoulder at the way the two fae squared off with the rest of the court looking on until I couldn't see them anymore, and then I immediately found myself lost when I turned back to the path ahead.

I'd been so consumed by the fae that I'd paid no attention to the court itself. Inside the walls, the forest grew tall and green as it did outside. Houses were built into the trees as well as on the ground, with a network of netted bridges suspended between those that crisscrossed overhead. The paths here were laid with a short, dense grass instead of cobble, and all the houses were grown in the same way as the fence.

There wasn't a glint of metal from a nail in sight, and I was sure no matter how closely I looked throughout this compound, I wouldn't find any.

No wonder the leader of these fae was so concerned with the

death of a few gnats. This whole place seemed alive, intricately connected to the forest and everything in it.

"Is Caldamir going to be alright?"

Armene looked back at me with a bit of surprise.

"Of course. Nyx is just a bit protective of his domain," he said, before turning back. "These days, we all are."

I expected to see more faces of the fae peering out at us from the windows or from behind trees, but either they were exceptionally good at hiding—or the entire court had met us outside by the gate.

The only fae in sight was the one now leading the half-stumbling mare beneath me. He kept his back to me, his hand curled tight around the reins he'd been forced to take.

I dared one last glance over my shoulder, and still seeing no sign of Caldamir, I leaned forward a little further in Rynn's saddle.

"What was it that you said before, about me being human?"

Armene kept looking straight ahead, but his shoulders stiffened slightly. "Of course, you're human."

"At home I was called fae-marked," I pressed on. "It's why Caldamir took me."

Armene muttered something like a swear under his breath, and this time it was his turn to glance over his shoulder toward where we'd left the other fae.

"I *knew* it. The moment I saw you, I knew it."

My heartbeat quickened as he continued, half muttering to himself. "The hair, the eyes, how did he think we wouldn't see it?"

"So, I do look like fae."

Armene didn't need to answer, his silence was as telling as any response.

I let out the smallest of sighs, almost out of relief. I didn't care so much about why Armene was upset about it. Let him and Caldamir fight, fighting seemed to suit the Mountain Court prince that'd kidnapped me from my home to take me here.

I was just glad to find out I'd not been tortured, branded as fae-marked for nothing.

Still, one question begged to be asked. "If I do look like fae, why haven't I seen any like me?"

Armene's brow drew into a scowl. "That's because they're gone."

Gone.

"Where did they go?"

Armene looked back over his shoulder at me. He seemed to consider me for a moment before tugging the horse away from one of the last buildings and toward where the forest grew thicker further in.

"That doesn't matter, not nearly so much as what they left behind."

I remembered the way the world had spun around me when I stepped down from the mare and felt my feet subconsciously dig a little deeper into her sides, much to her chagrin. She let me know her displeasure by swatting at my back with her long, tangled tail.

"And what was that?" I asked once I'd batted the itchy hairs back away.

"This," Armene said, suddenly coming to a halt, the shadows of the trees having grown close enough together to cast his face in darkness. He hadn't turned to face me, but he didn't need to. I followed his gaze as my eyes adjusted from the bright light of the clearing to see where he'd brought me.

"The Pool of Indecision," he said, nodding once as a grimace spread across his face. "The last great *gift* of the Starlight Court before it abandoned us."

CHAPTER NINE

I HAD SO MANY QUESTIONS.

So many questions—yet each of them vanished the moment I laid eyes on the pool for myself. I thought I felt magic in the way the forest reacted to Nyx, but this pool … it was different.

It had an ancient sort of feel to it, as if the magic in it came from some place inside of itself. The magic of the forest, Nyx's little display, was nothing more than a party trick compared to what lay before us.

The water of the pool itself was a color so violently blue that if it weren't for that deep, primal humming I felt once again, I'd have thought the fae dyed it. I'd felt that humming before, heard the roar of it in my ears when Caldamir pulled us from the human world into Avarath.

It was magic—real, tangible magic that was as dangerous as it was enticing.

The forest branches dipped low over the pool, their leaves barely skimming over the surface in some areas close to the shallows. A small break in the trees overhead allowed sunlight to filter down in steep beams to illuminate the water, but their light never quite seemed to reach the edges.

The water there was dark, too dark. It had an inky sort of stain just as unnatural as the blue in its center.

A set of old, twisted stairs had been built leading down from the edge of the water into the center of the pool, where the pattern of the rocks at the bottom hid small silver fish darting in and out of the crevices disappearing into the depths.

"A magic spring," Armene said, as if reading my mind. He'd still not looked at me. He was fixated on the center of the pool, at the way the light split and painted prisms beneath the surface. "Bathe in it, and you'll at last be able to step foot in faerie, at least for a time."

A slight shudder shook his shoulders, and I found myself looking at him more closely. I couldn't see his face from where I still sat perched atop the mare, but I wish I could. Caldamir had been able to read my face easily, but I was still learning to read theirs. I needed more practice, though it would be easier if the fae who kept insisting on being my keepers were just a little less … well … distracting.

I didn't know if it was real or if it was just the glamour, but it didn't matter. It didn't stop the way my heart practically lurched up out of my chest when Armene suddenly whirled on his heel and marched to the side of the mare, one hand outstretched.

He was no Nyx, but he was breathtaking in his own right.

His eyes had an upward tilt that contrasted with the permanent scowl that seemed to always be playing at his forehead. His cheekbones angled steeply downward toward a pointed chin and perfect, heart-shaped lips.

Lips that parted in offering. "Let me help you in."

"What?"

He wasn't looking straight at me, but I was still able to see the slight flicker of indecision on his face. "It's a pool," he said, annoyance creeping into his voice. "You have to get into it for the magic to work."

He was a picture, standing there before me with his hand outstretched in my direction. My body ached to climb down off of Rynn, but seeing him standing there like that, it made me ache in a different way.

A way that made me think better of accepting his offer.

"I'll get in on my own, thanks," I said, starting to swing one leg up over the mare.

Armene stopped me, one hand shooting out to rest on my thigh. Though layers of fabric separated us, I still felt my breath hitch at his touch.

"You can't step foot on the ground until after you've bathed in the pool."

I paused. "So, you weren't really offering?"

"I was offering."

"But I didn't have a choice."

Armene's eyes did lift to mine then. "Not if you want to live."

I wasn't sure what surprised him more in the moments that followed, the fact that I hesitated at his words, or when I actually reached out a hand and accepted the one he offered me. Armene carried me like I weighed nothing at all, one arm moving to encircle my waist as the other found its way up under my knees.

I, in turn, was surprised he didn't just throw me over his shoulder like a sack of potatoes and be done with it. That's what I'd always imagined of the fae. In all the stories of them, they were graceful and charming right up until the moment the deal was made. Once they'd tricked you, they turned into the true monsters they were.

But Armene didn't handle me like a monster. He carried me

with care to the slippery, moss-covered steps leading down to the water and then began his descent one step at a time until he stood ankle-deep, the crystal water lapping at the laces of his high-top leather boots.

"You can step in from here," he said. "Just, whatever you do, don't touch the dark water."

"Why not?"

The shadows at the edges of the water seemed larger here, up close. As inviting as the clear water in the middle was, the light playing across the surface so that it made patterns along the bottom down below, the outer darkness made me pause.

It was more than a shadow, it was an inky blackness as dark as the night sky—but without any of its tiny, twinkling lights.

"Just do as you're told, please. I'm not superstitious … but some rules are better left followed."

I leaned forward slightly, my neck craning over until I caught a glimmer of my own reflection in the surface of the water. I looked … rough … to say the least. My hair was matted to a forehead that glistened with grime and sweat, and the dark circles of my eyes had started to make me look like I was racoon-marked instead of fae-marked.

I didn't look like a girl who'd been riding through the forest for one night. I looked like I'd been lost in the forest for days.

Weeks, even.

The life was literally draining out of me here.

So there really wasn't much of a choice.

I finally drew back from my own sorry reflection to prod Armene in the center of his surprisingly hard chest. "Are you going to watch too, or am I allowed some privacy?"

Armene cleared his throat.

"Oh, of course."

He set me down with more of his surprising care, my feet

splashing into the water that easily reached up to my calves. Armene's eyes averted from mine as I hitched up the bottom of my skirts to keep from soaking them, but he was already trudging back up the stairs toward the horse before I could see if a blush had risen to match his sudden shyness.

Looking away from the pool was a mistake. I shouldn't have, not when Avarath still seemed unsteady beneath my feet.

Armene had barely disappeared over the top of the steps before I lost my footing.

There was one frightful moment where I thought I was going to pitch over the railing and straight into the dark black water lining the edges, but I somehow managed to pitch forward instead.

Ice erupted along every surface of my body.

I'd thought the water was cold at the shallower edges of the pool, but in the center when I surfaced, it was cold enough to make me gasp and splutter for air.

But for the first time since I'd arrived in faerie, I found it.

Air. Real, breathable, air.

There was no struggle to fill my lungs. From the moment my skin hit the water, that exhausted, tingling, *wrong* sensation abated. I felt a thousand times lighter, even as the heavy skirts tied around my waist threatened to weigh me down to the bottom.

More than a threat. They actually were.

Just as quickly as my breaths turned elated, they soured and became desperate. My hands reached out to try to keep my head above water, but it didn't work. They just got more entangled in the fabric, pulling me down deeper.

Through the rippling surface of the water, I could still make out Armene's form. He stood by the mare, his back turned to me like a stiff, unwavering soldier.

Surely he'd heard my gasping before, the splashing of my hands upon the surface.

So, he had to have ignored me.

Maybe this was it, the reason he'd brought me here. This was never a pool meant to save me. It was meant to end me.

But I'd not give up so easily, not just like that.

I tried to fumble with the ties of my bodice, but my hands were slick and the string slipped between them. The water in the middle of the pool was deeper than I expected, but the pool wasn't so wide. I knew even if I sank to the bottom, I could probably wade my way out to the edges.

If it weren't for that inky blackness waiting for me.

One more choking tug at the back of my throat and I didn't care.

Damn the inky blackness.

For all I knew, Armene's warning was just an empty threat. For all I knew, he wanted me to keep from the dark water because it might actually help me. It would be typical of a fae.

I started edging toward the dark, one sodden, tangled footstep at a time, and I knew in my heart that those threats weren't empty. Not when, with each inch I approached, tiny fingers of blackness started reaching out toward me.

Ready to pull me in.

Delphine.

The sound of my name echoed in my ears, surprisingly clear here beneath the surface of the water.

Delphine.

My name echoed out to me with a hauntingly deep note. It made a tingle race up my spine—and stay there. The water warmed as I drew closer to the dark edge, enticing me further. As if my burning lungs and watering eyes needed any more enticing. I could feel the slippery rocks beneath my feet and see the surface of the water drawing nearer with each step that inched me closer to the edge.

No matter how dark that edge was.

"Delphine!"

The third time I heard my name, however, it was different. It was broken, garbled, shouted from above the surface of the water instead of beneath. A second after it rang out, an ear-splitting crash erupted all around me as something massive lunged into the pool right beside me.

The darkness reached out to me one last time, those fingers almost grazing mine the moment before arms encircled my waist and pulled me, coughing and spluttering, up onto the stairs in a tangle of sodden skirts. Above me, looking down into my surely pale and bloated face, was one unlike any I'd seen before—on this side of the veil, or the next.

He was more muscular than any of the other fae I'd met, or maybe he was just the first one I'd seen bare chested. His skin was so dark it nearly rivaled the inky blackness that had moments before been trying to lure me into their warm shallows, but it was his eyes that were really the most striking. They were a bright and luminous gold, the pupils slitted down the center into two, mirrored half-moons.

Gold piercings glittered in his ears and brows, long braided plaits falling down across that muscular chest as he leaned closer to my face to look at me.

Right before I promptly vomited a lungful of water right into his open mouth.

"I usually like to get to know someone before I let them do that to me," he said, his one free hand reaching up to wipe the bottom half of his face. "Though I suppose we all have to start somewhere … and the story of how Tethys, Prince of the Sea, saved you from drowning before you vomited on him is going to make a good one."

His eyes travelled over me, a still-quivering mess in his arms, and a mischievous smile pulled at the corner of his lips. "You're not at all what I expected."

Armene appeared right above us, eyes wide and face flushed with fury as he and Tethys pulled me the rest of the way up and away from the black water to the grass at the top of the steps.

"I told you not to go near the edges!"

"Well," I spat after several hearty, spluttering coughs, "I chose that over dying."

"That was the wrong choice," he hissed back, one hand reaching up to tug at a loose strand of hair that had fallen out of his bun and into his face. "Do you have any idea what would've happened to you if you did?"

"No," I said, struggling to force the words from my searing throat. "Because you didn't tell me."

"Madness," Tethys answered, before Armene had a chance. That gold in his eyes glittered brighter than the gold in his ears for a moment. "All who touch the darkness go mad. As much as the water in the center of the pool is blessed, it's balanced out by a curse."

"Damned Starlight Fae," Armene muttered, pulling at his hair again. He'd started to pace, head shaking as he tried to work out what had just happened. "How often do humans have to breathe, anyway?"

Both Tethys and I stared at Armene in disbelief for a moment.

"A whole fucking lot more than you, apparently," I snarled at him, before pitching forward to hurl another stomach of water out onto the leaves and grass.

When I looked back up, both Armene and Tethys were watching me carefully.

"What is it?"

"How do you feel?" Armene asked, hesitantly.

I looked down at my hands on the ground, and despite myself, I felt a small rush. "Aside from nearly drowning, I feel fine," I said. A little woozy, a little unsteady, and still unsure of whether or not I should have just let myself drown.

But those things I didn't share with them.

Some things were best kept as secrets. Especially when that was the only thing left that I owned. That was the only thing left that was mine.

Armene straightened up, obviously relieved. He tilted his head up and Tethys followed him as they measured the angle of the sun in the sky.

"Still plenty of time to dry off. We should get her back before anyone comes asking questions."

Both fae turned to look through the surrounding woods, their shoulders rigid, as if expecting to see those same faces I looked for earlier. But there was no one. No one I could see, anyway.

I couldn't wrap my head around what just happened here at the pool.

It was more than the whispered words from the shadows, whispers that still echoed if I listened closely enough when staring into a shadowy corner between the trees. It was the way the two fae had acted.

Armene and Tethys, both.

They'd been … protective of me. The human.

I didn't know why.

I was insignificant to them. Of all the things we got wrong about the fae, that was one thing we'd gotten right. I was nothing more than livestock to them, a strange, lesser-than mirror image of what they were. I'd be long dead before they'd even realized I was really here.

But still, Armene had nearly pulled his hair out from the roots when he realized what'd nearly happened. And Tethys, I'd seen how close he swam to the edge of the darkness. I'd seen it reach for him too.

He took a risk, for me.

There was only one explanation.

They needed me for something. But for what ... I supposed I'd just have to wait to find out.

CHAPTER TEN

Both fae were eager to leave me in the care of one of Nyx's Woodland servants as soon as we returned, damp and shivering, to the court. I only guessed she was a servant from the slightly less extravagant drape of her gown, though from the way she roughly tore the wet clothes from my back, muttering the whole time, you'd think she was a queen forced to dote on a slave.

Which, in a way, I suppose she was.

My ranking here was quite obvious, something lower than the mare that was now making sighs of pleasure as someone outside the leafy house brushed the tangles from her mane and tail with much more care than was being taken with mine.

"Have you ever brushed your hair before?"

The question wasn't meant to be answered, a fact reiterated by the next tug of the brush that pulled my head back as far as it would go, and not without a small screech of my own in response.

The servant grumbled some more and reluctantly started working in smaller sections. "I don't think I've ever seen someone with so many leaves in their hair."

"It's not like I put them there on purpose."

We fell into a disgruntled silence—her with the fact that she had to disentangle each one of my white strands from where they'd gotten matted in the mud and dirt, and me with having to put up with her less-than-gentle touch doing so.

We'd been led to one of the smaller houses inside the cluster of living buildings that made up the court. This one wasn't suspended as high as the others, though I knew if I went to the window and drew back the vines, I'd likely break a leg trying to leap down to the ground—if the building would let me get that far.

Inside, the walls had fashioned themselves into intricately woven patterns of interlocking tree branches. Paintings hung on the walls depicting faerie beasts—or what I could only assume were faerie beasts. Most of them looked foreign, like strange versions of creatures I might've encountered back at home.

Others looked straight out of my nightmares, creatures that had no right to exist in this world or the other.

There were no candles here. The inside of the rooms were lit with more glowing fungi. Here, inside, they grew in elongated candle-like clusters that gave off a welcoming warm light instead of the enchanted blue I'd seen most often in the forest.

That familiar light did nothing to change the fact that something about the servant tugging at my hair seemed … off … in the cracked reflection of the glass before me. She worked with disjointed movements, as if she was unused to her body. Or unused to me.

That was one thing at least that we had in common. We shared a mutual discomfort that was, in its own right, comforting.

"How is it I understand you?" I blurted out, when another sharp tug was already forcing a squeak out of me.

She gave me a withering look meant to dissuade me, but it didn't last long. She melted a little, and with it, so did some of the stony exterior that had left her face looking drawn.

"Fae language is universal to humans," she said, finally. "Part of the glamour that still remains intact."

My heartbeat quickened at her words.

There it was again, this casual mention of their magic as if it were something from the past. I hadn't thought much of it before, but now it sent my mind reeling. Maybe the fae weren't as powerful as we'd been led to believe.

I leaned forward a bit and was promptly rewarded with a smack to the back of the head. "Hold still or I'll cut it all off and blame the pixies."

"So, this glamour …" I started. "Something's wrong with it, isn't it? You're not the first fae to say so."

Though not in as many words.

"I'm not a fae," she said, suddenly. "I'm a demon."

"A—a *what?*" I started and stood up, knocking the chair back so that it tumbled to the floor. Or it would have tumbled, had roots not shot up and caught it, gently returning it to its upright position before slithering back to their place as part of the floor.

"I just presented myself in the way Armene thought would be most pleasing to you."

"So … so you're Armene's?"

Her lips turned up in a grimace. "I serve the prince, yes, but not in the same way that you're now Nyx's … but you wouldn't understand."

Another fae prince.

"What's your name?"

That question had a far more extreme effect than I anticipated. She tilted back her head and laughed—a hollow, screeching sound that made me shrink back from her. For the first time, I saw the demon in her. It flickered in and out with each wracking of her breath, only to disappear again behind her smooth fae features when she locked eyes with me again.

"We're an ancient and powerful race, nearly eradicated by the fae long before they even came to your world," she said, voice deepening. "I'm one of the last of my kind. A kind controlled by their true names … so no, human, I won't be telling you that."

I swallowed, hard.

She pointed the brush into the chair and I promptly sat back in it, facing rigidly forward.

"What's your true form?"

Her hand stopped for a second, halfway down my back.

"You said Armene asked you to take this form for me. What do you really look like?"

The brush returned to stroking, the tangles growing less and less with each pass. "I wouldn't want to frighten you."

I turned in my chair despite the knot growing in my stomach. "I know what it is to be considered a monster. You don't need to pretend with me." I held out my palms on either side of the chair, remembering another one of Caldamir's warnings about Avarath. "There's enough glamour here to make my head spin. It'd be … nice … to see one thing for what it is."

She considered this for a moment, her eyes taking on a vacant stare as she fixated, unmoving, on the dim mirror in front of me. Then, as I looked on, the skin of her face drew back. The full head of luxurious hair grew sparse and stringy, colored similarly to mine if mine had spent a millennium uncovered in the hot sun. And it wasn't a *she* so much as it was a *he*. A he with long, boney fingers and nails just as long and twice as pointed. The tips of one poked into my scalp from where he clutched the brush in his hand just a little too tight.

It was all I could do not to draw back in fear, right up until I saw his eyes.

Black, like mine.

When our gaze met in the mirror, just for a second, I wondered if he was thinking the same thing.

"That should be enough," he said, straightening up and pointing to a gown that had appeared near the door. Someone— or something—must have delivered it when we were too busy speaking. "Stay here and no one will touch you. Leave, and I make no promises."

He moved with surprising grace to the door, where I watched his lithe, almost insect-like body pause for a moment.

"Waylan," he said, before leaving. "You can call me Waylan."

I WASN'T LEFT ALONE for long, but it was still long enough to find myself spiraling into some kind of existential crisis. By the time I'd pulled on the gown meant to replace the one I'd soaked in the pool, I'd begun to feel the press of walls around me. The way this place breathed made me feel like I was inside the stomach of a monster, a monster that had swallowed me whole and already started digesting me.

It wasn't just the building, this living house I found myself in. It was everything here. Avarath itself had swallowed me, but it hadn't yet decided what to do with me.

Or if it had, it had yet to make its intentions clear.

Only one thing was certain.

I finished lacing up the front of my new gown, something that under normal circumstances would've made even the visitors to the Otto estate balk. It was simple cotton, or whatever was closest to it in the fae realm, colored like the inside of an iris.

Even in its simplicity, it was finer than anything I'd ever touched, finer than anything I'd laid eyes on in the human world. Lord Otto's estate was the richest place I'd been, and he'd long since sold off anything of value and had it replaced with a cheap fake.

Still, even in the dim light of the mushrooms and the glow of summer sun peeking through the vines swathed over the window, I didn't look like a fae.

I didn't look as close to death as I did earlier, but there was still a pallor to my cheeks, a darkness coloring the line of my lashes. My mouth was dry, my stomach aching from a hunger I couldn't feel over my own anxiety. I was weak.

I could feel it.

Avarath made me ill. The very ground, the air, the reflection of the light on my skin. This place wasn't made for humans. I might be able to stand now, but it didn't change the fact that this place was poisonous to me.

If this deal didn't involve me dying, I'd find my way out of Avarath. I'd find my way back to my ungrateful village. Or maybe not. Maybe I'd find my way to other villages. Maybe I'd finally shave my head and bind my eyes, hide their blackness by pretending I was blind or something.

Or maybe other places would be more kind to a fae-marked girl once she'd escaped faerie and lived to tell the tale.

One thing was certain.

I didn't care what Caldamir had said. I couldn't stay here. Wouldn't. As soon as the deal was finished, as soon as I knew Sol was safe for sure, I'd find a way out of this place. The first chance I got to get out, I was going to take it.

I'd be the first human to leave Avarath alive.

CHAPTER ELEVEN

But first there was the pesky deal that'd brought me to the Woodland Court in the first place.

The same one that had a black-skinned fae with eyes like golden coins rapping on my doorway before the sky at the end of my first full day in Avarath had begun to turn pink at the edges. Those same eyes glowed at the sight of me, widening as his lips edged upward in a mischievous smile that made me want to knock some sense into him.

Or would, if he wasn't easily twice my size. Not to mention immortal in every way that mattered.

"Where's Caldamir?"

The question made that smile falter on his face, just a little bit. It was worth it.

"What, don't trust me to get you to the feast in time?" he asked, eyebrows crinkling in the middle of his forehead. His lip buckled out in a pout, but his mock disappointment didn't reach his eyes. Those eyes still sparkled in that same, impish way.

"I don't trust you for anything."

I shouldered past him, my footsteps barely carrying me

halfway down the stairs before he suddenly reappeared at the bottom. He'd dropped down from the leafy stair rail as naturally as breathing, one arm grasping the rail to swing his surprisingly agile body forward to block my path.

"And here I was thinking we'd be friends," he said.

I glared up at him. "Not a chance."

I tried to duck under one of his outstretched arms, but he stopped me.

"Where are you headed?"

Behind Tethys, the fae that had been missing earlier had started to filter through the treetops and wind along the pathways below. Their footsteps carried them in wine-drunk, curving patterns, but it was clear enough to see where they were headed.

I didn't need a smirking guide to lead me in the same direction all the fae were headed, and I told him as much.

"And here I was thinking you might try to run."

I stopped for a moment and glared at him a second time. "And have Caldamir go right back to Alderia and enslave my village? I think not."

The slightest look of surprise rooted Tethys to the spot just long enough for me to duck under his arm and start trudging forward on my own.

Without the fae to follow, I'd still have known where to go. From somewhere in the heart of the court, where all the paths and bridges ultimately headed, music had begun to rise. It was an enchanting sound, winding around each branch and vine like tendrils of a warm breeze.

It wound its way into the mind, muddling the brain and causing its own kind of drunkenness. The colors around me grew more vivid, the grass softer, the light brighter. The edges of my vision grew soft and unfocused, and I probably would've slipped entirely into the enchantment and been lost if it weren't for Tethys' voice, broken by years of sea air, that cut through it.

"So, you're really determined not to trust me, then. Even after I saved your life?"

"After you …" It took me a moment to shake the drunk feeling, and another to understand what he's just said. "My life wouldn't need saving if you stupid fae didn't build pools of indiscretion."

"Indecision."

"Same thing. It's the stupidest thing I ever heard of."

Tethys dipped his head and flinched, but this time I couldn't tell if he was jesting or not. "Careful now, they might be listening."

All around us, the fae had started to move together, converging toward one elaborately designed building in the center of the maze of trees and living houses. It rose up like a cathedral of narrow branches, great open windows in the place of glass panes.

At the very least, it was the closest thing to a cathedral that I'd seen with my own eyes. But that wasn't what stopped me in my tracks.

"Who's they?" I asked, tilting my head up to meet Tethys' eyes when he realized I'd fallen a step behind. "The … the Starlight Fae? Armene mentioned them before."

Something flashed across Tethys' vision. "What did he say about them?"

I just stared on, tight lipped for a moment. "These are the same fae that I look like, right? The ones that made me what the humans call fae-marked?"

Tethys' eyes wandered the pathway behind us for a moment, thinking, before grabbing me by my exposed arm and pulling me out of the pathway before three beautiful fae females could trample me in their path. They barely noticed me, which was hardly surprising.

Compared to them, I was insignificant, less worthy of attention than the gnats that had just about started a fae war this morning.

Still, I wasn't willing to be distracted.

"These fae, the Starlight Fae, are they responsible for whatever's going wrong with the magic?"

This time, there was no hiding the panic that flickered across his face. "Put that out of your mind. None of that might matter by the end of the night, anyway."

I straightened up, peeling my eyes away from him to glance once more at the wooded cathedral for only a second before setting my gaze on his again. "What exactly is happening tonight? What's this got to do with the deal that brought me here?"

"Finally, an easy answer," Tethys said, with a slight sigh. He took my arm, dragged me back toward the door, and didn't answer until we stood at the threshold of a long, crowded meeting hall. "They're going to make a sacrifice of you."

CHAPTER TWELVE

No wonder he said nothing else would matter after tonight.

There wouldn't be *anything* after tonight.

There was nowhere to run. No *way* to run, not with Tethys' arm still clutching onto mine.

I struggled against him, but all it bought me was a few stumbling footsteps across the mossy ground. Long tables stretched along the length of the room on either side. Fae were sitting on benches and swinging in hammocks and lying on the floor as other fae fed them strange red and orange fruits from their slender fingers. Compared to the Woodland Fae, Tethys beside me looked almost like an entirely different species.

A species that could drag me, probably without realizing he was dragging me, the whole length of a room before I had the chance to force a word out against it.

"I want to speak to Caldamir," I said, my breath hitching as I struggled to keep up with my own racing heart. I was drowning, but this time it wasn't due to the poisonous air or magical pools of water. "He'd never …"

"Who do you think arranged it?"

My mouth clamped shut.

Of course, he did. He'd tricked me, lulled me into thinking he wanted to keep me alive, when really, he just wanted to make sure I could live long enough to be made a sacrifice of.

I should have expected nothing less from the fae.

We came to a shuddering halt at the end of the two long rows, where a third table had been placed slightly raised above the others. The roots here piled onto one another writhing and reaching for the fae seated at the center of the table.

This time, however, even Nyx's preternatural beauty couldn't force the persistent thoughts from my head.

This was it. What they'd brought me here for.

The worst possible fate.

Male and female fae filled the table spreading out to either side, but only those closest to the prince of this kingdom didn't seem utterly and hopelessly infatuated with him.

Tethys gave a little eye roll as he half bowed to Nyx before giving me a slight push forward.

I, in turn, refused to bow. Not that I was given much of a choice, not when the roots beneath my feet sprung up to force me down. They pressed like knotted fingers into my spine until I had no choice but to fold at the waist.

They held me in place until Nyx waved them away dismissively. They may have been able to force me to bow, but they weren't able to force the scowl from my face when I once again faced the Woodland prince.

"Glad to see your spirits weren't damped by the pool. Armene here was just telling me about your little swim." Nyx's eyes grew hooded as he took me in again, taking his time. He picked the last cherry from a bowl and plucked the stem before popping it into his mouth. The fruit mulled between his lips before he leaned forward to carefully spit the pit back into the bowl. He didn't speak again until he'd set it aside. My resolve wavered only for a moment beneath the weight of his gaze. "You don't look mad."

"Looks can be deceiving," Tethys said, his arm finally dropping from mine before he launched himself up over the table to take the last remaining open seat nearest to Nyx. "After all, take a look at you."

Either Nyx ignored Tethys' comment or, more likely—I was starting to think—didn't understand it, because his attention never wavered from me. That was what kept me anchored in place long after Tethys' hand no longer stopped me from bolting.

That and the hundred other fae surrounding me, each one eager to do whatever Nyx bade them do … not to mention Caldamir and the others. I wouldn't even have made it to the end of the first tables.

From a distance, I could see the glazed-over look in the fae's eyes, but I knew that wouldn't last long. Not if Nyx didn't want it to.

"You look like you've seen a ghost, silly girl."

Nyx's jacket was left open, the shirt beneath it unbuttoned to reveal the smooth, carved surface of his chest. He leaned forward toward me, and for the first time, I noticed a simple necklace strung around his neck. It was a tiny root so thin that it had been twisted into a kind of choker that rested just above his clavicle.

Tethys caught me looking and leaned forward too, his eyebrows raising conspiratorially. "Nyx has been in and out of a relationship with a tree for the last half century."

When I didn't say anything in response, he added, "Well, she's technically a dryad. Which also technically makes her a tree."

"And also, technically," Nyx said, frowning. "We're not together anymore."

"Yet you still wear her memento ..."

"What? Was I supposed to throw it out just because we're not together?" Nyx asked. "No, seriously. Tethys," he said, concern flickering across his face as he twisted in his seat to face Tethys. "Was I supposed to throw it out?"

Tethys didn't answer him. Caldamir didn't give him the chance.

"I don't think Delph here cares what Nyx here has been using to get his cock wet. Even less what jewelry you choose to wear."

He wasn't wrong. It was the last thing on my mind at present, the princes' banter doing nothing to stop my knees from wanting to give out beneath me.

Nyx's eyes cut over to me, and then back to Tethys as they narrowed. "Hey you, what did you tell her? She's practically shaking."

He motioned with his hand, and the middle of the table parted like the walls of the court had earlier, splitting a path between the tables that led to the other side. As I watched, a kind of pedestal grew from the ground, forming in the space directly beside Nyx. Caldamir didn't look pleased at being pushed ever so slightly away, but it wasn't him I was fixated on.

It was what lay on the pedestal—another root, this one sharp as a blade.

"Come forward."

Nyx's next words were an order. I found it impossible to disobey him.

This was it. If he planned to sacrifice me here in front of all his gathered subjects, there was nothing I could do to stop him. All I could hope was that I died with what little bit of dignity I had left.

I might not be a hero to my village, but one day, Sol would know I was a hero for him. That was all that mattered. That was the image I held in my head as I stepped through the gap in the tables and onto the other side.

Overhead, the setting sun had illuminated the branches so that they appeared to glow with golden light themselves. Mirrors had been hung from the natural rafters, catching the light that radiated down on us in flashes like falling stars. Soon the sun would dip down below the horizon, but for that single moment, the whole forest seemed ablaze with its light.

There was a heat that radiated off of Nyx that I hadn't felt off any of the others. Standing this close to him was overwhelming. No wonder the others were drawn to him like a moth to a flame.

"Caldamir was kind enough to bring you here so that a deal I made with that lord of yours was finally fulfilled," he said, looking deeper into my eyes. "And so now, I fulfill it."

With that, he promptly reached forward, grabbed the knife from the pedestal, and slashed the tip of the blade across my outstretched palm before I could so much as try to draw back. The knife dropped with a clatter to the table, the entirety of the hall falling silent as he leaned forward and pressed his full lips to the cut.

His hand enfolded mine, cupping it around his face as he drew in the iron of my blood. When he lifted his face again, that perfect golden palette of his face had been smeared with dark red. He mulled my blood over in his mouth like the cherries whose pits he leaned forward to spit it into.

For the third time, I heard the familiar rumble of magic. That breeze from nowhere blew back the already wild tendrils of Nyx's hair as the bowl in his hands began to shake.

Caldamir, Tethys, and Armene leaned in to watch, their faces intent.

The pits in the bowl began to quiver and take form. Tiny wings unfolded and legs sprouted to form several gnat-like creatures that rose slightly to hover, for a moment, in the air above it.

All four of the fae princes' faces flickered with hope—but it was as brief as the lives of the small magic-born creatures. Almost as soon as these new small creatures had taken flight, they crumbled to black dust in the bottom of the bowl from which they'd been resurrected.

As soon as they did, the thrumming stopped. A sort of emptiness settled in its place, a hollowness that came with a bitter aftertaste.

Caldamir shattered the silence by slamming one hand down on the table. "It's not enough."

The other three fae fell back into their own seats.

"I told you it wouldn't be," Armene grumbled. He tugged at the sheer fabric wrapped around his shoulders, masking for a moment the disappointment on his own face.

The scent of blood and honey overwhelmed me as Nyx, beside me, tilted back his head and closed his eyes for a second, his nostrils flaring as he took a deep breath. When his head nodded back down to look at me again, I caught a hint of a familiar mischief I'd already grown accustomed to seeing in Tethys' eyes.

"At any rate, the deal is done."

My heartbeat still thudded in my chest. "That … that's it?"

Nyx let my hand drop to my side, but not before I caught him looking once more at the gash on my hand. It was already healing.

"How did—"

"Oh, I love you humans, you're always so naïve," Nyx said with a tinkling laugh. He grabbed my wrist again, tilting it up toward the setting sun. "You didn't think I was just going to waste all that pretty blood, did you?"

"It's fae fluids that allow us to heal. It can heal humans too, if they're so lucky," Caldamir snapped from my other side. His patience had thinned with the failed magic. He stared straight ahead, his head already sunk halfway into his cup of wine. "Not that any humans have ever been so lucky."

Together, Nyx and I watched the sliced skin of my hand knit back together until all that remained was a short, silver scar.

I wondered for a moment if the stories of the fae would've been the same had humans known this … or would we long since have found a way to trap fae, to use them for our own means instead of wishing them gone. I wondered if we'd hate the fae so much if we'd known they held this sort of power.

A power that might actually help us, and not just destroy us.

Nyx seemed to be the least affected by his failed attempt at creating new gnats to replace the ones Caldamir and I had killed. Tethys had fallen uncharacteristically quiet, while Armene, usually still and serene, had begun tapping his foot under the table.

The Woodland prince still hadn't let go of my hand. His thumb traced circles around the back of my hand, the last of the inner heat fading from him as his eyes lifted to rest on my face instead.

"It's been a long time since I laid eyes on a human, but not so long that I'd forgotten how they were supposed to look. I don't remember any like you."

"I don't think any of us do," Armene said, on his other side. His foot continued to tap anxiously beneath him. He cast first a sideways glance at me, and then at Caldamir. Neither of them spoke, but I saw the way Tethys watched them too.

Only Nyx remained oblivious, his attention still devoted to

my face as if I was some sort of puzzle he was trying to work out. The last of the sunset faded, leaving the mirrors up above to tinkle in an unseen breeze, their dancing lights extinguished in an instant.

It was only then that Nyx let go of my hand and sat back.

"At least this business is done," Nyx said, the weariness on his face seemingly unable to last more than a couple seconds. It was immediately replaced with that simple smile that seemed to most often occupy it. "Now, let's enjoy the last of the evening before we're all forced to return to the drabness of reality."

"What do you mean, done?" I asked, head turning from Nyx to Caldamir, and then to the other two fae seated beside them in turn. "I thought …"

"What, don't tell me you thought that I meant we had to kill you," Tethys said, leaning forward. "We just needed Nyx here to taste a little of your fear."

"A … a little …"

"For minor rituals, the fear is what really matters. You really think we're savages?"

"Yes."

Tethys let out a bark of a laugh, one leg slipping down from the edge of the chair where he'd wedged it up. "At least she's honest," he said, shuffling to rebalance himself. His golden eyes glowed again in the dying light as he took me in, in all my full chest-heaving glory. My heart had once again started to beat too quickly, this time, not out of fear.

"Such a shame, really."

I wanted to ask Tethys what he meant, I wanted to ask a thousand questions, but there was really only one that mattered.

"Then does that mean I can go home?"

It was Armene who flinched back when I said it, a look of

distaste marring his handsome face. But it was Caldamir who answered.

"Impossible."

"But, the deal …"

"It has nothing to do with the deal," Caldamir said, curtly. He still kept his eyes fixed on his wine glass, though it had long since emptied. He was taking the failed magic worse than the rest of them. "You wouldn't be able to make it to the bridge in time."

"In time for what?"

"Before Midsommar has passed, and the magic has once again slipped …" Tethys said, picking up some fruit only to let it tumble listlessly back down to the table "… through our fingers."

My mind was reeling. "Fine then. I'll just wait for the next festival. How long off could that be?"

A coldness had started to settle into the hall at the dying of the light. That far-off look in the fae's eyes had started to fade, a sharp hunger replacing it in the way they glanced at me. I wasn't the only one who noticed. Though Nyx remained blissfully ignorant, that same infuriating smile pulling at the corner of his eyes as it always seemed to, both Caldamir and Armene had started fidgeting restlessly with the knives on their plates.

Even Tethys sat up a little straighter, his muscles tensing at the ready.

"Just a couple months," Caldamir said, hand still twiddling the knife a little too close to where my now-healed hand rested on the table. I drew it back to my chest and cradled it, though it no longer so much as stung.

"What's a couple months? I can wait for that. I'll make the crossing then."

"It'll be too late by then."

A slight coldness followed his words, but I still pressed onward, despite the restlessness building around us. Caldamir's hand had stilled, his fingers wrapped tightly around the blade.

"Too late … how?"

"Because by then, you'll be dead."

CHAPTER THIRTEEN

By then, you'll be dead.

It wasn't the first warning of its kind that Caldamir had leveled at me, but this one stung the hardest.

"And why's that?" I demanded. "Why will I be dead by the next festival?"

"Because you're a human," Caldamir answered, his voice sounding suddenly tired. "Humans can't live in the fae realm. You'll be lucky to live until the end of the week … let alone the end of the summer."

I shook my head.

"But the pool—"

"The pool is only a temporary fix," he said, cutting me off. "It won't spare you from dying, only prolong it. You're only human."

"Yeah well, unless she's not."

It was Tethys that said it, still seated on Caldamir's other side. He wasn't looking at me now. He was watching the fae rising from their seats, a different kind of trance upon their faces.

"Not now," Caldamir said, something like danger in his voice. "It's not possible."

"I mean," Tethys said, ignoring him, "take one look at her and tell me you don't see it."

"Enough."

Caldamir stood, the chair scraping out behind him. "We need to get Delph out of here before the court gets too rowdy. Unless you're about to tell me your Midsommar rituals have changed, Nyx."

Nyx's beaming smile told him everything he needed to know.

"You sure you don't want to join in?" Nyx asked me, one hand reaching out to cup mine. He drew a finger along the inside of my palm, teasing at the tender new skin that had replaced the work-worn callouses. His eyes became hooded, and his lips parted, tongue darting out to tease at their upturned corners. "It'd be an honor to show you a *true* Midsommar at the Woodland Court. A proper birthday present for you, if you will, if Caldamir told us right."

It wasn't until I saw the hands slithering over his shoulders and onto his chest, those hands attached to the most beautiful of fae women who'd appeared behind him, that I understood what he meant. I'd misread the restlessness of the court.

My own heat rose in my cheeks, fueled even hotter by the fact that the first instinct that ran through my head *wasn't* to say no.

"Please, as if she wants to spend the night with you and a couple of saplings."

Nyx's head snapped up to glare at Tethys. Before he could say anything, however, Caldamir was reaching for my arm.

"We should go, now."

Nyx's lip stuck out in a pout, but then a second pair of hands joined the first, this from a dark male fae nearly as beautiful as Nyx himself. He knelt at the prince's side, and any hint of annoyance faded away from his face.

"Your loss. One of these years, Caldamir."

Armene stood up, as did Tethys... though Tethys without quite as much determination as the other two. I saw the way his eyes roamed the room, drinking in the sight of the debauchery quickly turning into something more.

"Thank you for your hospitality, Nyx," Armene said with a bow.

Nyx didn't answer. He was far too lost in the lips brushing across his skin and the hands pulling at the already scarce swaths of fabric draped across him. The cathedral around us gave a slight shudder as the sigh of wind passed through the open windowpanes.

The fae, in turn, responded.

The male fae kneeling in front of Nyx moved between his knees and nudged them apart, his hands searching for the ties that held his trousers in place. They moved hungrily, deliberately, egged on by the moan that escaped his prince's lips.

Caldamir took hold of my arm. "We should get going." His eyes met those of Armene and Tethys. "We've much to discuss."

Try as he might to pull me away, however, I remained rooted to the spot—too enthralled to move. I was hardly a blushing virgin, but I'd never seen anything like what was unfolding before me. It stirred that heat within me, the heat that pooled between my thighs and made a deep yearning tug at something primal.

Ties undone at last, Nyx's full length sprang forth with another moan. I barely had time to lay eyes on it in all its impressive glory before the dark-haired male leaned forward and took it up in his mouth. His lips parted to suck in the pink tip, his head moving forward and then back in time with Nyx's increasingly labored breaths.

The more I watched, the more impossible it was to look away—especially when Nyx's eyes opened again and found mine.

The female at his side undid one of the straps of her dress, exposing a perfect breast which she promptly brought to Nyx's lips. My own bodice felt suddenly tighter as the prince latched onto her and started to suckle like a newborn babe, one hand lifting up to knead her other breast while the second moved to dig into the hair atop the fae's head now bobbing rhythmically between his thighs.

All the while, his gaze remained fixed on me.

It wasn't just them, either—Nyx and his two consorts. In the matter of an instant, the entire hall had transformed into a writing mass of bodies. The air, once honeysuckle sweet, grew thick and cloying with the scent of sex.

Hands reached out to me, pulling at the hem of my skirts and the ties of my bodice.

The female at Nyx's side pulled free of his hungry lips and stepped forward to take my hand. Her dress, undone on both shoulders now, slipped to pool around her feet, fully exposing her willowy fae body.

She pulled me toward her out of Caldamir's grasp for an instant. Her body moved behind mine, nudging me closer to Nyx's sprawled figure.

"Join us," she whispered, placing her lips near to the back of my ear, her voice as thick as they honey dribbling from Nyx earlier. "We'll show you pleasure like you've never known before."

Emboldened by the female, the male kneeling before Nyx drew back, leaving the prince to groan in frustration as his manhood throbbed, wet and glistening, against his exposed chest.

He started to rise, eyes fixed on me too as he reached out, trying to pull me into his place. "We'll make it well worth your while."

Behind me, the female reached around to grope my chest, her fingers finding the laces of my gown and starting to undo them. Still, it wasn't until Nyx himself reached out a hand, breaths panting, that I nearly succumbed.

And I would have too, if it weren't for the sudden, stern hands that clamped down on both my arms and this time didn't let go.

"Come, Delph."

Caldamir pulled me out of the two fae's hands and whirled me around to face him, instead. "I can promise you, there's no worse time to make a deal with a fae than at Midsommar's end."

Behind me, Nyx let out a frustrated growl. "There you go, ruining everything, Caldamir."

Caldamir ignored him.

He was so close to me that I could see every line that furrowed the outer corner of his eyes, the only sign that he might be a single day older than me. This close, I could almost taste the wine he'd drunk still lingering on his breath.

He let go of my arms and instead held out a hand to me. "Come, Delph. Unless you really want to find yourself entrapped so soon."

Blame Midsommar, blame Nyx and the heat he'd stirred in me, or blame myself—I *wanted* to taste the wine he'd drunk. It was for that very reason that I only stared down at his hand for a moment before I took it reluctantly.

I didn't need a mirror to know my face had finally flushed red enough to be visible even here, in the fading darkness. I let

Caldamir drag me out of the hall, bodies parting at the last second to keep from being run over by him.

"I—I wasn't going to make a deal with them," I finally managed to splutter out when we spilled into the cooling air of the night. Outside the cloying air of the cathedral, my thoughts finally started to clear too. The moon had begun to rise, its silvery light casting a new set of shadows upon the ground.

"Are you so sure about that?"

It was Tethys.

He'd appeared a moment after us, and not without casting one last longing look through the door of the dining hall. From where we stood, we could still hear the sounds of coupling—the sighs and grunts and rhythmic motion of bodies joining together.

"Aw, lighten up love," he said, sidling up to my side and throwing a hand over my shoulder. "It's only natural to want to join in. It's a natural fae instinct."

"Shut. Up."

This time Caldamir's hands had balled up into fists at his sides. "End of discussion."

He pulled my hand again, and this time he wasn't gentle as he marched us back down the winding paths away from the crescendo of noise.

Tethys, it seemed, was not so ready to give in.

"No, Caldamir, it's not the end of discussion. You can't tell me you haven't been wondering the same thing."

"Just not now."

He pressed on, despite Caldamir's refusal to so much as look at him. "When, then? When it's already too late? Or have you forgotten already that you're not the only prince here with a duty to his people?"

Caldamir finally dropped my hand, but only so he could spin

on Tethys. I'd never seen someone move so quickly. In an instant, he was pressed up against the dark fae's chest, their eyes locking. Caldamir was several inches taller, but not enough to make Tethys so much as flinch back. If anything, he met Caldamir's rage with a fire of his own.

"You speak to me of duty?" Caldamir said. "What is it you think I'm trying to do? Why do you think I brought her here in the first place?"

Tethys still didn't back down. "I'm just saying … if she is what we think she is … then we need to act, fast."

"I have to agree with Tethys on this, as much as I hate to," Armene said, breaking his silence at last.

Caldamir took a step back, but he was hardly backing down. He angled his body between the two of them, as if trying to decide who presented the greater challenge.

"If you've been thinking the same thing I have," Armene continued, "then you know—you both know—this might be our only chance. We may never get another opportunity like this. It won't be long before others start to think the same thing we are."

Caldamir squared his jaw. "If they haven't already."

Neither Tethys nor Armene responded. The moon had grown higher now, its light catching on the fae's sharp, angry features.

"Is anyone going to tell me what's going on?" I asked in the silence of heavy breaths that followed. "Or are the three of you just going to fuck already?"

All three sets of eyes turned to me. The weight of it was enough to make me squirm.

"You should have some respect for your betters. Language like that—" Caldamir started, but I'd had enough.

"Won't matter if I'm dead," I said, squaring my own shoulders despite the way breath seemed to want to evade me. "I'm going to die soon, anyway. So, nothing matters. Right?"

Even Caldamir didn't have an immediate answer to that.

I pointed back toward the cathedral behind us. "What's stopping me from going in there and letting the Woodland Fae tear me apart?" All three of them flinched for a second, a sight that was strangely gratifying. "At least then, I'd die my own way. I could imagine worse ways to die."

"Unless," I said, moving to point at them instead while slowly taking a half step in their direction, "there's another reason you still need me alive. Something to do with whatever it is you're trying *way* too hard not to tell me."

Armene glanced over at Caldamir. "She deserves to know."

Much to all of our surprise, mine perhaps more than anyone, Caldamir agreed.

"Fine. We'll tell you everything."

CHAPTER FOURTEEN

I was interested to see the princes' quarters, but it wasn't far up the path that I realized we were headed back to mine. The other fae had started to wander out of the great hall, their drunken footsteps carrying them precariously through the swinging bridges crisscrossing overhead.

Caldamir shut the door as soon as all four of us had stepped inside the house, checking through the vines draped like curtains for any listening ears that might have wandered too close.

I crossed my arms over my chest. "This is getting more interesting by the second."

"We're only here because you asked for it," Caldamir reminded me, leaning up against the wall so he could keep an eye out the window with his peripherals. "Don't make me regret this."

I had half a mind to tell him just where he could shove his regrets, but for once, I managed to keep my mouth shut. I wasn't going to waste an opportunity to finally get some answers.

Armene had already sat backwards on the only chair, his legs sprawled out along either side as he leaned on his arms crossed over the high back. Tethys, meanwhile, had chosen the bed—but not in the traditional sense. He'd found a perch atop the back of the headboard, one foot propped up at his side, the other dangling over the edge.

Tethys saw my wandering gaze and leaned forward to pat one of the pillows beneath him. "Here's as good a place as any. Right where you belong, between my legs."

"Tethys …" Armene glared up at him through the dark strands of hair that'd made their way out of his bun.

I, in turn, ignored my aching feet and planted them firmly on the branches making up the floor.

Caldamir took that as the sign to begin.

"You know you were brought here to fulfill a deal, but that isn't the full truth of it."

My carefully measured breaths did nothing to stop my heartbeat from racing again.

"It's no secret to either realm that the fae haven't been visiting as often as we used to," Caldamir continued, "but there's a reason for that."

"The magic," I said, slowly. "There's something wrong with it."

"At least that's one thing we don't have to explain," Armene muttered. He'd taken on his own kind of vacant stare. He and Tethys both.

That's how I knew I wasn't going to like what Caldamir had to say next.

"The glamour operates on a system of what you call 'deals.' We'd hoped that completing one, something long-standing, would bring back a spark. But then when I saw you at Otto's estate, I had another idea."

"I knew it," Armene practically growled this time, his eyes

narrowed as he glared at Caldamir. "I *knew* you'd planned this all along."

"I'd hardly call it planned," Caldamir snapped back, before turning to me and squaring his shoulders. "I'd hoped it wouldn't come to this, but here we are. How much do you know about the fae realm?"

"Basically nothing," I admitted. "Everything I thought I knew has been wrong so far."

"Well then," he said, "I'll try to keep things short, but there are some things you need to know. A long time ago, there were more than four courts in Avarath. There were more than princes. We had a king."

"If you could call that wicked creature a king," Tethys muttered from his perch.

"Wicked or not, that king held the key to our glamour. Our magic. So, when he lost the war—"

"There was a fae war?" I asked, before biting my own tongue again, afraid that anything that came out of my mouth would ruin the chance I had of getting further answers.

"A great and terrible one," Armene answered. He was still staring ahead, but something flickered across his face as he said it. A haunted look, the look of memories he wished he could forget. "It nearly tore Avarath apart."

"In order to defeat the old king, one of the greater courts sealed him away so that only one of their own kind could re-awaken him. We were so blinded by the need to rebuild our kingdoms that we didn't realize what that meant until it was too late," Caldamir continued, his face fighting the same haunted expression. "When the war ended, faerie was left in ruins. We didn't blame the greater courts for abandoning it … not until we realized why. It wasn't until later—much later—that we started to understand the true consequences of what they'd done."

"The king acted like a conduit through which all glamour of this realm flowed. When we imprisoned him, new magic stopped entering Avarath. All that remained was what was here at the end of the war … and over the last couple centuries, it's been slowly dwindling away."

Caldamir fixed me with his stony glare. "The courts that abandoned Avarath knew that and left us here to slowly die with the glamour. And die we will. Slowly. Painfully. Unless we do something about it."

I didn't dare ask what he meant.

Tethys answered my unspoken question, anyway. "It was the death of a Starlight Fae who sealed him, so only the death of a Starlight Fae can release him."

All three of the fae were staring at me now.

"Please." My voice sounded small as I struggled to control it. As much as I wanted to know *everything,* I didn't want to waste time. I didn't want these three to descend back into fighting before I'd gotten any actual answers. "But what does this have to do with me?"

"I lied to you that first day we met," Caldamir said. "It wasn't your human blood that would make you hunted here in Avarath. We—*I*—brought you here, because there's a chance you're not just fae-marked. You're not cursed, Delphine. You're fae. Not just any fae … Starlight Fae. The last of their kind."

All three of their faces were stony now, serious—a far cry from the laugh that bubbled up and spilled over out of me, wracking my shoulders until I had to reach out and grab the wall for support.

"You find that funny?"

"I find it ridiculous," I said, only after I'd managed to regain my voice. I motioned down to my frame, utterly normal by human standards, but positively miniscule compared to even the smallest of fae. "White hair and black eyes don't make me fae."

"Not full fae, but a descendent, maybe," Caldamir said, something about his voice a little too careful. "Your village had a reason to believe you were fae-marked. The hair, the eyes … those are distinct markers of the Starlight Fae."

"Fae that spent altogether too much time in the human realm." Tethys' voice was the one that surprised me the most, however. For perhaps the first time since we'd met, there wasn't even a hint of some unspoken jest on his face. He stared determinedly at the wall directly in front of him, one hand absent-mindedly worrying at the rings on his fingers.

I shook my head, eyes narrowing. "No way. I'm not fae. It's not possible."

"Not all fae, no … but enough to count," Caldamir said.

"Maybe," Armene interjected. "Maybe enough to count."

I could feel the blood draining from my face, and with it, the room started to tilt around me. This time, when I reached for the wall, it wasn't to steady me from laughter.

"So, what you said earlier about me being unable to live in Avarath as a human, that was a lie?"

"No," Caldamir said. "If you are human, you'd die before we reached the Mountain Court."

The Mountain Court. Caldamir's kingdom.

"But if I'm fae … then I'll die after."

Caldamir paused for a moment before he nodded, however reluctantly.

I felt like I was going to be sick. "And this isn't another fear thing? Another cruel trick where you end up giving me a paper cut and calling it a sacrifice?"

"No," he said. "This time, the wording of the deal is very specific. It isn't only blood that must be spilled. It must be a life."

"Not just any life," I reminded him. "My life."

"Lord Otto never gave me up, did he?" I asked, suddenly. "You had something to do with that."

"Humans are easily convinced. By the time Lord Otto offered you up, he truly believed it to be his own idea."

I felt the slightest flash of guilt for the hatred I'd felt for Lord Otto when he'd showed up at my cottage, the deepest sense of cutting betrayal. He, like me, was just another victim of the fae.

"And I, more convincible than most." I shook my head. "Why should I believe anything any of you are saying?"

"It doesn't matter if you do. By this time tomorrow, we'll be well on our way to my court. You can come with us as a guest, or you can be brought as a prisoner. That, at least, is up to you."

Armene and Tethys both started at that.

"Tomorrow? Shouldn't we take some time to discuss things first? Consider our other options?" Armene asked.

Tethys nodded his head in agreement. "There's no need to be hasty. Like we all agreed earlier, Delph being fae changes everything."

"It's precisely for that reason that we *have* to leave right away," Caldamir shot back. "You think the other fae here haven't started to get the same idea? It won't be long before news of her spreads … and not all the fae will agree with us."

"Oh, I wonder why?" Tethys said, sarcasm heavy in his tone. "I know I'm really looking forward to having that king back on his throne again."

"I, more than any, have reason not to want him back," Caldamir said, fixing Tethys with what I was beginning to realize was his signature glare. "But I know this is the only way. So, unless either of you can come up with another way to bring the glamour back, then we leave at first light."

"This isn't the last we talk on this," Armene said, matching Caldamir's glare.

"And I don't expect it to be," Caldamir said. "There'll be plenty of time for talking on the road."

All three of their heads cocked to the side suddenly, but by the time I picked up on the rustling sound outside the door, Caldamir was already throwing it open to confront our eaves-dropper.

"Show yourself, Waylan."

The demon materialized beneath the stoop.

Caldamir shot Armene a dirty look. "Keep track of your pet, or I won't be held responsible for what happens the next time I find him creeping in places he shouldn't be."

The demon bared his fangs at Caldamir in what was supposed to be a smile, but it wasn't fooling anyone.

"That's enough for one night," Caldamir said, glancing back over at the rest of us. "If we're going to get an early start, we need to rest." He nodded at Armene as all three of them started getting back to their feet—which in Tethys' case meant jumping down onto the bed first, which he did with surprising grace. "Have your demon keep watch. Even the boldest of Nyx's fae won't dare approach with him guarding the girl."

"So, what happens now?"

All three of them stopped in the door, but Armene and Tethys looked to Caldamir to answer my question. Which he did.

"You make your choice. You ride in ropes, or you ride free. We have a duty to our people to fulfill. That has to come first."

"A duty that's dependent on me actually being fae," I said.

"Well then, if you're human, then none of this will matter anyway, now will it?"

That, at least, I couldn't argue.

CHAPTER FIFTEEN

FAE. THEY THOUGHT I WAS FAE.

It was the one thing worse than being cursed.

For all Caldamir's talk of me getting to choose my role as guest or prisoner, I sure felt like that decision had already been made for me.

The answers I'd been given weren't what I'd been hoping for, but they were something. It was enough to leave me pacing across the floor, my hands digging into the roots of the same hair that'd betrayed me. The same damned hair that had led to me being kidnapped by the fae in some insane attempt to save the same dying magic that had terrorized my world for over a millennium.

The same magic these fae princes were now trying to claim ran in my very veins.

The room around me was closing in with every step, the very air growing suffocating as it did when I first arrived. This time it wasn't the air, not in the strictest sense. But it still was Avarath. This place was smothering me, trying to squeeze the last bit of life from me with each moment I remained in it.

I couldn't bring myself to eat the food they'd brought to me —rations taken from the human world while they waited to see if I was fae or if I died. This way, they said I wouldn't at least be driven mad by hunger that couldn't be quenched after tasting faerie food.

No, this way, I'd just be driven mad by everything else.

I could see no way back to Alderia. No way back to Sol. No road that didn't end with my death here in the faerie realm. I should have known it was useless to imagine, even for a moment, anything otherwise. I'd known what I was giving up, agreeing to come here.

That knowledge did nothing to stop the crushing emptiness as the realization settled in a second time.

I fell back on the bed with a groan, only for Waylan to make an immediate tutting sound with his tongue from across the room. I sat up sharply, my face paling. I hadn't seen him come in, hadn't so much as heard a root rustle beneath his step.

"What's with the disappointment? I thought you'd be glad to see a *friend.*"

"I ... I ..." I considered lying to him for a moment, but then reconsidered. There was sarcasm, sure, in the way he used the term 'friend'... but then again, he was the closest thing I had here to one. Maybe it was because he was the only thing here that *wasn't* fae, and from the sound of what he told me earlier, probably had every reason to despise them as much as I did. So, I told him the truth.

"I wish I could have just a minute to myself," I admitted, pulling at the front of my bodice, already loosened as much as it could be and yet still felt like it was choking me. "I feel like I can't breathe here."

"You know, Armene would be very upset with me if you ran

away. I'd rather not have to deal with that situation, if it's all the same to you."

I went to roll over onto my stomach, ready to bury my face into the pillow and hope the exhaustion of the last two days would swallow me whole and take me away from this place. But then I had a better idea.

I narrowed my eyes up at Waylan. "You didn't exactly say no."

"I didn't think I could say 'no.' I have no say over what you do. I was told to guard the door, if I remember correctly, not you." He fixed me with a look that hid something wonderfully evil within. "The fae aren't the only ones who are … particular … with their words."

"I won't run away," I promised, sitting up suddenly. "I just need to breathe. I just need to remember I'm not dead. Not yet."

"You might as well be if you do run away," Waylan said by way of warning, but he did nothing to stop me when I stood and crossed to the window. The vines rustled gently in the evening air, the sweet scent drifting in from outside enticing me further. As if I needed any further invitation.

I did consider, for a moment, what it would be like to run away. Where would I go? Back to the bridge where we made our crossing?

There'd be no way for me to get back to Alderia, even if I did.

So, without any other place really to go, I set my mind on the one place I thought I might, at least, be able to once again catch my breath.

"You're my favorite, you know that?" I said, pausing with one foot swung over the sill. I glanced back once to the demon standing stoically guard at the door.

He bowed his head to me slightly. "As the creature here most likely to eat you if I was allowed, I take it as an honor."

I FINALLY UNDERSTOOD why they called this place the Pool of Indecision. I'd been warned of its effects, of the madness that would overtake me if I ventured into the dark, warm depths at its edge. More than a warning, I'd felt it.

I'd heard it.

Yet despite those warnings, I wanted to hear it again.

That was the second reason that drew me back to the pool. Almost as much as I longed for the clarity of lung my first plunge into it had given me, I wanted to hear the voice again.

Try as I might, I couldn't get the whisper of the pool out of my head. It had only uttered my name, but I felt as if there was something else it meant to say. Something meant for me.

Now that I knew this pool was made by the same fae that the princes claimed had blood running through my veins, I couldn't get it out of my head.

I half expected getting to the pool to be much more difficult, that the trees and roots would reach out to stop me, but something had changed in the court since the sun set on Midsommar's day. It had grown all too quiet. All too stiff. It was as if, with the setting of the sun, all the court had fallen into a dream-filled sleep. I still felt the ground beneath me breathing, it was just a touch further away. It was the moment the eyelids started to flutter before waking, but they never quite opened. The moment before you know you're about to let out a breath, a breath that never comes.

The tension only drove me forward.

It was surprisingly easy to pick my way over the bodies of the fae that had collapsed on their way back from the drunken feast. I guessed the pleasures of the great hall had finally gotten to them.

Once again, I was reminded of how little I knew of their kind. Caldamir, Armene, and Tethys might not look like the Woodland Fae ... like Nyx in all his splendid, graceful glory ... but they were still fae. They probably felt a tie to their world the way I felt a tie to mine.

And mine didn't reek of magic. The magic might be leaking out of Avarath, but it was still here, seeping out of every knot and hollow.

Yellow sunlight had given way to silver moonlight streaming into the pool. The way the trees aligned over this place made it so that no matter what time of day or night, some sort of light shined down into it in full. At night, however, even the clear teal middle of the pool was eerie.

That was to mention nothing of the blackness. It had seemed to grow since the day, reaching out its shapeless form further into the water. It quivered there, alive, waiting for me.

That almost-spoken secret still lingered at the forefront of my mind as I unlaced the bodice of my gown and left it hanging at the water's edge. I took several steps down, my feet feeling at the slippery surface as my skin grew accustomed to the freezing cold water staining the wood a dark brown.

It wasn't until I stood on the very last step that I pulled the shift from my head to drape over the end of the railing. Insurance, should I need it quickly.

The moment the water touched my skin this time, it was like starlight itself had erupted across my body. It tingled so fiercely it almost burned, stinging at the insides of my eyes until salty tears gathered in their corners when I emerged, spluttering, in the very middle of the pool.

It was hard not to believe, in that moment, that a pool like this could keep me alive until the next festival—human or not—

whatever the fae wanted to claim otherwise. More than that, it felt like it could keep me alive forever.

The water in the center was even more icy than it was in the daytime. My breath fogged in front of my face along the freezing surface, rolling in pale white tendrils toward the shadows refusing to be ignored.

That was the real reason I was there, after all—not only for the charmed water, but for the cursed.

Here, barely treading the freezing water, I was disappointed to hear not so much as a single syllable. Not that I could hear anything above my own chattering teeth, let alone a whisper.

"It only works when you're underneath."

My gasp nearly drowned me before I could turn to peer in the direction of the voice.

The gold of Tethys' eyes shone from the shadows long before the rest of him followed. He sat perched on a low-hanging branch by the edge of the pool, one leg dangling dangerously close to the inky black at its edge.

"What are you doing here?"

"Interesting question for you to be asking."

His eyes dropped down from mine to the crystal-clear water that did nothing to hide my nakedness beneath. I still instinctively dropped down a bit, as low as I could without swallowing more water than I already had.

Tethys' gaze made its way over to the stairs, where my shift hung like a ghost over the wooden banister.

"Oh my," he said, "I didn't think I'd get to see quite so much of you so soon."

His bluntness brought color to my cheeks as memories from earlier resurfaced in my mind. Tethys had been the most reluctant to leave Nyx's Midsommar revelry. Well … aside from me.

I would never have admitted it, of course, but if it weren't for

Caldamir's warning, I might have stayed. None of the persuasions of the other fae could have made me take my eyes off the Woodland prince.

Though for Tethys … I might've made an exception.

It wasn't until my eyes had drifted from Tethys' full lips to the defined lines of his upper chest, visible now above the loose neckline of the tunic tucked into his pants, that I realized what I was thinking.

What was I thinking? These were fae.

I'd be a fool to trust them with anything, let alone drool over them like some pathetic schoolgirl.

So, I averted my eyes, but not before Tethys saw.

Those eyes alit, glowing stronger than they were already, and before I could say anything he stood on the branch and stripped the rest of his clothes off in one fluid motion. It was impressive really, second only to the shape of his body in the brief moment I was able to see it before he dove into the pool at my side.

He didn't come up immediately. He stayed underneath the rippling surface, swimming a half circle around me with wide, skillful strokes.

When he did finally emerge, there was something wrong with his eyes.

For one moment, a thin milky film obscured their color. Before my heartbeat could consider quickening, however, the film pulled back.

And he grinned.

"You're even more beautiful than I imagined."

Something inside me seized up as I realized what he meant, my arms trying to snake protectively across my chest before I realized I needed them to keep my head above water.

"You bastard," I hissed, the slightest sound carrying across the surface as if it'd been shouted instead of whispered. "You can see underwater, can't you?"

"A perk of my court." Tethys let out a contented sigh and floated back up to tilt his head toward the stars. "My only regret is that it isn't daytime. Then, I'd have been able to see you better."

The rest of his body followed suit, the breadth of his torso breaching the surface to glitter in the moonlight. Only a thin film of water obscured his groin, not enough to hide the fact that even here, in the freezing water, his appendage remained impressive.

It was all I could do to keep from staring.

I was grateful for that same cold water, for any of the redness it might have dulled as it tried to spread to my cheeks again. I moved my strokes to carry me away from him, but Tethys just kept moving in his slow half circle, never drifting from me no matter how I tried to change my course.

"Be careful of the edges, unless you're certain."

I paused, pulling my eyes from him to glance over my shoulder. I hadn't realized how close I was getting to the edge until now, but I should have felt the way the water had grown less cold. I'd subconsciously thought it was just my body finally growing used to the temperature.

It was, instead, because I'd swam right up to the edge of that inky darkness.

"Certain of what?"

The water made little waves as I hastened to swim away from the black fingers snaking out toward me. I heard, in that moment, a dull far-off sound. It was indistinct, able to be dismissed if not for the whispers I'd heard earlier.

It was, of course, the sound of my own name.
Delphine.

"Underwater," Tethys said, from somewhere much closer than I expected. When I looked back from the dark water, I was met with the fae swimming close enough by my side to reach out and touch me. He moved through the water like a fish, every motion as natural and controlled as my own steps on land. I supposed it was to be expected from the prince of the Avarath Sea.

"If you want to hear what they have to say, you have to go under the water." He pointed down to the clear stretch of water beneath us, the reflected stars darting in and out between our own shifting shadows. "But you have to be careful. Some of the fae think the water here is cursed, that whatever it tells you down there will—"

"Drive me mad?" I finished for him, looking away only long enough to catch another glimpse at the rippling, black water. "You told me earlier, remember?"

My teeth had started to chatter in the colder water again. It was somehow even more freezing the second time around. All my muscles felt strained and stiff, my breath catching somewhere before it reached the bottom of my lungs. It was a small miracle Tethys understood anything I'd said between my short gasps for air.

"Why would you help me?" I asked, when I turned back to him.

"I don't know," he said, each word punctuated by a smaller stroke carrying him ever closer to me. "Maybe it's because I think everyone deserves to make that sort of decision for themselves. Or maybe it's because I like you."

"Why would you do that?" The question sounded stupid, but I was glad the cold made me blurt it out. I genuinely wanted to know, and not just because I kept finding myself having to remind myself to hate these fae.

He was close enough to touch me, and he did. He didn't reach out and grab me like I might've imagined. He was gentle. Soft. Surprisingly so.

His hand reached out of the water to trace the outline of my hair along my left temple. "Little human, I don't know."

His hand dropped back down to the surface of the water, and for just one second, he let it run a small circle around the top of my shoulder before pulling it away. "But I intend to find out."

I could feel the water changing course as it moved between our bodies.

We stayed like that, suspended as if flying for a long moment —hovering ever closer but never actually touching again. Tethys broke that moment with a smile, one so filled with mischief that it made me do the only thing I could think to escape before I was entirely and utterly lost in him.

I took his advice.

I turned away from Tethys and submerged, sinking below the freezing cold surface of the water. At first, I heard nothing but my own bubbles rising from my nose and corners of my mouth to burst up above.

Then I heard it, the same voice as before.

But it wasn't a whisper. It wasn't just my name.

"Delphine. We knew you'd be back."

CHAPTER SIXTEEN

My eyes flew open underwater at those words. I didn't have the benefit of Tethys' second eyelid, but it didn't take me long to start making out shapes in the midst of that darkness. Tiny lights popped up, stretching around the inside of that black water at the edge of the pool. Almost like stars.

The last great gift of the Starlight Court.

From within the starlit water, a new shape began to form. A blackness darker than all the rest began to move forward. The rounded shape of a head and shoulders strained at the line where the two waters met, but struggle as it may, it was never quite able to leave it.

"Come closer. There's something you need to know. Something only we can tell you."

The sound was surprisingly clear, unlike the bleary shapes my watering eyes were making out in the darkness.

I had no way to respond to the being—or phantom—and I was already running out of air. Part of me was afraid to surface. Afraid that the voice would disappear by the time I dove back down. Afraid that I wouldn't have the courage to dive again in the first place.

A curse supposedly waited for me in that inky blackness, one that the fae themselves feared. I was no stranger to curses, but this one made me pause. It was one thing to be cursed among humans, another among the creatures from which all curses sprung.

But then the voice spoke again, and any thoughts of turning away to surface disappeared, my need for breath suddenly not so urgent.

"There's another way out of Avarath."

This time when the darkness reached out to me, I reached back.

The moment I did, the very instant that the tips of my fingers grazed the ones beckoning to me, I was plunged into darkness.

It was unlike any darkness I'd known before.

I was weightless in it, floating in a void that wrapped around me like the tender caress of a mother with her newborn babe. All around me, those pinpricks of light pulsed with their own life.

I wasn't alone in this darkness, either.

That black shape grew larger, more defined until it formed the shape of a shadowed body. I couldn't make out its face, but I could somehow sense it meant no malice toward me.

How could it, in a place like this?

"Do you know why you were brought to Avarath, Delphine?"

I opened my mouth in an attempt to respond, to try to force something garbled through the water—only to find no water rushing in. I answered hesitantly at first, but my voice came out as crystal clear as the pool I had only begun to realize I no longer floated in.

"I have to die so the fae king can live. So the magic can come back."

"That's what we were afraid of." There was a darkness inside the voice too this time. Danger. "If you really want to save Avarath, you can't let that happen."

I turned slowly in the blackness, my outstretched arms unable to stop the slow spinning. Wherever I turned, the shadowed form remained in front of me, staring at me, staring *into* me.

For the first time, I felt something cold grab hold of me.

"But how am I supposed to stop that?" I asked, trying not to sound desperate. "I'm only human."

"Are you quite sure of that?"

I hesitated this time, turning over in the star-spinning blackness until I finally answered. There was no one here to lie to other than myself. This blackness had known my name before I spoke it. There was no telling what else it knew.

"I don't know anymore." I swallowed hard, only to find I couldn't, not from the lump that had formed in the back of my throat. "It doesn't matter, anyway. None of this does. I'm never going back to Alderia."

"Very little in life is certain," the voice said. Despite the darkness, I thought I made out its hand reaching out to me again. "But I can make you this promise. We can get you out. Stay alive, Delphine. Defy the princes, and we'll make sure you do not die in Avarath."

I reached out and took the hand.

The moment I did, the darkness started to recede and a panic welled up in me as quickly as any hope.

"How?" I asked, already feeling the space around me grow thicker. "How am I supposed to defy them?"

With each word, my voice grew more garbled. The shadow

receded into the stars, fading until it blinked out of existence without another word. The stars followed after.

The moment they disappeared, I was plunged back into icy moonlit waters.

WHEN I DID FINALLY surface in the pool again, it was with a gasp so loud I was surprised half the court didn't immediately come running. I coughed and spluttered, ignoring the water running into my eyes as my lungs dug deep for the air it had been deprived of.

Tethys swam just a few feet away, his face showing he was more than a little impressed.

"I'd just started to wonder if I needed to pull you out again."

I ignored his comment.

"Did you hear that?" I asked, between panting breaths. "Did you hear what they said?"

My muscles were cramped and stiff, barely able to keep my head bobbing above the surface of the water. It was hard to tell in the moonlight, but I had a feeling my skin was quickly turning the same shade of blue as the water.

Tethys stopped and looked down at me for a moment, as if realizing for the first time that I'd come to press myself up against his heated side. I only realized it then too, but I didn't care. I'd instinctively sought out the warmth, my body choosing immediate salvation over his eventual threat.

It was bold, but I felt bold.

After what I'd just been told, however vague, I had hope. For the first time since Caldamir arrived and announced my fate, I had a plan. A way out.

It was faint still, but it was something. And that was what I clung to.

That, and Tethys' shadow. His body was so hot that it warmed the water immediately surrounding him. It may have only been by a degree or two, but in the current freezing temperatures, it was enough to almost make me want to reach out and wrap my legs around him, removing any remaining space between us.

Almost.

"Silly girl," Tethys said after a moment, after he too had caught the breath that momentarily escaped him. "You have to actually go *into* the cursed water to hear what it has to say."

I blinked up at him out of confusion for a moment, somehow stopping myself from correcting him.

He hadn't seen me get dragged in.

Better that way, I realized. This was one of those secrets better left kept to myself.

"I … I decided I've had enough of curses," I spluttered, pretending for a moment to splash water into my eyes so I didn't have to meet his gaze. When I gasped to the surface again, I let a shiver wrack my body before nodding toward the stairs. "I think I've had enough of this freezing water, too."

"I could keep you warm you know, if you let me," Tethys said, his maddening grin making its return.

The water was cold enough that his offer was almost inviting.

Tethys swam by my side to the stairs, where I noticed the dark shadows around the edges of the pool seemed to have retreated a bit. I was too cold to care if he watched as I rose from the pool and reached for the dry shift to pull it back over my head. For once, I was grateful of the hot, sticky summer air. It would only be a few minutes before my shivering turned to quaking, and not long after that before my body finally agreed to still altogether.

If Tethys hadn't noticed the change in the water, too.

"Is it just me, or did the shadowy bits used to be bigger?"

My heart leapt up into my throat where it remained lodged. It was better for me if he continued to think I hadn't had any contact with the being in the pool. I doubted he and Caldamir would give me any freedom if they knew I'd been directly tasked with defying them—in exchange for the very thing they'd denied me.

My freedom.

"Oh? I didn't notice," I lied, praying internally that Tethys would just let it go.

He didn't.

"No," he said, that note of concern growing in his voice. "I *swear* it used to be bigger. That tree there used to dip right into it. I'm sure."

It was everything I could do not to show my obvious alarm. I tried to keep my breaths normal, measured.

"Is that so?"

He still didn't let it go. He started taking a step back into the water to take a closer look, but I couldn't let that happen.

I couldn't chance him getting suspicious. I'd been given a rare opportunity. I was under no illusions that I'd get another chance like this, a chance to do the impossible, to get back to Alderia.

So, I did the only thing I could think to distract him.

"Actually …" I said, suddenly turning back to face him. "Does that offer still stand?"

For a moment, Tethys only blinked his double eyelids back at me, confused. I banished any doubt of my intentions when I slowly, deliberately, moved the shift that hung in front of my naked body to hang it once again on the stair rail.

I stepped one foot back into the freezing water so that my head was now level with his.

"The offer to warm me," I whispered, leaning closer. Tethys stood stock still, unable—or unwilling—to move. "Unless, of course, you didn't mean what I think you did."

When Tethys did move, it was only to let out a long, slow breath. The heat of it warmed my face mere inches from his.

"I should warn you," he said, "I may be a prince, but I'm not so honorable as to turn you down."

This close, Tethys' breath was somehow salty like the sea, and his skin still glistened as if with tiny crystals. The gold in his ears reflected back onto his skin, casting tiny lights dancing across his jaw. A jaw so sharp it made my fingers itch to reach out and touch, if it only to see if it would make blood bloom across their surface.

With his one free hand, he brushed away a tangled strand of my hair that stubbornly clung to the side of my neck.

The heat of him burned deep into me, igniting a fire inside my core.

I took one more step down, further into the water, closer to him.

I blinked up at him for a moment, not at his eyes, but fixated on the lips that had come so close for a moment to hovering beside mine. I wondered what they would taste like, if they'd taste like the sea that Tethys carried with him. I swore, for a moment, that standing so close to him I could *feel* it. His body swayed ever so slightly against mine, his feet still standing on the deck of a long-forgotten ship.

I opened my mouth to tell him I'd changed my mind, that this was wrong, but I couldn't. I could have stopped it there. I had no doubt, honorable or not, that Tethys would have let me walk away.

But I didn't want to.

I wasn't in the habit of expecting gifts for my birthday, but after the one I'd just had, this time—I gave one to myself. I was still most likely to die in Avarath, promises of an inky black pool or not, but at least now I could say I didn't die without first tasting its charms.

There was no hesitation this time. No waiting to ask me questions, and certainly no waiting to allow me any more of my own.

His lips were just as I imagined. Soft and powerful as the sea. His hands moved around my waist, drawing my exposed body to his, lifting me up. They didn't stay there, either. They explored the flat of my lower back, the sharp inward curve of my waist, stopping only when they came to the shadow beneath my breasts.

My body ached for him. There was no denying it.

No denying him.

All I had to do was place my hands on his and pull them upwards for a new frenzy to overtake him. He needed no further invitation.

Tethys rose from the water in all his naked glory and swept me with him to the top of the steps. He dropped me, breathless, in the tangle of his forgotten clothes and clambered down on top of me, pausing only to remove each of his rings—one at a time—in careful, methodical movements. His eyes never left mine as they did. A flash of Nyx earlier came to mind, only for more need to flood my body.

I reached for him, trying to pull him in for another fevered kiss, but he stopped me short.

"Unless you want me losing one of these rings inside you,

you're going to have to be a little patient," he said. "But I promise you, it'll be well worth the wait."

And it was.

The moment he tucked the last of his rings into the pocket of the same jacket sprawled beneath us, Tethys shoved me down onto the flat of my back and crushed my lips beneath his. One hand supported his weight so he didn't crush the rest of me while the other, with the same tenacity as the tide, moved to nudge my knees apart.

No, not nudge, force.

He wasn't rough, but he wasn't gentle either. His hand moved with practiced precision, stroking the outside of my sex first in long, teasing lines, then moving inward to the swollen bud at its center and pressing harder, forming circles that coaxed a moan of pleasure from my lips.

He hadn't let the sound die in my throat before he turned it to a gasp by slipping a finger inside me. His teeth bit down on my lip until I let out another soft cry. Only then did he draw back his face from mine, and only enough to lock eyes with mine.

"There, just like that …" he whispered, panting. "I want to get a good look at you while I can. I want to see what your face looks like before I fuck you, because I can promise you—you won't be looking at me the same way after."

Another finger joined the first then, nudging further into me and hooking up to find a place inside me that made my sex pulse in response. I tightened around him, thighs clenching as I tried to hold back, only for Tethys to force them apart again.

"I can feel you're close," he grunted, lips parting. "Come for me. I'm not going to fit inside you until you do."

So, I did.

I couldn't have stopped it if I tried.

As soon as the wave of pleasure dulled, he rolled me onto my belly and pressed his hardened member to my opening. He dipped his head down so that his lips brushed first between my shoulder blades, then trailed across my shoulder until they were behind my ear.

"Tell me this isn't your first time. I wouldn't want to hurt you."

"It's not," I said, trying to steady my trembling lips. "There was another."

"Good," he said. "Now I'm going to make you forget him."

And he did. Both his hands moved to balance his body over me, steadying himself before he pushed the tip of himself inside.

He let out a soft grunt of his own pleasure, his panting breaths a measure of his carefully restrained power as he eased the rest of his length in inch by inch—or what of it would fit, anyway. It was only then that he began to allow himself to rock in an upwards circular motion, the shaft of him withdrawing and then pushing back faster each time.

I buried my face into the pile of clothes to muffle the involuntary gasp that followed each one of his strokes.

It wasn't my first time, sure, but in Tethys' hands, it might as well have been. He made my fumblings with Leofwin seem positively innocent compared to how he took me. He dominated over me, giving pleasure as much as he took it.

As soon as I'd been stretched enough to take him in, he spread my legs wider, pushing my hips further apart before he began truly thrusting.

The sheer size of him should have hurt, but my body welcomed him with another shaking orgasm instead. It wracked my body, building in my core until it exploded out of me with quivering thighs and shaking knees.

Not just me, either.

Tethys plunged in with a final, fierce burst of passion before he met his own release. I knew when he met it from the way his hands dug into the earth on either side of me, soil and dried leaves forced between his curling fingers as a feral growl rumbled from the back of his throat.

Where I collapsed, exhausted, to the ground—he was practically writhing with newfound energy when he took me into his arms.

No matter how still he lay, it was like something inside him constantly begged to move. Just as he made love, his body rocked with that energy. It was a rhythmic, unceasing motion that had his hands moving to slide between my slick thighs again by the time I'd barely caught my breath.

"Did I make good on my promise?"

"Promise?" I asked, rolling over to look up at him. He was all I saw, all that consumed my thoughts until they slowly, ever so slowly, began to return to me. I wished they wouldn't. I wished I could forget them, forever, and only lay here in Tethys' arms. Lay here where I felt safe, even if here, in his arms, was really the most dangerous place a human could be.

And for me in particular—human or fae—more dangerous still.

"My promise to warm you," he reminded me, salted lips moving to tease me with a kiss on the corner of mine. "Or do you require further fire in your belly?"

His hand dove the rest of the way up to bury itself between my legs again, his fingers teasing much like his lips had moments earlier.

I was tempted to take him up on the second offer, to forget again everything else but the feel of us wrapped together. But that wasn't going to happen.

Not when Tethys happened to look up from me to spot something up ahead that made him swear.

"The sun'll rise soon," he said, scrambling to get back to his feet. "I hope you know I'd enjoy nothing more than to lay with you here until then, but I'd hate to make Caldamir jealous before we've even left."

"Jealous? Caldamir?" I let out a scoff. "He doesn't seem the type capable of the emotion."

Tethys shot me a sideways glance. "I think you'd be surprised what we're all capable of."

He offered me no chance to respond, in its place offering a hand up instead. Between the two of us, we were soon laced up and brushed down enough to start the short trek back without arousing too much suspicion.

I, meanwhile, was already dreading the look on Waylan's face when he saw what I'd already managed to do to my hair.

"Let's keep this little excursion to ourselves," Tethys said as we walked back toward the edge of the inner forest. We paused for a moment and looked at the way the moonlight caught on the edges of the trees overhead. The humming that had filled the air earlier and faded almost entirely away. The magic was there, but it was buried deep down.

Midsommar had come and past, and with it, the glamour had retreated.

"What?" I asked, emboldened by the sight of Waylan peeking out of the window up ahead. "Really that eager not to tell Caldamir about what we did back there?"

Tethys let out a small breath. "You're not subtle at all, you know that?"

"It's one of my strong points."

"Yeah well, I'm even less eager to tell him I let you back into the pool," he said, hands still shoving ring after ring onto his fingers from the depths of his many pockets. He stopped me though, before we parted ways. "I hope I won't come to regret that. I shouldn't have told you what I did. Caldamir would skin me alive for that. But I'm glad you didn't go into the blackness. It … wouldn't have been good for any of us if you'd touched it."

What I didn't tell Tethys, however, was that he was worried about the wrong thing. I hadn't just touched the blackness—I'd made a deal with it.

Caldamir had warned me of this, or tried to, anyway. Not all deals were signed with contracts, neither was it always obvious they were deals at all. At least this time it was clear. I didn't need to see the details of what I'd just agreed to in writing to know a deal was exactly what it was.

By the time the two of us left, I was the only one who'd looked back at the pool.

The only one who'd seen that the black water had not only receded, it'd disappeared completely.

CHAPTER SEVENTEEN

There were a thousand reasons why the next few hours my mind fought back sleep.

Against all odds, all warnings, all precedents—I'd been told there *was* a way back to Alderia after all. A way back to Sol.

It was foolish to think I'd be welcomed into my village with open arms, but I didn't care. If I survived Avarath long enough to get back, I could survive anything. I *would* survive anything. I'd never take that blessed normalcy—cursed or not—for granted again.

I did eventually fall into a dream-filled slumber, one that made it all too difficult to wake when the time came.

It was Waylan who finally forced me to rise from my bed, long after Caldamir had started threatening to tie me up and throw me over the back of his mare himself and be done with it. I had half a mind to let him this time, if only out of spite, until the demon's lizard-like skin appeared in my face.

"He's serious, you know," he said, solemnly. "Dangerous precedent to set. And here I was thinking you were a fighter."

I let out a groan, but reluctantly sat up. My hair had dried wet, turning into another bird's nest of a mat at the back of my head. The sight of it made Waylan's hands twitch toward the brush he'd already packed in the bag slung over his shoulder. *That* was what finally made me leap out of bed and start pulling my dress back on.

I'd managed to avoid it last night, but I wouldn't put myself through that again. Not now. Not willingly.

I'd barely pulled the top of the bodice down over the sheer part of my chemise before Caldamir burst through the door, color staining his cheeks the same hue as the sky behind him. The sun had barely begun to rise, still sitting low enough not to break through the line of trees that surrounded the court.

Behind him, on the ground, Armene already sat on a massive black stallion with hair that matched his own in both color and coarseness. Tethys was fiddling with the reins of a smaller, dappled mare that had a flighty look about her. Her eyes rolled in her sockets, and with each breath that flared her nostrils, so did a set of gills that cut behind the creature's jaw.

Caldamir's mare Rynn was there too, but this time she'd been saddled differently. I knew immediately what the longer leather seat meant.

"What, you don't trust me to ride on my own?"

"I don't trust you for anything," Caldamir said, mirroring a similar sentiment I'd found myself expressing all too recently. "I've been honest with you already. That should be more than enough."

He eyed Waylan for a moment, glanced over the room, and since I apparently wasn't moving fast enough already, grabbed me by the wrist and starting pulling me out and down the stairs after him. It was all I could do to hold the laces of my gown together to keep it from flying apart.

"Can't you wait just a minute?"

"No. We should be going before the rest of the court wakes. There'd be more than a few fae who'd rather not see our journey succeed."

Just like the creature in the pool.

I stumbled back, my hand somehow slipping out of Caldamir's. He grasped at air in the moment my hand left his, as if he'd forgotten how much smaller I was than he.

"Why not? Don't all the fae want your precious glamour back?"

He didn't waste time reaching for me again, but I was too fast for him. I dodged out of his way and back a step toward the house behind me.

"Now is not the time for this," he said, voice low. The third time he held out his hand palm up, though he was practically twitching to grab me.

"I could scream, you know," I said, "alert the whole court. Then it'd be a lot harder for us to slip away."

"If we promise to tell you on the ride, will you just get on the damn horse?"

For one second, I let my eyes lift to roam the sleeping court up above. Soon, I was sure the revelers from the night before would be waking—or maybe not. I wasn't sure if there was such a thing as fae hangovers, though from the wine and revelry of the night before, it'd certainly be warranted.

I'd seen the hunger in the fae's eyes before, I'd sensed their power, felt their lust firsthand. I didn't think I'd like to be on the receiving end of their hatred, whatever the reason. At least Caldamir and the others needed me alive, for now. They wouldn't kill me right away, and that was something. That was more than something. It was insurance. It gave me a chance, something that staying here any longer couldn't guarantee.

The creature in the pool had promised to get me out of here if only I stayed alive. I'd been told to defy the princes, but surely, that could wait. For now, I needed their protection.

"Fine." I reached out my hand to Caldamir.

The moment he took it, he pulled me forward sharply and hoisted me up onto the back of Rynn in one fell swoop. He rose up behind me in the saddle, his body melding into the back of mine. His thighs were huge, spread on either side of my hips, cradling me so that I probably didn't need to hold on to the front horn for support. With Caldamir at my back, there was no chance of falling. Not unless he did first.

No chance of slipping away either.

"And Waylan—"

"Stop worrying about the demon," Armene said, pulling up beside us. "He'll meet us whenever we stop. They have their own way of traveling."

True to his word, Waylan was already gone. Though not before, I discovered, he'd somehow placed the brush in my lap without me noticing. I'd never felt so threatened by something so mundane in my life. By the time our three horses had passed through the gate and out onto the narrow path winding around the court, my hair didn't have so much as a snarl—I'd made sure of it.

If I was somehow going to make it out of this whole thing alive, it wasn't just the fae I was going to have to watch out for. Though, from the way the princes rode out of the court with heads bowed and necks swiveling to look over their shoulders at every snapping twig, the fae might be a bigger threat than I thought.

These were Nyx's people, the same fae that had welcomed us into their court only yesterday. I supposed things had changed since then. For me to stay alive, it wasn't Caldamir, Armene, and Tethys that presented the most immediate threat.

So, with that in mind, I stayed silent. I ducked my head when they did, held my breath when I heard them holding theirs, sat in stillness when all around me stopped moving.

We rode in this tense silence until the court had long since dropped away behind us and the little brook had grown into a broad stream. The water flowed in steady rivulets between thick, slippery stones. Sometimes the horses ventured into it, letting their hooves grind into the stones and the water splash up onto their knees.

We stopped eventually, the princes dismounting one at a time to splash their faces with water and refill the flasks at their hips. Gnats buzzed heavily in the air, but I noticed no one reaching for them—not even to bat them out of the way.

I guess Nyx had gotten to Caldamir in the end.

The horses bickered amongst themselves, mostly in their own language of sighs and sniffs, punctuated occasionally by the most disturbing kind of human laugh. It only sounded human against the background of their whinnies. On its own, it was the kind of sound that might illicit nightmares instead of a swat on the head by the back of Caldamir's hand.

"Wait too long, and this happens every time," he said, shaking his head to match his mares as he slid her bridle back into place after a particularly long rest. She'd given him the runaround for the last ten minutes, avoiding being re-saddled until the very last minute. The bridle she now reluctantly took from him wasn't an ordinary bridle with a bit, it was more of a simple leather contraption meant to give a gentle tug in the right direction. Explained how she was able to speak so clearly—when she chose to.

The last thing Caldamir did before we started up again was kick one of the wayward rocks turned over by the horses back into its place at the edge of the stream.

"Never can be too careful," Caldamir said, finally swinging one leg back up onto the mare and up behind me. I'd grown so used to the feel of him already that I melted back into the shape of his hard stomach before I realized what I was doing. By then, it was already too late.

I shifted uncomfortably in the saddle, all too aware of the press of the fae's body up against mine. I'd assumed at first that Caldamir's beauty was due to his kind's glamour, that it was another tool in his arsenal to lie and deceive. It felt all too real now to be any kind of magic.

As soon as Caldamir had stopped squirming, each movement giving me too vividly a picture of what lay beneath his fine silks, I was more than ready for a distraction.

"So, now you'll explain, right? Tell me why we had to sneak out of there like common criminals."

"Nope."

Caldamir's tone was so matter of fact, I thought for a moment that I'd heard him wrong. Right up until I felt his arm tighten a bit around me and he leaned in to speak into my ear, the tingle of it making a kind of electricity alight at the base of my skull. "I'm not telling you anything."

I jerked away. "I knew I shouldn't have trusted you. You tricked me!"

"I don't trust you. You don't trust me. Now we're even."

The horse swayed beneath us in a way that I swore was something akin to a belly laugh. Rynn tried to cover her snort with a whinny, but I knew better and dug one of my heels into her side in retaliation.

She let out another snort, eye rolling back just to narrow itself at me.

I ignored her.

"I'd hardly call it that," I said to Caldamir. "It's not the same."

"But oh, it is. Let this be a lesson, Delphine of Alderia. Never agree to anything with a fae unless there's a deal."

I kept my face forward and my voice even. "Right, and never make a deal with a fae."

"Ah see, you're learning."

The slightest smile pulled at the corner of my mouth.

If only he knew.

CHAPTER EIGHTEEN

I MIGHT NOT HAVE GOTTEN A STRAIGHT ANSWER OUT OF CALDAMIR, but the question broke the uneasy silence that had stretched out for far too long. The princes' banter made the hours pass quicker after that, until the sun had started to set directly in front of our eyes.

The same magical quality of the Midsommar night wasn't there, but a glimmer of it still remained. It was crazy to me how quickly I'd grown used to the magic of the forest, how soon it became so normal that it faded into just another forest to me. Compared to those we had back home, this place was a wonderland. The trees still towered over us like great monsters guarding the tightly winding path. Birds in brilliant colors flitted overhead. The stream bubbled in its narrow confines.

There was an undeniable hope in the air, and more than anything, that was what disturbed me. All throughout the day, I'd caught all three men sneaking glances at me from time to time. I couldn't see Caldamir's face, but I could feel the way his breaths caught, the way his heartbeat quickened … even the way his cock grew excited, swelling against my lower back every so often until he'd managed to get himself back under control.

With Armene, it was different. Guilt was the first expression to cross his face each time I caught him looking at me. Guilt for taking me. Then guilt for the fact that it didn't change the color that rose to his cheeks. An anticipation. If it wasn't my life they planned to exchange for their magic, I'd understand.

Tethys too, had his own complicated look when I caught him staring.

Most of the time, Tethys' face remained the same—as if he was thinking of a secret he just remembered, something he had no intention of telling anybody. It was the look of someone dangling something invisible in front of you, something only he knows of … and yet he knows you'd kill to be let in on too.

This time, I was in on the secret. We both were.

But once I caught him looking, his face peering over at me from between two trees that had separated us in the curving path, it was a far more pensive look that'd taken over.

It was gone as soon as it came, flickering away the moment he realized he'd been caught. In that moment, however brief, I missed the curve of the smirk on his lips. Tethys' face was made for mirth, not the conflicted, almost sad look I'd caught him sending my way.

If it weren't for Caldamir's body supporting mine, I would have long since needed to stop for the night by the time we actually did. By the time Caldamir called for us to halt again, this time to make camp, I'd given up trying not to lean on him and had practically already fallen asleep against the solid wall of his chest.

It was for that reason that I didn't hear the first sound, the first sign that something was amiss. I was jostled out of my half-dream state with the unceremonious disappearance of the support behind my back as Caldamir dropped to his feet and started unloading the bags.

I didn't miss the second sign, however. While the fae were busy unloading their packs, I'd taken to lazily scanning the surrounding forest. Everything about Avarath felt like I was looking the wrong way into a mirror. It was eerily similar to my world, but everything was off somehow. It was more than the appearance, it was the scent, the feel, the very tingle of the air.

I could only imagine this world before the glamour had drawn back.

It was as I was watching that I saw it—a shadow flickering through the trees. It was at the very end of my line of sight, just far enough to make me wonder if I'd seen it at all, or if I'd imagined it.

I didn't imagine the sound, though. Nor did I imagine the cracking of branches coming from the same direction a moment later, or the way the birds alit, their discontented squawking ringing through the forest.

"Caldamir   "

He was at my side in an instant.

"What is it?"

The concern on his face was almost charming, right up until my hand lifted to point into the forest.

"Something's following us."

All three fae—Caldamir, Armene, and Tethys—sprang into immediate action.

While Armene and Tethys drew their weapons, Caldamir pulled me down from Rynn's back and instructed me to stay down. The three horses moved in to huddle around me, their massive sides like great living walls.

Caldamir grabbed a longsword and went to stand alongside Armene's hammer and Tethys' double blades. The rustling

came again, a little closer this time—but from the opposite
direction. No sooner had the boys whirled to face it, however,
then something else made a noise, this time to their left. Then
the right.

Each time it drew closer, moving faster than any one of them
could turn to face it.

"Protect Delph," Caldamir ordered, and all three of them
moved to surround the horses, backs facing in toward the center.
"It sounds like a fiend ... maybe more than one."

A fiend. I'd been told stories of the creatures back in Alderia.
They were the nightmares of the nightmare realm, creatures of
supernatural strength, size, and intelligence hell-bent on destruction. They'd ridden with fae on their first arrival to our lands,
trumpeted the warring courts with flashing teeth and claws that
could rip a human to shreds in a single swipe.

But like the fae, fiends had long since fallen into myth. Before
the high fae stopped arriving, the fiends had long since stopped
crossing between worlds.

I crouched down to peer out from between the horses' legs,
but the underbrush was too thick to see what the fae were
looking at beyond. All I could see was their tensed shoulders
rising, their hands gripping their weapons, and then—with the
growing sound of something crashing ever closer—everything
suddenly dropping back down to their sides as a familiar voice
rung out from between the trees.

"Did you miss me?"

It was Nyx.

"I nearly shit myself for that?" Rynn muttered, low enough
that the Woodland prince didn't seem to hear—but he *did* hear
the giggle I had to stifle between my fingers.

Tethys' mare flared her nostrils and let out a short sigh.
"Almost? I actually did."

"Shut up," I hissed at them, already struggling to straighten back up to my feet. "You're going to get me in trouble."

"You mean more than you already are?"

It was the first time I'd heard Armene's stallion speak. He looked at me with doleful eyes as he took a graceful step forward, clearing a path for me to break out of their formation. He had a solemn look about him, much like his owner.

Once again, the Woodland prince struck me dumb with his beauty.

Nyx was standing at the edge of the path, a broad, child-like smile spread across his face. He stood, arms wide, as the last of the princes lowered their weapons. He carried with him the glow of sunlight in his hair and on his skin, even when the sun was barely visible above the horizon.

The other fae, especially Caldamir, didn't match his excitement.

"We could have killed you," Caldamir said.

"With those toys? Here, in my forest?" Nyx's eyes shone as he pointed back over his shoulder toward another fae emerging through the woods. "Maybe you could have, if you had my bow."

"A bow he made *me* carry, mind you."

I was taken aback by the voice. I'd thought the massive fae emerging behind him was a male at first, given the towering, broad stature—but upon further inspection, I was wrong. It was also apparent she was *not* a Woodland Fae, not from the heavy armor she wore and the hardened look in her eyes. She didn't look like she spent the majority of her days lounging about in the treetops and her nights rolling around in their roots.

She looked like Caldamir. She looked like a warrior.

She towered above all the other fae, intimidating right up until the moment she locked eyes with Caldamir. She dropped down to one knee then, head bowing as the many weapons strapped to her back made enough noise to draw any creatures or fae that might have been lurking in the forest straight to us.

"My prince."

An odd expression crossed Caldamir's face. "Tallulah. I didn't call for you."

She straightened up, face shining at his recognition. "You didn't need to. I've come to escort you back to the Mountain Court. Your people need you."

Caldamir chewed on the inside of his cheek. "We're already headed that way."

"Are you?" She didn't mean to sound facetious I realized, as her head swiveled around the forest—only for her steely gaze to settle on me.

"What's that?"

Caldamir let out a sigh. He held out a hand toward me, palm open.

"This is Delphine. She'll be traveling with us back to court."

Tallulah's eyes were narrowed at him when she looked back. "What's wrong with her? She doesn't look like she's going to make it back to court."

"And as you've probably guessed," he said to me, ignoring Tallulah entirely, "this is my personal guard."

"Yes, that's right. The guard who's supposed to stay with you, not be left twiddling her thumbs as you go off to—where was it this time?"

No one answered her right away, so she turned back to me. "Where was it he got you?"

"Alderia."

Her eyes practically bugged out of her skull. When she whirled back on Caldamir and the others, even Nyx's grin dimmed a little, especially when her gaze finally settled on him.

"You sent him to the human realm? And for what? Do you have any idea what could've happened?"

Her hand tightened on the strap holding up the many weapons attached to her.

"Do I need to remind you who you're speaking to?" Caldamir asked.

"I'm very well aware of who the selfish man-children in front of me are," she snapped back. All four of them shrunk a little in their boots. "You all have a duty to your kingdoms. You're the ones who need reminders of who you are." She finally turned back to Caldamir, her body sinking noisily and less gracefully than I'd expect of a fae, back down to one knee.

"I will follow you to the ends of the earth, my lord. I am your sworn protector. But you have to let me protect you."

"If you want to protect me," Caldamir said, "then you should protect Delph." He stepped back as all eyes turned back to me. "She's the one who holds our future now."

Tallulah's face screwed up. "Surely not. A puny human like her?"

"These are trying times."

She looked me over again, the doubt only deepening on her face. "I'll say."

"Still, not nearly as trying as it will be if the magic keeps draining away. You think we have trouble holding power now? Just imagine."

"I imagine it every day," Tallulah said, solemnly. "I imagine it each time I put on my armor, each time I remember when once a single swipe of my blade would cut a fae in half."

She looked down at the weapon in her hand, as if for a moment she was considering hurling it off between the trees. "Now it takes three."

I swallowed, hard.

"Well, now," Nyx called out, his feet shifting uncomfortably beneath him as if he'd not been the center of attention for too long, "if we're all quite certain we're on the same side … mightn't we want to get moving?"

"Actually," Caldamir said, shooting the Woodland Fae a look of annoyance. "We were just settling down for the night."

"Settling down? But … but you've hardly gotten started."

For a moment, the other three princes stared at him in confusion, until suddenly Tethys let out a frustrated sigh. He'd climbed up to the bottom branches of one of the trees, his gaze turned steadily behind him.

"It's the Woodland Court. We never left it."

True to his word, when I looked between the trees carefully now, I could make it out too. It was faint, hidden in the dense leaves of the forest, but it was there—the great wall of trees surrounding Nyx's court.

My head started to spin. We'd left the court behind hours ago. *A whole day.* I'd been sure of it.

We should've been miles and miles away from the court, not barely outside it.

But then, there *were* signs. The brook, most notably. I should have noticed something was awry when it had narrowed back down to a bare stream trickling alongside us.

Caldamir swore and Armene covered the top part of his face with one hand, as if shading himself from the discouraging sight. Nyx was the only one among us who looked completely unfazed.

"See? What would you do without me? Now hurry up. We wouldn't want to waste an entire day."

"Spoken like someone who didn't spend that whole day traipsing in one, gigantic circle," Tethys said through clenched teeth.

"You're right. I was far more productive than that."

Nyx stuck a couple fingers between his lips, and out of the forest behind him came two horses and a mule. All three were saddled and hanging with bags of fresh fruits so ripe, I swore I could smell them from where I stood.

Too bad I was still resigned to eating little more than stale bread brought from the human realm.

The horses were for Nyx and Tallulah, but the mule, it seemed was saddled for me. I'd grown so used to riding behind Caldamir that I was almost disappointed to discover I'd be riding on my own from here on out.

The last thing I was going to do was let onto this fact, however.

"Come on now," I said, reaching forward to touch the mules' bristly nose, hoping he didn't sense my secret disappointment. "What should I call you?"

"That one's dumb," Tallulah said, interrupting me as she hoisted herself up onto the back of her own mare. The horse let out a disgruntled sound and tilted its head back to nuzzle at the shape of the many weapons still strapped across the guard's back.

"Oh, shut up," she hissed at the horse, but still promptly pulled two massive maces off her back and shoved them into my arms.

I caught one, but the other fell to the ground, nearly crushing my foot in the process.

Not that I could have caught it. The first was already bowing me under the weight.

"Careful with that," Tallulah said. "Those are made of the finest metals the Mountain Court can forge. I've known fae able to cleave stone with it, to say nothing of what it can do to one of us."

Tallulah saw the startled look on my face, I know she saw, but she just tugged on her horse's reins and trotted forward to discuss battle plans with an ever-more-annoyed Caldamir.

I struggled to get the first mace into the mule's saddlebags, but the second one was absolutely hopeless. Every time I managed to get the mace up off the ground, already a feat in and of itself, the mule stepped forward at the last minute so that instead of dropping into the second saddlebag, it thudded to the ground gradually closer to my toes each time.

It was Nyx who finally dropped from his saddle as he passed in the procession, soundless and with the grace of a gentle breeze, to pick the mace up and slip it in successfully—all while holding the mule firmly in place. It looked no more difficult than if he had stopped to pick up a leaf.

Our eyes met for a moment, before he climbed up into his own saddle. A pink blush rose in his cheeks, and with a shy flutter of lashes far too long for any man to have the right to be in possession of, he nudged his horse forward to rejoin Caldamir and Tallulah still arguing about plans up ahead.

"This stupid forest," Caldamir was saying. "It turned us around. Made us waste an entire day."

Nyx had nearly made it to their sides, but Caldamir's comment left him distracted a moment.

"And you said all the magic was gone." Nyx stopped, one hand reaching out to rest lovingly on the trunk of a young sapling. "But my forest still holds on."

The tree rustled at his touch, but what he didn't see was that the moment he let go and rode forward, the tree slumped a little. A few leaves browned and fell from the top, drifting down in slow, sad circles to the ground.

"How he manages to lead a court is beyond me," Armene

said as he rode up behind me. Tethys lingered still a few paces behind.

Unless I was mistaken, he was watching me.

For all his talk of Caldamir being the jealous one, too.

I'd just managed to settle into the mule's worn saddle myself, but it still took another couple moments to get the thing to start moving. He ignored my gentle nudges until I was forced to go less gently, only for the creature to nearly throw me off when he finally lurched into motion.

Armene was kind enough not to comment on my rough riding. He pulled back up to my side, the horse and mule barely fitting side by side on the path.

Now that Tallulah had settled in at Caldamir's side, a new question begged to be answered.

"I thought I'd heard her wrong before, but is it true, then? You can actually kill a fae with a sword?"

Armene cast me a sidelong glance. "If you had the right one. But even our weapons would be useless in your hands. It takes a great deal of skill—not to mention strength—to kill a fae. Right weapon or not."

"Are you trying to insinuate something?"

"Not at all," Armene said. "Just giving you a little friendly advice. Here, if you want to be useful, take this. It'll be a far more productive tool in your hands."

With that, he tossed me a flint. "And before you ask, no … trying to burn a fae to death isn't going to work very well, either."

I wrinkled up my nose at him, not that he saw it, and asked another question that'd been hounding me ever since we left the Woodland Court. "Where's your demon, Waylan? Wasn't he supposed to join us?"

Armene pressed his lips together. "Probably went on ahead to Caldamir's court." He sucked on his cheeks for a moment, his voice dropping to a grumble. "Use a single wrong word with that demon, a single word, and he takes advantage of it every time."

I was the last one to complain. It was that very thing that had given me the ability to slip back to the pool. It gave me the ability to make a deal—and with it, regain the possibility of getting out of Avarath.

However slim that possibility was.

CHAPTER NINETEEN

With Nyx among our party, I swore the forest moved right alongside us. By the time we made camp that night, my flint quickly lighting a roaring fire with the dry leaves for kindling, we'd ventured further in those last few hours than we had the entire day before.

Like Nyx had said, not *all* the magic of Avarath had faded yet.

Not enough to keep the forest from reacting to its prince's presence.

Not enough to keep from poisoning me in my sleep, either.

I felt the fae's concern before I felt it for myself. I woke in a tangle of my own skirts, the pallet having done little to prevent the cramps that made me groan with every waking movement, or the ache that exploded in my head when I sat up. The sun had barely begun to rise, but the birds had wasted no time swooping low overhead with their morning song.

Nearly a dozen of them had found Nyx in the dim light, pecking at him gently until his eyes fluttered open and they took off to hover around him, offering him small gifts of seeds and berries. Each one of these he took with a grateful half bow, the bird in question taking off with a delighted noise—doubtlessly to seek out new offerings.

Nyx didn't see me watching until the last of them, a hummingbird no bigger than the tip of my thumb, buzzed off in a blur of red and turquoise feathers, a final drop of honey still lingering on the tip of the prince's tongue.

He was a picture, a window into a dream I wasn't entirely sure I'd awakened from. Sleep pulled heavily on my eyelids, and vision, still blurred and dimmed with rapid blinking, gave everything a soft, feathered appearance.

I was jealous, in that moment, of Nyx. I fixated on the drop of golden liquid, imagined the sweetness, the stickiness—but more than that, I was jealous of what he was.

He wasn't a monster, not in this realm. I was merely rumored to look like one of these creatures, and I'd been ostracized and hated for it. But here one of them was, an actual, living fae, and nature itself treated him like a god.

Nyx caught me staring, and before I could figure out for sure if what I saw was even real or dream, he suddenly did that part for me. It had to be a dream, because he leaned forward, grabbed me ever so gently by the shoulders, and kissed me.

His lips were soft and sweet, but nothing compared to the honey on the tongue he pressed to mingle with my own. It was hot and thick, brought fresh from whatever hive the humming-bird had been brave enough to rob.

I should've pulled back, should've grabbed whatever weapon was closest to me and used it to shove him off of me. But it was a dream, after all.

So, I didn't.

I kissed him back. I let my tongue savor the taste of him, the feel of him.

His lips pressed harder, his tongue seeking mine out long after the honey had melted away between us. We would have stayed this way longer if it weren't for the rustle of other bodies moving, the sounds of them stirring that roused my own consciousness back to life.

I drew back from Nyx, spluttering, eyes wide and hands flying up to clamp over my mouth. The dreamy, soft-focused quality of the air sharpened in one instant as I was dragged back to reality—and all the pain that came with it.

Our palettes had been laid together with the rest of the fae's beds spread out around us. Weapons, drawn and ready, were laid at each one of our sides, filling the small gaps where the grass and rocks peeked out around the sparse bedding. The moment I realized I was not dreaming, but was actually kissing Nyx, the gorgeous prince of the very woods that surrounded us, I was so startled that I fell back onto one of the weapons closest to me.

It was, unfortunately, not one of the maces pawned off to me, but rather one of Tethys' knives. They were too short to be called swords, but too long to be simple knives. They were also too sharp.

Just resting my hand on one of the blades for a second left a long gash along the back of my hand. It was far deeper than the cut that had spilled my blood at the ritual, the line of it severing a vein all too happy to spill a head-spinning amount of blood in an instant.

I sucked in a gasp of breath at the pain, which had the rest of the party leaping to their feet in an instant. Their first glance at me did them no favors, with their sleep-blind eyes catching me with blood spurting from a wound on my hand.

"Where is it?" Tethys grunted, stumbling forward on his hands and knees as he reached in his half-sleep state for the same daggers that had just cut me. "Who did this to you? Let me at 'em."

Nyx alone had fallen back, away from me, his shoulders shaking with a quiet laughter that made me want to grab the knife and stab him with it. Not that it would do anything. He'd start to heal by the time the dagger pulled from his flesh.

Tallulah was the one who first realized I hadn't actually been attacked. The other fae were still fumbling for their weapons when she took a step toward me, eyes squinting up, before holding out a hand in a motion meant to make the others pause.

"It's just a cut," she said, blinking the last of the sleep away and straightening back up to stretch. "Though we might as well get going now."

Caldamir came to my side anyway, crouching down beside me and grabbing my wrist hard enough that it started to staunch the flow of blood. I half expected him to lick the wound as Nyx had done yesterday, but he didn't seem eager to taste my blood.

He leaned forward and spat on the wound twice—but nothing happened. Not right away. After a moment, the blood started to flow less quickly, and then stopped. But the wound didn't close up, the skin knitting together as quickly as it did before. It was sluggish, painfully slow, much like the rest of me.

Caldamir was scrutinizing my face a little too closely when I looked up from the wound.

"Come on," Tallulah said, tossing a piece of bread onto the pallet next to the two of us. "It's just a cut."

"It's not the cut that concerns me."

Within seconds, five faces peered back at me, each one more grim than the last.

"She could just be tired," Tethys said, but even he didn't sound very hopeful.

"What are you talking about?" I asked, speech slurring as my annoyance rose. "What's wrong with me?"

Nyx reached into his bag and took out a mirror that must have taken up half the space inside it. He held it out to me so I could see myself, and for a moment, I was taken aback.

I'd never seen myself so clearly. I'd gotten a glimpse in a real mirror here and there, tiny things back at Lord Otto's estate that were embedded into the few family heirlooms that remained, and then again in the dim light of the treehouse back at Nyx's court.

But this was something else.

This wasn't the polished metal that gave me a warped, dim reflection of myself. This was so bright, so clear, that I wasn't entirely sure I wasn't looking into some kind of portal.

But that discovery was slightly overshadowed by the fact that, though this was my first time truly seeing myself, it only took me a few seconds to see something was wrong, too.

It was the eyes.

My eyes.

All around the outside of my eyelids, tiny black lines had started to form—growing outward from the lash line like spiderwebs.

I was being poisoned from the inside out.

Maybe I wasn't fae after all.

I should have been made happy by that fact, but I wasn't. That was what made me the most worried of all.

Two days ago, I would've been appalled to learn I was fae. Now being fae was the only thing that might keep me alive.

Just long enough to get me killed.

By our fourth day in the forest, I'd found myself growing jealous of Waylan, the demon whose ability to travel on his own had probably long since carried him to a dry bed without strange creatures peering down at him through the damp foliage at night.

The dark lines around my eyes had continued to grow, spiraling out beneath the pale surface of my skin—but I wasn't dead yet. I was tired and sore, but so was everyone else. Nyx was the only one among us who seemed to awaken refreshed and well-rested each day, but I had a feeling that had more to do with the creams and lotions he lathered over himself at the end of each day when he thought no one was looking.

Not that I was looking.

Nothing had passed between us since that first morning, since the kiss that'd drawn attention to the darkness spreading through me like poison in the first place. I'd made sure of that, placing my pallet as far away from him as I could each night when we laid down for a few precious hours of sleep.

Even less had happened between me and Tethys, not for lack of the fae's trying.

He'd quickly gotten over his mood from the first day and had instead devoted most of his energy to trying to lure me off the path at every opportunity. I spent most of my remaining energy resisting the urge to follow him.

Not that there was much energy remaining.

I hadn't been getting much sleep at night.

No matter where I moved, only one thing was certain, and that was that Tallulah somehow found her way to squeeze her pallet up against mine. I caught her looking at me more than all the rest, and only she didn't so much as glance away when she got caught. If anything, she just stared harder.

It was like of all the dangers we could encounter on our

journey back to court, I was the one she was worried about the most—even more so than the increasing signs that we might not be the only high fae traveling these twisting paths.

They, not *we*.

I wasn't fae. Not yet.

"Two or three of them, from the looks of it. They can't be more than a half days' ride ahead of us now," Tallulah said, straightening up from where she'd bent over a set of footprints pressed into the soil. "I'm no tracker, so it could be less. We need to keep our eyes peeled."

"That's the same thing you've been saying for the last two days now," Armene said, his horse taking an uncertain step beneath him, mirroring the look of annoyance on his face.

"Yeah, well, it just means we need to pick up the pace if we want to catch them."

Armene was more anxious to get to the Mountain Court than the rest of us. I wondered sometimes if it was because of Waylan. He hadn't been at ease since the demon disappeared.

"But do we want to catch them?" I asked, the question drawing Tethys' glance in my direction. Nyx had fallen to the back, Tethys' usual place, because a couple of deer had started riding along with us. He'd taken to chatting with them in a strange tongue that disturbed the horses otherwise.

"Better than being surprised," Tallulah answered.

I couldn't argue with her there. She tugged the ropes she'd unceremoniously tossed to me earlier before spurring her horse forward up the path, kicking a clod of dirt up into my face in the process.

Only Tethys noticed, and I caught him covering his face with a false sneeze to try to keep me from seeing the delighted grin that flickered across it. He waited until Tallulah had ridden up ahead and out of earshot before his own horse sidled up beside me.

"What's she so afraid of?" It was everything I could do to keep my voice down. I pulled up my sleeve to prod at a dull, purple bruise on my forearm that was still healing from the first day she dropped a mace into my arms.

Tethys made a face. "You, I think."

"What?"

"Oh, please, don't try to tell me you haven't noticed," he said, tilting back his head. "You're a lot of things, but you're no idiot."

"Noticed …" I trailed off as I went to glare at the back of Tallulah's head, only to see Caldamir riding right beside her. She was glued to his side during the day, his or mine—but when she rode beside me it was with a lot more suspicion.

And a much less gentle touch.

I whirled back to face Tethys. "Wait, she and Caldamir?"

"She wishes."

I sat back a bit in my saddle, and for a moment, I watched the two of them up ahead. It was pretty clear to anyone looking on that Caldamir didn't feel the same way. I felt sorry for Tallulah, or would have, if she hadn't worked so hard to treat me like a criminal these last few days. I had no doubt in my mind that if Caldamir hadn't strictly ordered her to keep me alive, she would've already found a way to make sure I wandered off into the forest not to return.

"Well … well she doesn't have to worry about that from me," I said, finally forcing myself to look away. Now staring at them felt invasive, like I was watching something I hadn't been invited to see.

"Doesn't she, now?" Tethys sat back on his horse, eyeing me with the kind of look that made me squirm beneath the weight of it. "And here I was starting to think maybe she wasn't the only one who should be worried."

"Whatever it is you're thinking, you can put it out of your mind."

"Can I now? That'd be a lot easier if you'd so much as looked at me in the last five nights. Is that typical of you humans, to use a male once and ignore him ever after?"

"I'm not ignoring you," I said, keeping my voice low for a very different reason this time. "I've been a bit preoccupied, you know, between being your prisoner and trying not to die."

"Ah well, none of that stopped us before."

"Besides," I continued, "it's not like we've had a moment alone."

"And?"

"And what?" I asked, finally glancing over at him.

"All I'm saying is that I don't think the others would have such a problem with you and me coupling again. It wouldn't be the first time some of them would've had to choose to close their ears or join in."

I swore my mule understood for a moment, because he nearly tripped and threw me—his shock matching my own.

"What are you suggesting?" I hissed at Tethys, embarrassment making my skin grow hot.

"Oh, don't suddenly go shy on me now. I saw you on Midsommar. You didn't want to leave that orgy, either."

My skin flamed hotter.

"I don't know what you're talking about," I said, forcing myself to sit up straighter. I nodded ahead at the horses winding further and further on up the path. "We should hurry up. We're falling behind."

"Actually …" Tethys said, slowing a little to look over our

shoulders. "It isn't us who's fallen behind. Whatever happened to Nyx?"

The words had barely left his mouth when a cry rang out behind us. Not just a cry, a scream.

It was Nyx.

The sound of his screeches now sent all the horses bolting several paces. The only creature that stood still was my own trusty mule—and only because the scream had made him halt altogether, nearly throwing me over his shoulder once more in the process.

For one pivotal moment, I forgot the only true task set to me —stay alive.

Of course my mule obeyed me for once, turning at the slightest nudge on the reins and bolting off back down the path where Nyx had long since disappeared behind us. To my back, there was the sound of crashing footsteps and hooves as the other riders struggled to get their horses back on the path after me.

I expected to turn the first corner of the path and see Nyx screaming about being hand-fed by a butterfly or something, but there was no sign of him. There was, however, the very last flash of a deer leaping into the bushes off the path.

So, of course, I followed it.

As soon as the mule had crashed its way through the thick line of underbrush, the deer was already plunging into another. I followed it this way through several lines of trees, each time making sure to check over my shoulder to keep track of where the road was.

Until I didn't.

Until I saw a flash of something red, of long curly locks and a terrified face—and I dug my heels into the mule a little too hard, and this time, he'd had enough.

This time when his hooves skidded to a stop, he did it so suddenly that I wasn't able to catch myself. He stood still at the edge of a patch of brambles while I flew over it.

I was lucky, really, that I didn't land directly in the middle of it. The spines of the brambles were long and wicked, their hooks reaching out to me with hungry knife-like edges. I landed instead on the other side of what turned out to be a wall of hedges surrounding me and Nyx by three sides.

Because he was there, on the other side, his horse now missing as well.

He lay in the middle of the brambles, a stunned expression on his face that should've been on mine as well. I struggled not to freeze at the sight of him, my instincts both begging me to draw closer to him when at the same time those instincts were telling me to run.

Though run from what ... I didn't know.

All I knew, as I reached for Nyx's hand, is that we'd made a terrible mistake.

We hadn't stumbled this far into the forest.

We'd been led here.

CHAPTER TWENTY

I'D GROWN FAMILIAR ENOUGH WITH THE FORESTS HERE TO KNOW when something was wrong.

And something was definitely wrong.

It was more than the way the brambles grew like a perfect wall up around us on all three sides. It was a feeling. It settled over us like rancid air, a sourness that the stooped branches of the trees overhead.

The moment our hands met, the dazed expression on Nyx's face turned to me. His eyes stared vacantly into mine for a moment, looking through me instead of at me.

From somewhere behind, on the other side of the brambles, I heard our names being called. They were familiar voices. Caldamir. Armene. Tethys. Even Tallulah called out after us, the crashing sound that followed a sure sign of the underbrush meeting a swift demise at the end of whatever weapon she'd chosen to swing.

The voices might've been familiar, but they were also already fading. They were moving away from us, not toward us.

"Come on, Nyx," I said, wrapping my second hand around his too and starting to tug. The motion finally jerked him out of his daze, his head shaking a few times as he cleared it. As soon as he had, he suddenly sat up to stare hauntingly ahead.

"That's right," I said, moving back a step and pulling on him again. "We're halfway there."

Nyx shook his head one more time before allowing me to help him back to his feet. Whereas I'd managed to avoid the brambles altogether, Nyx hadn't been so lucky. I guess his considerable weight had made it harder for his mare to throw him over the bushes, leaving him with two shallow scrapes along the back of his neck.

The discovery of which left him devastated.

I thought at first that the staggered, horrified steps that carried us even deeper into the forest were for the brambles' sake. I'd seen the way he reacted when he heard about the gnats. Maybe the brambles were sentient too.

It wasn't until he finally stumbled into a tree, one hand outstretched to support his hunched over body, that I realized what it really was.

"I—I must be hideous."

"Wait, what?"

He held out a hand to stop me from drawing nearer. From where I stood, the marks on his neck were already beginning to fade. They were barely small pink scratches now.

Nyx covered his face. "I never wanted you to see me like this."

I stood stock still on the dry forest floor in complete shock. "What the hell are you talking about?"

Nyx finally straightened up only to spin around furiously on his heel to face me. He pointed deliberately at the now almost invisible lines fading away.

"You know, before the glamour left us, you never would've had to see that. Or this. Or these."

His eyes averted shamefully away from me as he pointed at some unseeable defects on his flawless face. "I used to be beautiful."

The voices calling our names had faded even further. Not only were they still moving away from us, but we'd moved further away from them.

"Nyx, I can honestly say you're the most beautiful creature I've ever laid eyes on," I said, trying without much success to keep the annoyance out of my voice. "Human or fae."

His face lit up, that same rosy blush rising up to color his cheeks that I'd caught once before. "You … you really think so?"

"Yes," I said, genuine for just a moment. Then I heard my own name, the sound so distant it struck a panicked nerve inside me. "Now, can we get going?"

It took some time to find a break in the brambles that we could pass through. By the time we'd stepped through to the other side of the forest, something about the area didn't look right. The trees here were darker and grew closer together. The earth was littered with thick, undisturbed years of fallen leaves.

Feet rarely trod here, if ever.

We listened hard for the sounds of our names being called this time, paying closer attention to the next few distant reiterations, and my heart immediately sank.

They'd started to come from other parts of the forest. I heard it over my shoulder, then up ahead in the bushes. The closer we came to the source of the sound, the further away it sounded the next time we heard it. It wasn't until the sound of it started to sound … off … that I finally realized what it was.

I stopped dead in my tracks, Nyx taking several more steps before he realized I'd fallen behind.

"Birds," I said, swearing and stamping my foot as I turned in a slow circle, eyes scanning the trees overhead. "They're birds. We've been following birds."

As if on cue, a flock of the winged creatures made a loud squawking sound as they alit from two of the trees overhead. They fluttered in a dark silhouette against the pattern of leaves, a smattering of feathers slowly floating down after them. It was the only sign of them that remained once they'd taken off.

Not before I saw enough of them to marvel at how strikingly similar they looked to the birds known for their own mimicking cries in the human world. I plucked one of the fallen feathers from the ground and turned it over in my hand.

Dense, pinkish-colored bushes were growing here in the forest. I'd not seen them anywhere along the road. I knew I'd remember if I had, as if we needed any more reminders that we were well and truly lost. Nyx would never admit it, I knew, but I also knew the look on his face. He, unlike the other fae princes, was not so good at hiding his emotions.

"Mockingbirds, they call them in Alderia," I said, turning the feather over once more. "Just … a lot bigger."

Like everything in Avarath, it was a little *more*. Similar, but different.

Similar, but *more*.

Nyx looked a little more serious as he came to stand at my side, his eyes drinking in the same thing mine were. "Some of the courts used to use them as spies," he said, picking up one of the other feathers. "It's been a long time since I saw one in my forest."

When he looked back up, the feather disappearing—tucked away into one of his many pockets—there was a new, resolute look on his face.

"My forest," he repeated, nodding once. With that, he plunged headfirst into the rose-colored bushes. "This is my forest. We're going to be fine."

WE WERE NOT FINE, it turned out, though it took us several hours of wandering for Nyx to be ready to admit it. I'd discovered this hours earlier, of course. I'd known this since the distant sound of my name being called had long since dissolved into the harsh trill of the birds overhead, the mimicked sound of it repeated over and over until it no longer resembled a name at all.

It was even more haunting that way.

For Nyx, however, it took longer. It took until we finally stumbled upon the last remnants of a drying puddle and Nyx caught sight of his reflection in it for him to fully crumble.

His hands rose up suddenly to the back of his neck, his fingers fumbling with something I couldn't see until he'd collapsed on the edge of the muddy water to get a better look.

"It's ruined. It's all ruined."

I was exhausted, my patience for Nyx's … oddities … already worn too thin. He was supposed to be the protector, but here he was, skin turning pale at the sight of a few stained drops of blood on his collar.

Blood that was decidedly red, not blue, as if I needed yet another reminder of the many falsities we'd been fed about the fae in my world.

"First the glamour, and now this?" Nyx was saying. "This simply cannot do."

He suddenly got back up to his feet, and before I could say anything, he'd started tearing off the pieces of his wardrobe. The laces were made of such delicate silks that they broke at the slightest touch—or maybe I'd just forgotten that however delicate this fae might look, he was far from it.

Whatever was true, one or some combination of both, it was only a matter of seconds before Nyx stood bare chested in front of me, his lungs heaving air furiously in and out of his shuddering form. The remains of his waistcoat and shirt hung limply in his hands when we heard a new sound.

It was soft at first, the gentle cracking of leaves swaying in the breeze. It was the flutter of petals drifting down from a top branch. It was the crinkle of leaves unfurling.

Something moved in the shade under one of the trees along the edge of the puddle. A shapeless mass started to form, roots reaching up from the ground like small seedlings searching for light.

A look came over Nyx, a strange one—some mixture of recognition and terror—as a shape formed in the swirling mass. It grew from the ground with each step, forming first long, shapely legs, then thighs that rose into an hourglass body swinging back and forth with each exaggerated step.

It was a dryad. A sentient tree.

"Oh, Nyx … here I was thinking I'd have to do all the undressing."

The dryad's voice purred with a sensuality I didn't expect to hear coming from a tree. Not that I expected any sound to come from a tree, no matter how human she looked, how velvety soft her birch-tree skin had grown.

It took me a moment, right up until I saw the way she looked over the fae prince, to realize who she was. More importantly, what she'd once been.

Nyx turned to face her head on, chest still heaving—this time, from a new kind of fear.

"Betula," he said, the sound of her name barely hissing between his lips. "I can explain everything."

It was the jilted lover. This was the dryad Tethys had tried to warn me about.

CHAPTER TWENTY-ONE

And jilted she most certainly was.

There wasn't one drop of kindness in the glare she fixed Nyx with. Though her lips curled up, colored that same rose color of the bushes that had first started us down her carefully laid trap, there was no mirth there.

It was a smug, cruel smile.

"I'm surprised you dare venture into my forest, after how you've treated me."

Nyx's shoulders rose and fell, his Adam's apple bobbing in his throat as he struggled for an answer. "I didn't mean for things to end badly."

"End?"

All false sweetness drained from the tree-woman's voice. Roots burst up out of the ground, ready to grab and carry her over to where Nyx stood between us. He braced himself as she came to a halt just inches before him, her long reed-like hair billowing out around her in an angry cloud.

"If only you'd ended things, I might have been able to forgive you." Nyx flinched at her words, but I saw the way he averted his gaze. "But no. Instead, you left me here to wait. I waited for two *years* for you, Onyx."

"You didn't have to wait that long."

"You know I did," she hissed back. She drew herself up, more roots growing into her so that her body swelled and grew until she was taller even than Nyx. She jutted out her chin in defiance as her arms opened wide, fully exposing the naked curves of her body. Though she was made up of the forest itself, I still found it difficult not to blush as I looked on.

This dryad was, in essence, as real as any human.

"I wasted my youth on you," she moaned. "I'm no longer the green sapling I was when we met."

Nyx had started to back away, head tilted back to look up at her. "No, Betula, you're not. But I'm not the same boy, either."

"Yet you still wear the token I gave you," the dryad said. One of her hands reached out to briefly touch the root that dangled around Nyx's neck. The mournful look on her face turned to hatred in a flash, and she tore the chain from him with a loud snap. "You still deserve to pay for what you did."

The dryad started to move in a slow half circle around him— that was when she spotted me.

"Don't mind me," I said, holding up my hands and backing away. "I won't get in the way of a lover's quarrel."

"Delph," Nyx said, the plea in his voice low and desperate. I don't know what he expected me to do, though. She was a literal tree, taller than either of us, and from the sound of it … her anger at him sounded pretty justified.

"See," Betula said, when she'd circled around to stand directly behind Nyx. "Even your new woman sees it."

As justified as her anger might be, what she did next was not.

Her hands wrapped around Nyx's chest, forming to the shape of his body as she slithered over his bare skin. She pulled him up to her surprisingly soft form, pressing her face up to the back of his ear. Her teeth, naked roots, shone in the dim light as she bared them.

"Let me remind you of what you're missing. Let me remind you of all you've lost. Let me make you feel small, like you made me feel."

Her hands wrapped tighter as new roots burst from the ground. They snaked up Nyx's legs, trapping him further. But that wasn't what worried me. It was when the roots moved further upward, forming long fingers that started to undo the ties of Nyx's pants, that uncertainty flooded through me.

"That's enough, Betula," I said, though my voice was so small, I didn't think she heard me. Her finger-like roots only moved with increase fervor, her intent growing ever clearer as her eyes rolled wildly in their sockets.

She might not have heard me, but Nyx had. It was as if he was drawn out of a trance himself, something brought on by the fear of having a woman-turned-monster-tree wrapping around his body.

Nyx's muscles strained against Betula, but the dryad only continued to grow around him. She looked less and less human by the minute as new roots grew out of the ground around her. By the time Nyx's pants had finally fluttered to the ground, exposing his naked body to her wandering roots, she was well over twice his size.

But she was still a tree, after all.

There were many things Nyx and the other fae deserved. Sometimes, I thought they deserved death.

But they didn't deserve this.

I didn't think twice before grabbing the flint Armene had given me out of my pocket. The moment the black stone flashed,

I saw the sinews of Betula's skin ripple. The moment the two stones drew together, I saw her start to turn.

All it took was a few more strikes of the flint, one spark, one tiny orange flicker, and Betula was suddenly drawing back. Nyx fell to his knees, completely naked, gasping and choking for air. Meanwhile, Betula's eyes widened at the flint in my hand, a new kind of hatred flashing across those wooden features.

"You said you wouldn't stand in my way," she snarled, root teeth gnashing together with each word. Her anger had twisted her entire body, made her forget to make it appealing.

"That was before you tried to rape my poor friend here."

Nyx looked up from where he remained sprawled on all fours, his face aghast. "Is that what you were really going to do?"

The innocence of him in that moment—it broke my heart. Even when he was in the midst of it, how did Nyx not see? Surely, he wasn't so naïve.

"Betula … tell me that wasn't what you were going to do."

A single tear gathered at the corner of Nyx's eye, spilling over to stain the flushed cheek beneath it, and even Betula melted. Her form shrunk down until she'd returned to the small, shapely woman that had first approached us. Her roots retracted into the earth, leaving the ground a mass of scarred earth in their wake.

That was when Nyx struck.

Naïve or not, he knew what he needed to do.

He held out his hand behind him, reaching toward me as he shouted for me to throw him the flint. Behind him, Betula started to grow again as she realized it was her turn to be tricked. Her roots leapt from the ground, reaching for him with more ferocity than before. This time, she was going in for the kill.

But when Nyx turned back, she was too late. Just a moment too late.

The next sparks that showered from the flint alit on the soft birch of her skin, smoldering and smoking enough to give Nyx time to scramble back. He struck the flint again, this time sending the sparks into her roots. The heat of it made them curl and whither back, and Betula stumbled.

It was enough for Nyx to turn on his heel and run—but not before reaching out to take my hand and drag me with him.

For a moment there, I'd half expected Nyx to burn down the entire forest to get away. I'd seen the dry leaves, the kindling waiting to go up in flames. But I'd also seen the way it pained Nyx to save himself, that each spark made him flinch back as if he wasn't burning his attacker, he was burning himself.

For a while, our wild escape made it difficult to tell what was making the most noise—us, or our pursuer. For she did pursue us. She followed us like a banshee, her roots digging into the soil and bursting out to try to trip us with every step. Leaves lashed out to whip at the backs of our arms and legs. Blossoms that same wretched rose color swirled through the breeze trying to blind us.

But still, eventually, the sound around us dulled. The crashing and thudding fell away until the only remaining sounds were those of our own panting breaths.

Only then did I realize how my lungs burned, how my calves stung, how my eyes felt as if they'd been lacerated with a thousand tiny cuts.

Only then did we allow ourselves to collapse onto the forest floor, our bodies intertwined as Nyx reached for something to cover his nakedness. That something ended up being me.

"Nyx …"

"Stop," he said between gasping breaths, holding up one hand. "Let me make sure she's truly gone."

Nyx spread his arms wide to either side and plunged his hands into the soil, his eyes rolling back in his head, lids fluttering some place between open and shut. A vein popped in his throat, near the back of his jaw where it pounded with each of his heartbeats, growing larger and larger until I feared for a moment that it might burst. I started reaching for Nyx, ready to make him stop—when he dragged his hands back out of the dirt and collapsed back a second time.

This time, his body was covered in a thin sheen of sweat.

What could be seen of it beneath where I straddled him, anyway.

"Is she gone then?" I asked, hardly daring to breathe.

His gaze lowered from the treetops to come rest on mine. He nodded, once.

"Even better, though," he said, taking another gasping breath. "We're not as lost as we thought."

I felt myself melt into him. We lay together in silence for a moment, the adrenaline fading with each rise and fall of our breaths.

"You could've used that before, you know," I said, peering up at him from where my head had found a resting place on his chest. "That's a handy little trick that."

"I wasn't sure it would work," Nyx admitted. He turned his head in a circle, his eyes scanning the forest as I'd so often seen him do. "The magic gets harder the further away from the court you are. And these days, even there it's hard to pull the tiniest spark."

But he'd pulled a spark, as he called it, and we were saved.

More than saved.

That spark had alighted in each of us something more, or

maybe it was the adrenaline, maybe it was the rush—but this time, it was me I found closing the gap between us. There was no honey on Nyx's tongue to bait me in, but I didn't need bait.

"Delph …" The sound of my name on his lips like a sigh was the only honey I needed.

Nyx lay on the dried ground, lips parted and hair splayed around him like a halo. The faint sheen of sweat still lingered on his skin, highlighting every perfect curve of his body, every angle of his face. His eyes had gone soft and hooded, as I hovered in the inches above him, one hand lifted up to gently cup the side of my face.

His hands were softer than I imagined, with a sort of hidden strength that made a fire alight in my lower belly. I knew he could crush me with that single hand if he wanted to. I was no more than a toy to him, a lesser being, and yet …

And yet it was I who hovered above him, one subtlest shift away from our naked bodies pressing together beneath the halo of my skirts. That's all it would take for us to share the heat that had begun to pool between my legs, to satisfy the ache in my body that had grown there ever since I laid eyes on him.

It wouldn't be the first time since arriving in Avarath that I'd let a fae take me. The memory of that first time brought back the same furious yearning that had led me to lay with Tethys that night. Not all the fae made me feel this way, flushed with insufferable, unquenchable heat.

Only the ones who were determined to kill me made me feel that.

As Nyx did now.

The Woodland prince's chest rose beneath me and stayed there for a moment as he took me in. It was a long moment before he let out that breath in one long sigh. That hand cupping my face dug into the hair behind my ear, his long fingers intertwining between the strands.

His other hand moved to my shoulder and began tracing down the curve of my side, pausing for a moment to press into my waist before it slid down again to rest on my hip. His fingers played along the ridge of my pelvis, feeling the shapes there without daring to move further down.

Never before had the cotton gown felt so thin. It was all that remained between us, two thin layers that did little to conceal Nyx's growing excitement—or my own, I was sure.

Both our breaths had grown ragged again, Nyx's even more than mine.

He reached for me hungrily, his hips bucking forward a bit to press harder into me. It took every bit of my remaining energy to stop him.

"Nyx, are you sure this is what you mean to do?"

He blinked up at me in that angelic, naïve way of his, and promptly broke the spell that had fallen over us with the next words that slipped from his perfect lips.

"Is it because of Tethys?"

I sat up, hands pressed between Nyx's chest and mine.

"What? No. It's because of the dryad ... you ..." I stumbled over my words, my concern over Nyx's state of mind suddenly overshadowed by what he'd just said. "What do you mean by that?"

"You and Tethys, you mated."

I glared down at him in growing horror. "We ... we what?"

"Do humans not call it that?" A look of confusion crossed his face as he said it. "It means that—"

"I know what it *means*," I hissed through clenched teeth.

"Oh, I see what this is about," Nyx said, propping himself up on his elbows. "You're embarrassed."

"How can I be embarrassed by something I didn't do?"

"Please, we could all smell it on you."

My cheeks had never burned so hot. I remembered the last conversation I had with Tethys. There was no point in denying it now. Not if all the fae already knew what had passed between me and the Prince of the Sea.

"Does that make you jealous?"

"Should it?" he asked, genuinely. His hand stayed steadily on me, eyes meeting mine with a soberness not usually found in him, even on the best of days. "Have you decided you want to only be with Tethys? I've heard humans are strictly monogamous."

"Not that it matters, given the fact I'll be dead soon, but no."

Nyx somehow completely missed the point of what I said.

"Well then, I've no reason to be jealous." His brow furrowed up for a moment, his eyes lifting from mine to stare up at the treetops waving above our heads. "Though I think I'm starting to understand what you were saying before. I should have listened to Tethys. I never should have worn that damned necklace."

"I ... I don't think what Betula did had anything to do with you wearing that trinket."

"Either way," Nyx said, "if it's all the same to you, maybe it's best if we don't mate tonight, after all."

And here I was, thinking my cheeks couldn't burn even hotter.

There was no point in correcting him.

I let out a sigh, rolling over off of him and tilting my head back to let the cool night air rush in. The last of the adrenaline rush faded, and with it, the fearsome desire that had overtaken me.

I didn't remember pulling Nyx's head onto my lap, but

somehow in the moments that followed, I came to cradle the prince there between my crossed legs. One hand had started to absentmindedly stroke the hairs at the side of his face, twirling each one into individual curls that came to lay along his ruddy temples.

He was by far the fairest of the fae princes, and yet nothing compared to the illustrations of fae that the humans of my world had long since committed to memory. Armene and Tethys looked like different creatures altogether. That left only Caldamir, and he, compared to Nyx, wasn't much better off. Caldamir looked like he'd never learned to laugh, where Nyx here looked like he'd never stopped. Strange to think both these creatures were princes, each one tasked with leading a people.

I'd never been given responsibility over so much as one. That would have required someone to trust me, even for an instant—and that was never going to happen, not back in Alderia.

As if reading my thoughts, the Mountain Fae was the next thing on Nyx's tongue.

"If it wasn't for Caldamir, none of us would be doing this, you know."

My fingers still moved in their little circles, taking another stray hair and winding it, winding it, winding it and then watching as it fell to join the other, perfect curls.

"I sometimes forget there was a time before he came and got me," I said, quietly. "Avarath will do that to you, I guess."

"No, no, not that," Nyx said, brow furrowing. His forehead still glistened with sweat. He was clearly exhausted. He'd taken on that far-off look from earlier, each blink of his eyes making it harder and harder for him to focus up at me. "We weren't expecting this to be so hard."

I froze a little, looking back down at the fae between my

thighs. He was drifting close to slumber, his words slurring dangerously near to the truth.

"What about Caldamir and this being hard?" I asked, already feeling a pit start to form in the middle of my stomach.

"He's the one who keeps insisting on going through with this. He's the only one. If it were up to the rest of us, now that we've gotten to know you, we'd find another way."

I was frozen in place for real then, as Nyx turned listlessly over on his side. He pulled my skirts to cover his bottom half again as he settled into a satisfied, dreamless sleep with promises to reunite with the rest of our party in the morning.

But I wasn't going to get any sleep.

Not after what he'd just told me.

CHAPTER TWENTY-TWO

I DON'T KNOW WHY NYX'S WORDS LEFT ME FEELING SO BETRAYED. IT was Caldamir who kidnapped me in the first place. Caldamir who'd played the obvious ringleader all along.

Still, somehow Nyx's claims left a weight on my shoulders I couldn't shrug off.

I was there when he, Armene, and Tethys had all agreed that this had to be done, that my sacrifice was worth regaining hold of their glamour once again. Had really changed so much in the days since then, or was Nyx—the only fae not present that night—mistaken?

He had to be mistaken.

Nyx, pretty as he was, was not the brightest of the fae princes. It was more likely that he'd misunderstood, or never understood, what we'd really set out to do. I could imagine the others trying to shield him by sparing him the gruesome truth.

A truth that, in the past few days, I'd begun to forget myself.

I waited until Nyx had long since fallen into a deep slumber before I searched the surrounding forest, always staying within sight of the fae until I found a small, dark puddle of water reflecting the still darker sky overhead. Only a few stars glittered back at me, peeking out from between the thick branches.

The lighted flora of the forest illuminated my face enough to make it out in the water, if only barely. The dark shadows around my eyes were made darker by the poisonous lines still spreading out from their lids.

I'd been given a promise in the pool that night, made a deal to defy the princes in exchange for being taken out of this place, but how was I supposed to do that? In order to defy the princes, I first had to live long enough to be given the chance. I could die of being human any day now, well before we ever made it to Caldamir's Mountain Court. I wasn't enough of a fool to think I'd survive a single day alone here in the forest. I'd seen the way it twisted the minds of the fae, glimpsed the kind of deadly fiends waiting within. I needed the princes' protection to stay alive, but at what point were they more of a danger to me?

I peered past my reflection in the pool, trying to focus on the dark water itself. No shape formed in the pool when I reached a hand out to it, my hand making tiny ripples that spread through the surface of the water.

I glanced over my shoulder once to make sure Nyx was still asleep before I leaned closer to the water and whispered, "Are you there?"

I felt silly. I didn't know who I was trying to summon, didn't know if this was any way to go about it. I had no name, let alone species to call upon. When nothing responded, I leaned a little closer.

"It's been days. What do you expect me to do?"

Again, nothing.

I looked over my shoulder to make sure Nyx's chest still rose and fell with sleep before I tried once more, acting on a hunch.

"If you really are the Starlight Fae, and I'm one of you. Then I deserve answers."

Nothing.

Anger and frustration welled up in me. I had no reason to believe whatever creature had made the deal with me before would answer, let alone that this was the way to do it. Both Tethys and Armene had warned me of this. That pool was nothing but a curse. I'd been mad to believe the words spoken to me that night, madder still to try to contact those who spoke them again.

This was nothing more than a futile prayer. The futile prayer of a desperate, angry woman.

"Fine then," I hissed into the water, knowing full well I was speaking to no one other than myself. "Let the princes kill me. I don't have the strength to do this on my own. Better to die by their hands than be torn apart by faerie beasts in the forest. You're the true villains here, giving hope you have no business to give. Whatever it is you're afraid of, I hope it comes to pass a thousandfold."

Desperate and futile as it was, there was a strange satisfaction in saying it aloud.

I lifted up my hand and plunged it down into the puddle, intending to splatter the dark water into a thousand tiny muddy droplets—only for something beneath the water to grab hold of my wrist and pull me in instead.

"Who are you, to threaten us?"

The world tilted and me along with it until I came face to face with the dark figure in the pool.

It wasn't like before. I wasn't pulled into the blackness fully, wrapped in its warm embrace outside of time. I was still fully aware of my body hunched over the puddle, could feel the cool air where the water soaked my shoulders.

"I—I didn't think you were listening."

"We're always listening for the cries of our own kind."

My heartbeat quickened. "So, you are the Starlight Fae then?"

"We've been called by many names," he said. "That's one of them."

His hand gripped mine tighter for a moment. "Don't tell me you dragged me all the way here just to ask me that. Every moment we spend speaking, the longer it takes for us to get to you."

"I can't do this on my own," I said, keenly aware of my half-exposed body on the other side. "I can't defy four fae princes when I'm barely fae myself. What am I supposed to do, wander off into the forest on my own?"

"That would be unwise."

"Then tell me what to do."

The figure pulled me a little closer, but I still couldn't make out anything more than the solid wall of black in the shape of a fae. "That part is up to you. Staying alive is your end of the bargain, Delphine of Alderia. You do that, and I promise you we'll uphold our end."

"But how long? How long do I have to stay alive?"

"Long enough for us to reach you."

"That doesn't help me," I snarled back. I kicked my foot in frustration, immediately regretting the thud of it on the dry ground. I couldn't hear what was happening outside the pool, but I could feel the shift of something nearby.

Nyx. It had to be.

I'd woken him.

The fae in front of me sensed the change too, even before I felt the rumble of footsteps nearing me on the other side. I knew how I must have looked to him, that it wouldn't be long before another set of hands wrapped around me to pull me back.

Before that could happen, the fae let go of me. I started floating upwards, back, out of the darkness for one moment, but I lashed out and caught his wrist, and he didn't pull away. Not immediately.

"Please, I need a date. I need something to strive for. I can't do this forever. But give me a day, and I can do it."

Nyx's arms finally did reach me, started pulling me back.

The fae in the pool hesitated a moment. "Stay alive until the new moon sets, and we will come for you."

"The new moon? But that's nearly two *weeks* away. There's no way they'll keep me alive that long."

Nyx was pulling harder. My hand was slipping.

The fae in front of me pried his hand free of mine, uttering one last useless reminder before the image of him shattered with the pool as I was pulled free. "And you've already survived nearly one in Avarath," the fae said. "That's more than any mortal before you can claim."

The forest spun back into view with a spluttering gasp. I spat dark water out of my lungs and across my front, aided by several swift slaps on the back courtesy of Nyx.

"What were you doing?"

The Woodland prince tilted my chin up to look me in the face, concern patterning his own. I, in turn, glanced back at the puddle, but the remnants of it were already drying up.

That was all I'd get out of the Starlight Fae.

"Nothing," I said, "I just, I just fell asleep."

I thought the lie was pathetic, that Nyx would immediately become suspicious of me, but he only nodded his head in commiseration.

"I've fallen asleep in puddles like that too before," he said, "but I don't have to breathe like you do. I made it halfway through the night before I realized it. You should be more careful where you choose to take a nap. Maybe next time choose a tree. Or a nice rock."

This time it was Nyx who made me do a double take. "Don't worry," I said, taking his hand to lead him back toward our previous sleeping spot. "I won't be falling asleep in any puddles again any time soon."

I let Nyx spend a few minutes stomping through the underbrush, breaking apart any water he was worried was deep enough for me to fall asleep in before he once again curled up in my lap.

The display was as sweet as it was simple.

None of the other fae would have believed my lie for a second, and for that, I was grateful for Nyx. Twice, now, I'd gotten away with an encounter with what I now knew was the Starlight Fae.

Twice now, I'd been given hope that there really was a way out of this godforsaken place.

And now, at least, I knew how long I had to endure this madness.

TRUE TO NYX'S WORD, we were no longer lost in the forest thanks to that single spark of magic he pulled the day before. We'd barely set out in the direction he pointed us in before we started seeing signs of others nearby; a smothered campfire, bits of old string, boot prints still fresh along the edge of a bank, sunk in despite the dry soil. It didn't look like remnants of Caldamir and the others' encampment, but at that point, I don't think either of us cared.

Right up until a strange scent started permeating the air.

Nyx caught on to it long before I did. We'd been following

along a rough, unmarked trail for about an hour when he first smelled it. I saw the moment he caught the scent for the first time, because his face screwed up in such exaggeration that it was almost comical. He stopped in his tracks, tilted his head back and took a deep breath that ended in a choked snarl.

His eyes narrowed and his head snapped back down to glare forward.

"No …" he started, head shaking. "No, it can't be."

He didn't stay to tell me what it was he smelled, what it was that had creased his perfectly smooth forehead with worry. He just took off, leaving me standing stunned as tree branches swung back to slap me in the face.

"Nyx—" I started and then paused. Just for a second.

I'd smelled it, too.

Something rotten—something too sweet and sour and smoky.

Something up ahead had died, and it was this that I followed long after Nyx's thudding footsteps had left me behind, right up until I broke through another thick patch of underbrush and came to a stumbling, crashing halt.

We should've been at least one more day's journey to the edge of Nyx's woodlands. We might have been, once—back when there was a day's journey left of them.

Something had wiped out miles upon miles of Nyx's forest. As far ahead as I could see, the ground was turned an inky black. The edge of the forest rose like a wall of its own out to either side, curving ever so slightly around the far-off line of mountains.

It was the first time I'd gotten a glimpse into unobstructed Avarath. It was not a pretty sight.

This was not the kind of destruction caused by a fire. It was deeper than that.

The trees hadn't turned to ash in a blaze, they'd withered instead into dried out husks of themselves. The grass had rotted away, exposing roots that had died as they tried to free themselves from the ground—as if the ground itself had been poisoned.

It left the ground looking like a sea of dirt, the trees captives, unsuccessful in their escape and left like bloated white corpses upon its surface.

And that was to say nothing of the actual corpses.

Deer. Rabbits. Birds. Elk.

Something larger, like a fiend, rotted just off to my right.

They all lay unmoving with ribs exposed to the air as even flies and carrion refused to pick at their spoiled meat. The scent in the air was more than rot, however. It was as if the air itself had spoiled long ago, and this was just the aftermath.

"What … what is this?"

"This," Nyx said, from where he stood frozen, "is what happens when the magic truly leaves Avarath."

He turned to me for a second, eyes glazed over. "I never should have used magic to get us out. I should have let the two of us die there, in the forest."

"Nyx …" I started, but he wouldn't let me finish.

His gaze turned ahead again, his head shaking from side to side as if he couldn't believe what he saw with his own eyes. "I'd never have drawn that spark if I knew this would be the price."

Nyx fell to the ground at the edge of the forest just a few paces away. His knees sunk into the black, ashen dirt. Hair fell over his eyes, covering his face—but I knew what I'd find there.

I knew it from the way his shoulders wracked with sobs, how his hands turned to curled, gnarled claws where they grasped at the dirt. I knew it from the way he tilted his head back and let out a heart-stopping scream, so filled with anguish that my heart broke for him a hundred times over.

This time, Nyx's scream had the opposite effect as the first. Where the first one broke apart out party, this one drew us back together.

Voices broke out from the tree line, followed by the crashing sound of leaves and broken branches under hoof, right until Caldamir and Tallulah broke out of the tree line still on horseback.

Tethys and Armene followed soon after, accompanied by two more men in black hoods that I didn't recognize.

Seemed they'd caught up to the fae Tallulah had been tracking.

They all stumbled to a halt too as they took in the missing forest before them.

Tallulah was the only one fixated on something beyond the wreckage. While everyone else was dropping down from their horses to examine the scorched earth, her hand rose to point at something in the distance. I followed the tip of her finger, eyes searching the line of dark gray mountains until I saw what she did.

There, set into the tallest peak, something glimmered among the stony walls. The high afternoon light had caught on the smooth walls of a tower.

There was only one place it could be.

The Mountain Court.

The place I was set to meet my end.

I wondered, when Nyx turned to Caldamir with a look I'd never thought I'd see on him, if what he'd told me the night before still held true. I wondered, if now that he'd seen what it was to lose his precious forest, if he'd still prefer to keep me alive.

CHAPTER TWENTY-THREE

THERE WAS NO CHOICE BUT TO TRAVEL STRAIGHT THROUGH THE broken, rotting remains of the forest. The whole thing was like a skeleton, with the great white-bleached trees making up the exposed ribcage of some giant monster rising up along us as we rode in silence.

They rest of the party had managed to retrieve Nyx's horse and my mule both, who'd had the good sense to wander back in the right direction after they'd thrown us over the bramble wall. My mule begrudgingly took me back, though his burden had grown considerably lighter now that Tallulah had taken to riding with *all* of her weapons, her eyes constantly shifting over to the two newest members of our party.

The duo was the most unremarkable pair of fae I'd met yet. I hadn't spent much time paying attention to the fae of Nyx's Woodland Court, and when I did, I was mostly interested in the shapes their bodies made intermingling together during the Midsommar celebrations. If I thought back, I couldn't remember them individually, their faces all blurred together into the same kind of high-cheekboned mix with eyes in different shades of blue and green.

I'd quickly learned upon meeting Caldamir, and then coming to Avarath, that the fae weren't what the picture books and old tapestries made them out to be. More than just their appearance —which up until the prince's arrival I'd thought would be strikingly similar to mine—they were a far more complicated people than I'd ever imagined.

The two males that had joined our party where no exception.

I wouldn't call them ugly, for by human standards they'd be far above average on all accounts, but compared to the other fae I'd seen, however well I remembered them, these two were positively plain. Their faces were emotionless, their voices bland and unfeeling. Even when they spoke to each other, always in hushed tones that were hard to make out, it was difficult to tell whether they were pleased or not. From the sound of their voices, it was impossible to tell whether they'd been traveling for a few days, or a few years. Their dark cloaks bore something that looked like it might have once been the emblem of Caldamir's court, but the threads were worn to the point of unraveling. These might be his fae, but they'd been gone a long time.

Long enough that even Caldamir didn't remember them.

No one had said as much—no one had said much of anything since we rejoined—but I could see it in the way he snuck furtive glances their way more often than he did mine. There was a questioning look on his face, as if he was trying to remember something that he couldn't quite put his finger on.

Armene, meanwhile, was far less subtle with his suspicions.

"I don't trust them," he said as soon as he settled down by our campfire at the end of our first day traveling together again. His eyes shifted over to the smaller fire our two companions had made a few yards off. He didn't bother keeping his voice low. He hoped they'd hear him, hoped they turn their hunched shoulders to meet his gaze, provide some kind of assurance either way. "Who's out traveling this time of year?"

"Lots of fae travel for Midsommar," Nyx said, shifting glances in his direction.

Nyx's face stared blankly into the fire. He hadn't spoken much since we'd discovered the ruined forest. The lighthearted joy in his face had faded, the look replacing it far more pensive.

It didn't suit him.

"Not the kind that don't stop to spend it with a nearby court," Armene argued. He finally peeled his gaze away from the newcomers' silhouetted forms, only to fix it on the fire alongside Nyx instead. He shrugged up his own shoulders and hunched forward, brows furrowing. "They would've been at the court in time. Who passes up the opportunity to enjoy a Woodland celebration?"

"As I recall," Tethys said, appearing suddenly beside the log where I sat, "we did."

"Yeah, well," Armene said, "we had good reason."

"And maybe they did too." Tethys flopped down onto the old branch beside me and stretched out his legs with a contented sigh. "We're not the only fae struggling to find our place in this new world. You think we're the only ones who've noticed the magic is going missing? Just because our advisors think it's best left alone doesn't mean there aren't other fae out there looking for a solution. We're just the only ones who may have actually found one."

"Please don't tell me you're stupid enough to be talking about that right now," Caldamir said, appearing out of the darkness next, a dark shape before an even darker sky. He dropped an armload of branches into the fire, so dry that they almost immediately turned to ash.

"Tethys is over here flapping his mouth as usual," Tallulah grumbled from where she sat across from me in the shadows. She was the only one not sitting in the light of the fire. She'd preferred to stay back, pulling a log of her own up behind our inner circle—creating a sort of armored shield between the two camps with her own body.

"Well, unless you'd like to spend the rest of our days in Avarath watching helplessly as all our lands turn to ash too, then you'd best learn how to shut that pretty mouth, Tethys."

Tethys only grinned. "You think I have a pretty mouth?"

Caldamir picked a hot coal out of the fire with his bare hands and flicked it at the Sea prince, promptly wiping the grin off his face as he fought to bat it off him in time before it burned an already larger hole in his tunic than it already had.

He finally settled down at the fire alongside the rest of us, though he made no sign of relaxing. He leaned in close enough to the flames that I was surprised he didn't flinch back from the heat.

There was a determined look on his face that I'd become all too familiar with over the last few days. Each day that drew us closer to his court—and my death—the reality of it was settling in for all of us.

We'd managed to make it to the old border of the forest by nightfall, but only barely. The ghosts of the ruined land still lingered in our peripherals, those bone-like trees standing out against the blackness surrounding us on all sides. After days spent traveling the forest, I was surprised by how uncomfortable I felt exposed in the dark emptiness of the plains. In the forests, I'd felt eyes on me constantly—but out here, it was a different feeling. A different kind of exposure.

Anything that stumbled upon us here would have to do it intentionally.

As some already had.

I cast a glance at the fae seated at their own fire, and once again caught them just as they were looking away from me. They had that same hungry look in their eye that I'd seen in some of the Woodland Fae, one that once again made me subconsciously shrink a little in my seat. It made me think that of all the warnings about the fae that I'd gotten wrong, the rumor that they sometimes ate humans might not be one of them.

Because the way they looked at me carried none of the tenderness that I'd spotted on the faces of the other fae seated around me. Well … all aside from Tallulah.

Strangely, it was this realization—and not the fear of our fae newcomers—that suddenly made the heat of the fire become unbearable.

I stood, motioning for the others not to follow even though I felt the weight of their eyes on me with each step I took away from the fire. I didn't go far, just far enough that I couldn't make out the dim voices around the fire from one another.

The air out on the plains got colder at night. Not cocooned by the trees of the forest, the fading of the sun gave way to an almost chilly breeze that carried the scent of the ruined forest far beyond its borders. It was a constant reminder of what was to come, should the fae fail in their quest.

This place was a constant reminder of what I was supposed to be, what I meant to them. To all fae. A burden. A blessing. A hope.

Hope was never something I'd associated with myself before, but I'd never imagined it to feel like this. So … so hope*less.*

"You really shouldn't be alone out here."

Caldamir appeared at my side, as I knew he would. He couldn't leave me alone, wouldn't let me out of his sight since we'd reappeared. He hadn't said as much, but I knew he'd feared the worst when I'd plunged after Nyx. Though the worst for him didn't mean my death. It meant losing me. Dead, or alive, it was all the same to him until I lay on his sacrificial pyre … or whatever other way he planned to murder me once we arrived at the Mountain Court.

"I'm not alone, I'm with you."

A low grunt issued from the back of Caldamir's throat. "That isn't what I meant. There were once fiends out here that could just swoop down and carry you off, you know. There might not be the numbers there once were, but all it takes is one. Out here, you're totally exposed—"

"Like I'm not exposed everywhere I go?" I cut him off.

Despite Caldamir's warning to Tethys earlier to quiet, I couldn't help myself. I kept my voice low, but he still flinched at the words that followed.

"I understand the fiends. I really do. But why are you so worried about the other fae? Finding out about me, about what you plan to do to me, I mean?"

"Fae are dangerous. I thought even humans knew that."

"But it's more than that," I said, resisting the urge to stamp my foot out of frustration. "Why would they risk that when I'm with you? With all of you? You're princes, surely they wouldn't want to anger you. Or do princes mean something different than they do in our world?"

Caldamir gritted his teeth. "No, we're pretty much the same."

"So, what is it then?" I insisted. "You promised to tell me back in the forest, but then you didn't. Don't you think I deserve to know?"

He made another grunt, but it wasn't completely dismissive.

So, I continued. "Some fae don't want the magic back?"

"Some fae just aren't willing to pay the price."

"The price? What price? I'm the one who's going to have to die." I didn't mean for it to, but my voice had risen well above my well-intentioned whisper. "You do realize that I don't get anything out of this deal, right? I don't see why I shouldn't just … just …" I flung my arms wide, feeling the breeze pick up as I did, rustling at the hem of my soiled dress. "Why don't I just let the fiends take me, then?"

The words were goading, as I intended. Of course, I had my own reasons not to let the wild fiends kill me now … but Caldamir didn't know that. None of them did. Any fears I had of Nyx recounting the story of me in the puddle had died with his silence at the sight of his ruined forest.

The moon was but half of a silver coin overhead, crawling ever forward toward the new moon with each waning day. The sight of it was a stark reminder of just how long I was still expected to stay alive on my own.

One week left. One week too long.

Though Nyx and I had spent but one night in the forest, Caldamir and the rest of them had spent three looking for us. It was yet another strange way the forest had twisted around us. Though, for once, I didn't mind.

It had brought me one day closer to my deliverance, bought me just a little more time.

And with it, a little more boldness.

I pushed onward, provoking him. "Why not take my chances with the unknown, if you're just going to kill me as soon as we get back to the court?"

It worked.

"Because then your death would be in vain, and you would die," Caldamir said, drawing closer, "that, I can promise you."

When I still didn't look at him, he grabbed me by the shoulders and forced me to look into his eyes. "You act like your life before I took you wasn't suffering. I saw the way you were treated. I saw the scars on your back. You should be thanking me for taking you away from that living hell."

This time, it was *him* provoking *me.*

"Thanking you?" I let out a scoff, the incredulity dripping like tar from my tongue. "Oh, *thank you*, Prince Caldamir, for taking everything from me. Is that what you want to hear?"

"I've done more for you than you know. I've killed for you."

I paused.

"What are you talking about?"

I'd never seen Caldamir like this before. His face had gone white with fury and unable to stand still, he'd started pacing in front of me. His hands moved in short, jerking motions, as if he didn't know what to do with them.

"Otto's man. I painted the cellar red with his blood." Caldamir suddenly stopped right in front of me and pulled me closer then, so close that I could feel his breath on my face. It smelled sweet, like the honey I'd once tasted on Nyx's tongue. "And I'd do it again."

"I don't understand you," I hissed at him, my heartbeat quickening at his touch. "You'll sacrifice me in some ill-fated attempt to get your magic back, but you'll kill a man who once took a switch to me a little too hard?"

He hesitated at that, just for a moment.

"That's different."

"How's that different? Don't get me wrong, I've no love lost for Raful—that's the name of the man you killed, by the way— but how can you stand here and say that was justified?"

I took a deep breath. "Why would you claim to kill a man for me when you plan on killing me yourself?"

"That was a man. If there's one drop of fae blood in you yet,

I'll not suffer another—fae or human—to lay undeserving hands on you."

The utter hypocrisy of it all finally broke me. Really broke me.

For a long moment, Caldamir and I stood at an impasse, his eyes searching mine for something he couldn't find.

But I found what I was looking for, found what I'd been trying to drag up ever since his arrival in Alderia to kidnap me in the first place.

I found hatred.

I couldn't find it in me for the fae, try as I might. But I found it for him.

For this specific fae. For Caldamir.

A muscle spasmed in his jaw. His lips quivered dangerously close to mine, close enough that for one, brief instant, I thought he might be about to kiss me.

Fortunately for him, one of our new traveling companions chose that moment to appear from the shadows. We'd been so preoccupied that we hadn't heard him approach.

"Everything alright out here?"

Caldamir's hands dropped so quickly from me, it wasn't until he took a step back that I even realized he'd let me go. "Everything's fine," he snapped, his tone announcing very clearly that he was anything but.

He turned to catch the rest of the campfire staring our way, half risen from their seats, hands already reaching toward weapons. Caldamir raised his voice, nodding toward the second guest at the fire adjacent to ours, making sure everyone heard him.

"Make sure to get some sleep, because from here on out, we ride hard. No more detours. No more hesitating. We've already wasted enough time."

"Wait …" Armene said, stepping after him. "Does that mean what I think it means?"

Caldamir's face was stony when he turned back. "Don't tell me you believe the stories about the valley?"

Armene was silent as Caldamir turned away and walked back toward the camp, where Tallulah was already starting to work to dull the flickering flames for sleep. "I never took you for the superstitious type."

CHAPTER TWENTY-FOUR

Superstitious or not, it didn't take long before I understood the hesitancy in Armene's voice when he mentioned the valley. Though in all truth, it was less of a valley and more of a canyon. From the edge of what was left of Nyx's forest, the plains had appeared to stretch on flat to the base of the mountain—but I couldn't have been more wrong.

The first light of our third day on the plains made visible what nightfall and distance had hidden from us.

The old edge of the forest was lined with a rocky, gently sloping terrain dotted with wiry brush and patches of green. Tall grass grew between boulders, on the edge of streams, and really wherever it could get a foothold in the rocky soil.

At the very edge of my vision there was a large swath of green, but something about it had seemed off for days. It was too smooth. Too perfect. It was because the plains didn't simply slope down to the edge of the mountains. There was something in between.

A massive crack in the ground ran from one end of the plains to the other, plunging down so far that the bottom of the crevasse must've been shaded in darkness all but one or two hours of the day.

The sides of it were so steep that it made me dizzy to peer inside, and even dizzier to imagine climbing down.

"Please, please tell me we're not climbing down."

Armene grimaced as his gaze followed mine. "Not quite, but the journey through isn't going to be much better."

He nodded on up the path to where Caldamir had led the others a few paces ahead. "There's a path through not far from here, though ..." he licked his lips, that same shadowed expression crossing his face that'd been there earlier. "There's no saying whether or not it'd be better to add a couple days and take the long way around."

Armene pointed out a long arm jutting out to our left. "There's a break there we should reach just before nightfall, it's steep but not this steep. It'll let us pass through."

I pulled my mule's reins to ride further away from the edge, as far as I could without resorting to climbing over the boulders that had grown larger as we approached, and for once, he was all too happy to oblige. From further back, the whole canyon had the appearance of a giant cross scarring the land.

"What is this place?"

I leaned forward a bit to take another peek down, and immediately regretted it.

"Well, the glamour had to come from somewhere, didn't it?"

Armene smiled just a little bit when my head snapped back to look at him. "It's just a superstition."

"Speaking of superstitions," I started, peeking up ahead to see if Caldamir was close enough to overhear yet. He was not. "Why don't you want to pass through the valley, really?"

Armene wrinkled up his nose. "You know, the early fae tried to build bridges over it, but the fiends always destroyed them before long. Eventually we just realized the bridges weren't meant to be built."

"Or maybe that you weren't meant to cross through it."

The gentle smile on his face pulled wan. "Now you're getting it. Sometimes nature tells us what she wants. Sometimes, we're better off listening."

"You talk about superstitions a lot for someone who claims not to believe them," I said.

He rode on in silence, but I saw his smile turn up once more.

The crevasse was dark, sure, but on the other side of the crevasse the plains came alive.

The base of the mountains gave way to rolling hills lined with long, grassy fields. The further from the mountains, the greener and softer they were. There was a place far to the south where I swore, for a moment, I almost caught a glimpse of a glittering sea—but I knew it was nothing more than a mirage. The mountain range extended too far, and then the hills stretched out from them even further.

Still, those green plains and rolling hills were a far cry from the barren plains we'd found ourselves picking through for days now, with nothing but the occasional boulder to shield us from an unforgiving sun. The only fae among us who seemed unbothered by it was Armene.

This was his element, after all, as Prince of the Sands.

By the time evening was fast approaching, he was the only one with energy left to ride on ahead with one of the trackers to scout out the opening to the so-called valley. They disappeared for a while as the rest of us slowed to wind along the narrow path until it dipped back around a rising set of boulders. On the other side, our path joined a new one—this one plunging straight between two sheer walls on either side.

It was just as Armene described. The rock walls were smooth

and colored with streaks of red and white, making it look like the path wound straight into a massive monster's maw.

The path only led a few feet in before it turned enough to hide the rest of it from view. Up at the top, this close to the edge, the boulders surrounding the edge of the crevasse had grown precariously large and close to that edge. One wrong step trying to peer up ahead, and it'd be all too easy to send one of those boulders tumbling down to block the path.

Or crush anyone unfortunate enough to stand below.

Once we were inside with the horses, there'd be no way but forward.

No going back.

More concerning still, was that there was no sign of Armene at its entrance.

Only the scout waited for us at the mouth of the path, perched on one of those boulders. One foot hung lazily down over the edge, but that didn't hide the way his glance went straight to me—and lingered there just a moment too long, as it always seemed to do—as soon as we arrived.

"Armene went on ahead," he called down, when Caldamir drew his horse up beside the entrance. "Insisted on double checking it was safe."

Caldamir's face worked silently for a moment as he took in the sight of the path. It was obvious to all of us that he was having doubts, if only for a moment. His head tilted up to the sky, already starting to color orange with sunset, and he swore.

"Stupid fae," he muttered, glancing over his shoulder at the rest of the party as we filled the narrow path behind him. Nyx and Tethys were last, their faces pale and dripping with sweat. They were taking the terrain harder than the rest of us, neither of them used to the dry, barren air.

"I told him he should wait, but he wouldn't listen," the scout said, though the words drew a strange look from his companion.

"We should wait for him to come back," the companion said, a little too quickly. "Bad luck traveling through that canyon at night. Wouldn't want us to get separated."

Something about his tone struck an uncertain cord with me, but since none of the other fae seemed to notice, I chalked it up to my own fears and said nothing.

"We're already separated," Caldamir snapped back, head shaking. He wiped his brow with the back of his hand, dragging down the skin on his face as he tried to think of what to do next. "No, we can't wait. We'll get through the first part by nightfall. Armene can't have gone too far ahead."

His words carried a confidence that didn't match the look on his face.

"Maybe you should go in first, on foot," Tethys called from where he remained astride his horse, his own face wrinkling up in displeasure at the narrow walls of the canyon. "See if Armene got stuck or something."

"No, no, I don't think that's a good idea."

"And I thought you weren't the superstitious one," Tethys said.

"I'm not," Caldamir said, adamantly. "I just don't fancy any more of us getting lost." He nodded down the canyon path. "But if that'll ease your mind … then I'll prove there's nothing to fear."

He swung down off the back of Rynn, and ignoring her irritated snorts, plunged in after the missing member of our party before anyone else could accuse him of something so close to cowardice.

It was strange without him here. It left us unbalanced, too

close to even with our peculiar companions. Just three of us—Nyx, Tethys, and Tallulah—to their two.

I didn't count for anything. If anything, I balanced us out completely, taking away the one of our number who'd need to protect me in a fight.

"No reason to sit around here, acting as if we're not going through that canyon," Tallulah called out, after a moment. Still, no one moved with haste. It seemed no one was particularly eager to follow the two princes who'd already been swallowed by the canyon's walls.

Tallulah fell back to my side as the slow process of dismounting began. Her horse dwarfed my mule, leaving the already tall fae towering over me. Her shadow blocked out the mid-morning sun, the chain mail helmet she never took off sending blinding little pricks of light into my eyes.

"Nyx told us what you did back in the forest, you know. That must have taken a lot of courage. I've seen an angry dryad before, and even I didn't dare mess with it. I hope I didn't offend you the other day, when I called you puny. I only called you that because you are."

It wasn't an apology, not in the strictest sense, but I had a feeling that was as close as it got with Tallulah. At least, where I was concerned.

She hopped down from her mare with a tired grunt, glanced once toward the scout only just starting to clamber down from his place on the rock, and stealthily slipped a knife from one of her belt loops.

This, she handed to me.

In her hands, it was barely a hunting knife. In mine, it was almost a short sword. It nearly dwarfed the full length of my forearm.

She kept her broad back between us and the scout as she

pretended to tighten something on her horse's saddle, but really she pulled out a strip of leather which she looped through part of the knife's sheath and then proceeded to slip her hands beneath the front panels of my gown, tying the strip of leather up high enough to hide it beneath the laced-up bodice. I didn't dare move. I'd always imagined if Tallulah chose to get this close to me, she'd be slipping a knife between my ribs, not concealing one at their side.

"None of my holsters will fit you. They'd slip right off to the ground. Lot of good a lost knife'll do you."

"And what is this supposed to do?" I asked, realizing too late how ungrateful I must have sounded. "It's not like it'll kill a fae."

"Not in your hands, it won't," she said. "But if a fae really wants to kill you, then you're out of luck."

She glanced once toward the canyon walls. "Besides, it's not the fae I'm so worried about in there."

My throat went a little dry as I followed her stare. Even though we were literally marching ever closer to my death, I didn't need a reminder that just about every living thing in Avarath would be all too happy to make that happen a little sooner.

"It'll keep you safe from fiends. Unless you run into a great fiend, then you're really fucked."

She tilted back her head then and roared with laughter, as if it was the funniest joke she'd ever told.

I, meanwhile, just tightened the leather strap of my new holster a little tighter.

"What's a great fiend?"

Our short window of privacy came to an abrupt halt as the second scout led his horse up to our side.

"We knew she was human, but we didn't know she was

dumb too." He eyed me for a second with a mixture of pity and, unless I was mistaken, disgust. "If we run into a fiend of any kind, at least we know who it'll pick off first."

Caldamir chose that very opportune moment to reappear.

"No more putting off the inevitable, we need to get going," he said, breaths panting from the heat as he started preparing Rynn to follow him in this time. "I'd like to come to the cross-roads before dark, but we should catch up to Armene sooner than that. After all, how far could he have gone?"

CHAPTER TWENTY-FIVE

Further, it seemed, than Caldamir thought.

The walls of the crevasse stretched higher and higher overhead until they stood like towers on either side. The path was narrow, just enough for us to file through one at a time, but in some parts even that was difficult.

One hour passed, and then two, and still no sign of Armene. We hadn't so much as seen a horse dropping, though the first scout had assured us he took his stallion along with him. The path up ahead was too quiet, but still I didn't worry until the sky had started to darken overhead.

It would be nightfall before long, true darkness falling soon after, and still there was no sign of our lost prince.

I was wedged between Tallulah and one of the scouts, with Caldamir and Nyx up ahead, and Tethys at the rear with the second scout. Even the horses, happy at first to be eased of their burdens, began to grow uneasy. They went from muttering about claustrophobia and how little it would take for them to bolt and run one of us over into full on wordless grumbling.

Their tails twitched and switched at their backs irritably, catching any fae standing too close with strands of stinging hair.

Eventually, just as we were all starting to grow a little too restless, the crevasse started to widen out. At first, I was just glad to be able to reach out my arms to either side and not touch stone, but then it suddenly widened out a lot. The walls took a sharp turn out, revealing a star-shaped center with narrow paths leading out from each point.

From up above, the paths had appeared to form the shape of a cross, but from here, there had to be at least a dozen paths to pick from, each one as cramped and uninviting as the last.

We'd finally come to the crossroads Caldamir had mentioned —and with it, at long last, we finally found the first sign of Armene.

Not a moment too soon. Within minutes, we'd be plunged into darkness.

"Ah, finally," Caldamir said, standing from where he'd stopped to kneel to look at something in the dirt. He held up a small metal object that glinted in the light. "It's his. At least he went this way."

I recognized it too. It was the small silver pin that he used to fasten his gauze head wrap.

All eyes swiveled around the small space, but it was one of the scouts who suggested what we were all thinking.

"Perhaps we stay here for the night?" he asked, glancing nervously around. I noticed that his eyes lingered down one of the paths in particular, but I didn't see anything when I tried to follow his gaze. "Or at least until your Sand Fae—"

"Prince Armene," Caldamir said, an edge to his voice. "You'd do well to remember that."

"At least until he's come back."

Once again, Caldamir stood center stage as all of us stared wordlessly, waiting for his reply.

One look at Nyx, and it was clear what he wanted. He'd taken to nervously scratching his arms, his head glancing over his shoulder all too often, making him appear skittish. He'd been like this since we left the forest, since the moment we'd laid eyes on the swath of land that'd been destroyed.

It was like some small part of him had been destroyed, too.

That was why I was surprised when it was he that suddenly straightened up, tugged on his mare's reins, and started down the path ahead. "No," he said, pausing just long enough to look up to the darkening sky. "We should keep going. Like Caldamir said, we've already wasted too much time."

"First, let's make sure we're headed down the *right* path," Caldamir said, hoisting himself up onto his horse. "Then, let's make sure we have some light. Tallulah, grab the torches."

Tallulah nodded and went to her horse, starting the arduous task of unloading weapons in order to access the bags' other contents.

I watched from my mule as Caldamir climbed upon his mare.

"And how do we know which is the right path?" Tethys called from the back. He was holding an empty water skin, his lips cracked with thirst. *Prince of the Sea*. We'll, he'd certainly found himself far from the sea now … and he was feeling it. We all were.

"It's the only path a horse can still ride through from here," Caldamir said, riding up ahead to check the path that Nyx had started toward a moment earlier. He'd barely ridden ten feet in before Rynn came to a grinding, frustrated halt.

"I could tell you if I was going to fit," the mare said, foot stamping into the dirt when he tried to urge her forward, anyway.

"Well then, lead the way."

Caldamir dropped the reins and waited as Rynn backed out of the path and started circling the rest of the paths, pausing at the mouth of each one it turn until, at last, she pushed forward on her own. She went just far enough to nearly disappear, leaving only her twitching tail flickering in the last of the fading light.

"This is it."

Caldamir didn't doubt the mare once. He just turned in his saddle and motioned for the rest of us to follow.

"Where are the torches?" he called back to Tallulah just in time for us to turn and look back at her as she paused, suddenly, and a horrified look came over her.

"Armene," she said, quietly. "They must have been with him."

Any fear of remaining in the dark lasted only as long as it took one of the scouts to draw Caldamir's attention instead.

"We have some," the scout said, rummaging through his bag, only to produce two. One of these he gave to his companion, who settled in at our back. The other he held, lighting it only as he climbed back onto his mare and ushered her forward, pushing past Caldamir to take the lead.

Caldamir didn't like it, none of us did, but the only other choice we had was to wait, alone here in the darkness, and that was a choice none of us seemed eager to make.

Especially when it turned out that we weren't alone.

It was Tethys who noticed first. He'd tilted his head up to the darkness once it'd finished falling completely, trying to spot the stars up above in the tiny crack of sky. His face screwed up, as if something was wrong.

"What is it?" I asked, glancing up after him.

I saw him trying to work something out, then the moment it dawned on him what that thing was.

"They're not stars," he said, quietly. His voice barely dared to rise above a whisper, even when Caldamir looked back, confused, and he had to repeat himself. He pointed up toward the tiny pinpricks of light up above and swallowed. "They're fiends. It's our torchlight reflecting off their eyes."

Hundreds of eyes peered down at us from up above. Tiny, white pinpricks of light.

They were scattered like stars all along the walls, indiscernible from the real things twinkling between them.

The only one who seemed unfazed was Caldamir.

"That's right. Just fiends," he said, nodding once toward the scout at the head of our party. "Now, unless you'd all like to stick around here and find out what kind, we best be going."

Caldamir's tone did nothing to stop the way my heart was beating at the top of my throat. It pounded in my ears and sent my stomach lurching with every crunch of dirt and stone under my mule's hooves, thinking it was the sound of some creature climbing down from the darkness instead.

We continued onward, remaining on horseback this time, though in a markedly new kind of silence. I tried not to look upward, but I couldn't help myself. Even with the flickering light of the torches ahead and behind, I often found myself in the crux of darkness. Two narrow turns was all it took to leave me floundering for a moment, alone with my mule, between two faint flickers of light and nothing but fiends hanging in between.

I thought I caught a flicker of one once, a great bat-looking thing at least half the size of me, before I was pulled back down to the path by an unexpected voice at my side.

It was Caldamir.

He and Tallulah had switched places, so he now rode directly ahead of me.

"It's better to ignore them," he said, gesturing up toward the sea of monsters over us, but without actually taking his eyes off the flicker of the torch up ahead. "There were plenty of fiends in the forest, you just didn't see them there. There's really no need to be afraid."

"It's not *them* I'm afraid of," I said, though that wasn't entirely true.

"Bullshit," Caldamir countered, stunning me.

I stopped in my tracks, or would have, if my mule ever once obeyed what I told him to do. "What?"

"Of course, you're afraid of them. I'm afraid of them. Fear is natural."

I bared my teeth, even though I knew he wouldn't see it here in the darkness. He was insufferable, Caldamir.

"There's an innumerable number of fae creatures watching me from overhead," I said through my gritted teeth. "But they're not determined to see me killed, specifically. They might want me dead, but it's more in a general sense. They want everyone dead."

"You think I really like this?" There was a change in Caldamir's tone. Frustration. Anger, even. "You think this is what I really want?"

"Yes, I do."

"Then why would I try to kiss you? You do remember that, don't you? From the other night?"

Of course, I remembered. I could still feel the heat of him on my skin. Feel the press of him against me. But I also remembered the hatred that had boiled up out of me. The hatred that had stayed, simmering on the surface of my mind, ever since.

"Lucky you didn't," I growled, a guttural sound from the

back of my throat. It wasn't anything like the feral growls of the fae, but it was close enough. "If you had, I would've bitten off your tongue."

"It only would've grown back."

"And I would have relished every moment of silence while it did," I said in response.

"I think you're confusing me for Tethys."

"And I think," I said, nodding toward the light that had disappeared around another bend in the path, "that I'm not confusing you at all. I think you just want to be the hero. You don't want to admit that maybe, just maybe, you're the villain."

"Is that really what you think of me?"

He turned back to look at me, but it was too dark for me to make out his face.

I didn't have to wait until we'd rounded the corner, until I could make sure that he saw the hate I felt plain on my own face when I answered.

But I did, anyway.

"Yes," I said, setting my jaw once we were once again in the flickering torch light. "That's exactly what I think of you."

Caldamir stared in silence for a moment before turning word-lessly away. He didn't have to spur his mare on, Rynn did it herself, overtaking and joining Tallulah and the scout in their cluster up ahead.

The path had begun to grow wider, but I felt no less claustro-phobic, not when there was now an ever-pressing ceiling of crea-tures moving in from overhead.

Caldamir rode on with his shoulders pulled back a little too tight. I watched on, eyes glued in an angry glare at his retreating back until I couldn't see him anymore.

I couldn't see anything.

It took me a moment, a moment too long, to realize it wasn't just because he'd turned the next corner.

No.

There was no flicker of shadows on the walls up ahead. Only blackness.

The torches had been extinguished. Both of them.

And I knew why, even before the hands of the scout wrapped around me and pulled me screaming up into the darkness … just as the fiends descended.

CHAPTER TWENTY-SIX

My screams were lost in the shrieks of the fiends and the clash of steal as Caldamir and the others fended off their attack. Or, I only hoped they were fending off the attack. By the time their shouts were fading down below me in the canyon, I was too far up to tell if it was because they were losing the battle, or because they were being driven away.

At least I wasn't alone when the scout dumped me onto the floor of the shallow cavern. Armene was there too.

Not that he would do me much good.

He was bound, hand and foot, by some kind of thick rope.

Mushrooms and lichen glowed so bright along the inside of the cave that I could see the way Armene's eyes rolled in their sockets at the sight of me. He tried to say something, tried to cry out, but the only noise that made it past the gag on his mouth was a muffled shout directed at the scout who stepped into the cave after me.

"How did you …"

I trailed off, already realizing the answer before a third fae, a stranger dressed in the same worn scout's uniform, appeared behind him. Dust and dirt exploded at his feet as the remains of a heavy coil of rope collapsed from where it was slung over his shoulder.

A bird flew in from the window, a garbled scream croaking from its throat before it alit in the spot where the rope had previously occupied. The scout turned to his companion and nodded.

"It's time. They're long gone, now."

I looked between the two fae and the familiar black and white bird, and I knew they'd been responsible for leading Nyx and I astray in the forest, too. When that hadn't worked, they're lured us here.

Lured me.

Nyx had said that the birds had once been used as spies. It seemed they still were.

The scout whispered something to the bird and then sent it on its way, surely to deliver some kind of message to the scout still down in the canyon with the rest of our party. Or what was left of it.

That was when I recognized the emblem on his cloak.

This one wasn't as faded and threadbare as those on the other two—who I was willing to bet had been picked at to make them look like they bore the remains of the emblem of the Mountain Court.

But none of them had. They all bore, instead, the image of a circle engulfed in flames.

The symbol of the truth-bringers.

So much had happened since my encounter with the two women bearing the truth-bringer's symbol back in Alderia on Midsommar's Eve, that until now, I'd completely forgotten it. Now, with the two men bearing down on me and Armene, it was all I could think about.

"I know that symbol," I spluttered, crawling backwards on

my hands to match each step they took toward me. "The truth-bringers despise the fae, they're heralds of your destruction."

The two scouts paused, exchanging broadening smiles that did nothing to warm my heart.

"*We* are the truth-bringers," the newest one said, when he looked back at me. "Not the other way around. We warned the humans of the fae's destruction. We told them to steer clear of the fae, to not trust the words of their deals. And yet … here you still are."

I shook my head, confused. "I don't want to be here."

"Well then, that makes all three of us."

I scrambled back another foot, the knife Tallulah gave me falling to the ground with a dull thud, useless at my side.

Not that it was useful before. Not in my hands. It would've barely nicked the fae in front of me.

The two scouts saw the blade and laughed, knowing as well as I did that there was no point in reaching out to take it from me.

"I almost feel bad for what we're about to do," the first scout said, cocking his head at me. "I'd forgotten how pathetic humans can be. It feels kind of unfair, killing her like this."

Behind me, Armene's muffled cries grew more desperate. I flinched at the sound of them, at the way his hands scraped the dusty floor in his frustrated attempt to right himself from where he lay.

"Then don't kill us," I said, stumbling over my words. "You could let us go."

"We have every intention of letting the prince go," the newest scout said. "We have no quarrel with him, with any of the princes for that matter. We're not here to start another fae war. We're here to make sure that the king is never put back on his unholy throne."

"I—I want that too," I said. "I don't want to die."

"But you have to, if we're to make sure no one tries to use you again in the future. As long as you live, you pose the single most threat to the peace here in Avarath."

I opened my mouth to respond, but I had nothing to say to that … because they were right. Even if I didn't have enough Starlight Fae blood running through my veins to actually undo the spell holding their king under the mountain, as long as I lived, so would the hope in me that I might.

The two scouts advanced, drawing swords from their belts in preparation for the blood they were about to spill.

I had no way to defend myself. No words. No weapon.

Fortunately, it wasn't up to me to defend myself anymore.

Armene had grown quiet for a moment, but I didn't understand why—didn't notice until he suddenly lunged forward, using the rope still attached to one of his wrists to loop around the neck of the scout closest to me.

It still took me a moment longer, a moment spent frozen as Armene pulled the rope so that it dug into our assailant's neck, leaving him gasping and choking, to understand how he'd gotten free in the first place. It was the mess of bloody cuts already healing down the length of Armene's forearm that gave him away.

It seemed my knife wasn't so useless after all. It may not have been able to kill one of these fae, but it could, at least, cut a rope.

The other scout lunged out to try and pry Armene off of his companion, but the prince's iron grip refused to let go. The three of them became a writhing mass of bodies, the shape of them difficult to distinguish from one another beneath the swirl of glowing lights. It was all I could do to keep from getting caught up in the tangle of it—right up until I had no choice but to get involved.

The second scout, having finally realized he wasn't going to get Armene to let go of his companion, stumbled back to get his bearings again. That was when he remembered the sword in his hand.

He raised the blade, preparing to swing at Armene's exposed and unprotected back, when I lunged at him. I collided with the back of the fae's legs, but the motion didn't so much as make him stumble.

It did, however, remind him of my existence—and the true reason they were here in the first place.

He spun on his heel and struck me. Hard.

The blow might have been enough to finish me if I wasn't already reeling back from my failed attempt to topple him. I fell back into the dust and dirt, head ringing so loud that Armene's mouth appeared to yawn in a silent scream as he looked on.

A new fury rose inside him, lighting a rage that twisted his features into something feral. With a single, deft movement, the prince snapped the neck of the fae still struggling in his arms. By the time the second scout had understood what just happened, Armene was upon him too.

He tore the sword from the fae's hands as if it was no more than a wooden plaything, then took the scout by the neck and pinned him up against the wall so that his feet dangled a good half foot above the ground.

The scout stared in horror at the limp body of his companion, his voice barely choking out beneath the pressure of Armene's hand on his throat. "You killed him. A fae. That breaks royal code. You know that?"

Armene's hand only pressed harder.

"You *dared* attack a prince of Avarath and really thought you wouldn't have to suffer the consequences?"

His face hovered mere inches in front of the scout's.

"Are you going to kill me too, then?"

"No," Armene said, after a moment. "Only so that you can live to warn anyone else who might try to stop us. We'll not hesitate to do what needs to be done. For Avarath."

He let go of the scout's neck and used the tip of the sword to keep him pinned to the wall instead. He kicked a stone up to the edge of the wall beside him then gave the scout a slightly less than gentle nudge with the heel of his boot.

"Step up onto it and put your hands up above your head, palms together."

A strange look flashed across the scout's face, the closest thing to real fear that I'd seen on a fae yet. "What?"

"Do as I say," Armene snarled, pushing the tip forward so that it started to cut through the layers of the scouts' waistcoat, "or I won't hesitate to run you through."

The scout did as he said, his hands shaking as he lifted them up and placed them overlapping above his head.

I tried to get Armene's attention then, calling his name out only for him to wave my words away, his eyes fixated on the scout in front of him.

"Armene…"

He had no time for me, however. Not when he was focused to solely on the scout in front of him.

"Higher," he instructed, jaw set.

The scout followed Armene's instructions, though his whole body was quivering now.

A moment later, I saw why.

Armene drew the sword back from the scout's stomach, but before he could so much as breathe a sigh of relief, the prince let out an ear-splitting scream of rage and lifted the sword overhead to plunge it straight through the scout's hands, hilt-deep into the stone.

Though I saw it with my own eyes, I'd not have believed it if Tallulah hadn't already told me it was possible. So was the true strength of the fae.

The scout's own scream was still echoing through the cave when Armene kicked the stone from beneath his feet, leaving him to dangle on the very tips of his toes or else let the sword cut further into the flesh of his hands. He cried out once more as blood trickled in long rivulets down his arms, but his own healing powers worked against him, mending the flesh of those hands as quickly as the sword cut into them.

The prince stepped back and nodded once, admiring for a second his own gruesome handiwork.

"Now, feel free to pull yourself down whenever you like, but you won't be climbing out of this cave anytime soon," Armene said, with a matter-of-fact air that bore no sign of the cruelty he'd just committed—justified or not.

"Why not just kill me?"

"You deserve to suffer," Armene said. He started to turn back to me, but froze when the scout's next words hissed out between his trembling lips.

"All this for your little human whore?"

Armene didn't move for a long moment. He didn't speak for longer still. When he did move, he moved with a contemplated, terrifying patience. He produced a small, sharp knife from his pocket, and moved to stand directly in front of the scout.

"Armene, please …" I said again, but he ignored my plea a second time and reached for the scout's mouth. This he pried open, his hand forcing his jaws to widen before he moved to conceal what he was doing behind his broad shoulders. The cave once more echoed with the sound of gurgled choking, but by the time Armene stepped back, the scout made no sound.

From the look of the blood dripping from both Armene's hands, he couldn't.

He'd cut out his vocal cords.

"For that, you'll suffer in silence. By the time your companions are able to make sense of your screams, you'll have the Mountain Court army to contend with should you wish to face us again. That is, if the fiends don't get to you first."

Armene finally turned away from the scout, one hand wiping his small blade clean on the front of his already blood-splattered clothes. His hair had fallen loose from its bun, cascading over his shoulders in dark locks longer than mine.

He knelt to pick up a fallen torch from the ground, but his fingers—still slick with blood—struggled for a moment to light it.

"I'll have to answer for their lives, but that's a price I'm willing to pay. We should hurry now to catch up with the others. It shouldn't be too difficult."

"Armene," I said again, this time, my voice faint. "That's not going to be possible. Not for me."

"That's nonsense. You'll …"

As soon as he stood, torch sparking to life in his hand, he saw why.

The same blade that had almost saved me, that had freed Armene, had just as quickly become my downfall.

I'd fallen straight onto it when the scout threw me back. I'd been too stunned to know it until the adrenaline of the moment had passed and the pounding in my head had turned into a different kind of throbbing.

It had impaled me deep into the back of my inner thigh, leaving blood to spurt between the fingers I pressed along the hilt's edges. No matter how hard I pressed, only more blood seemed to ooze in inky dark red onto the floor of the cave.

My hands were shaking when I looked up to meet Armene's face.

"I can't stop it bleeding," I said, my voice faint. "I feel like I'm going to pass out."

He dropped to his knees beside me, hands reaching out toward the blade but stopping short of actually touching it. I was all too aware of how exposed I was to him. The blade had penetrated me about as high up as it could while still embedding itself in my actual thigh.

"Loss of blood will do that to you," he said, moving more slowly this time as he gingerly started to peel back more of my blood-soaked skirts. I flinched back from him, only to nearly pass out from the pain of moving.

"There goes any thought of trying to turn you over," Armene muttered, waiting for my breaths to return to normal before he returned to his slow, methodical movements. I sat as still as I could while the prince pulled back the last of my skirts and left me—as well as the wound—fully exposed.

His eyes flickered up to mine for a moment.

"Now is not the time to be shy," he said with surprising tenderness. He reached out one of the same hands he'd just used to mutilate another fae and took mine in it. He held my gaze and gave it a squeeze, before his brow furrowed slightly. "There's a way I can fix this. I can make you live, but I'll not do it without your permission."

"How—"

Armene's tongue darted out between his lips. "I think you know the answer to that."

And I did.

The memory of Nyx healing my cut hand at Midsommar came to mind, of his tongue lapping at the wound he'd created until the skin knit itself back together. Caldamir had healed me too, but his method wasn't the one that the memory of nearly made me pass out again, this time, from the surge of heat that accompanied the realization of what Armene was suggesting.

"No, no," I muttered, even as my speech grew more faint with each word. "You can't."

"So, you'd rather I let you bleed out?"

Armene had already started unraveling the fabric of his hood, laying the stained gauze aside as he reached for the laces of his shirt beneath.

My head swam again. "I—I—" It was impossible to think, not just because of the blood pooling beneath me, but because of how with each ticking second the gorgeous, murderous fae was moving closer and closer to the space between my spread legs. "It's too intimate."

Armene's eyebrow arched up at that. He stopped moving, his arms already hooked between each one of my bent knees.

"So, you'd rather die than let me between your legs?"

"It's not that," I said, gasping a little as another throbbing pain shot through me. "It'll take too long now. It's just, it's too much blood."

"Please, Delph," he said, a sly smile pulling at the corner of his mouth. "I'm not afraid of a little blood. And if it's going to take me a while … well then … it's a good thing I have the stamina."

I considered, for a moment, allowing myself to bleed out on the floor. It was only natural to feel embarrassed of the situation I found myself in, but I was more than that. I was ashamed—less ashamed of the fact that a fae prince was inches from my sex, offering to lick my wounds to heal them, but more from the fact that blood wasn't the only bodily fluid rushing toward the place that prince lay awaiting instruction.

I should have been focused on the single task of staying alive, but all I could think of was how it would feel if Armene didn't stop when the bleeding did.

"Come on, Delph," Armene said. "Pretty soon this isn't going to be an option anymore."

"Oh, fuck me," I snapped, too overwhelmed with another burst of pain to care how my words sounded. I threw back my head with a grunt, my face twisting up as I fought back the next wave of pain that tried to tug me into unconsciousness. "Just do it, Armene. Do it now."

"And I thought I'd never hear you beg."

And with that, Armene, Prince of Sands, dove his face between my thighs.

CHAPTER TWENTY-SEVEN

It wasn't long before my gasps of pain had turned to sighs of pleasure.

Armene hadn't lied when he said he wasn't afraid of blood. He was deft with his tongue, so skilled that it wasn't only the magical properties of his fae saliva that dulled the agony. My head rushed with sensation—a mixture of adrenaline, fading pain, and near overwhelming desire.

He worked the blade from my muscle and skin, inch by excruciating inch, until at long last he pulled the final length of it free. The feeling of him removing it from my body came with a near orgasmic release—followed almost immediately by an actual one.

For Armene didn't stop when he finished healing my wound. No. He'd only begun.

By the time the prince resurfaced from my skirts to pour the remains of his water skin over his face and chest, it wasn't pain I was panting from. I reached to grab him by the collar, to pull him to me. He obliged, allowing himself to be dragged, drenched and dripping, on top of me until our faces were mere inches from one another.

"I don't want you to stop," I whispered at him, still breathless and shaking. "I want you to have me. All of me."

Armene stopped just before we kissed, our lips hovering so close together that I could feel the faintest whisper of them on mine.

"There's nothing in this world or the next that I want more," he growled back, voice husky. "But I can't give that to you. Not tonight."

I let go of Armene and he fell back onto the dusty floor beside me.

"Why not?"

I found myself shrinking back, arms moving to cross over my chest. I knew I was foolish to feel insecure, that it was this same creature that'd just spent the better part of the night first healing and then worshipping my body, but I still felt the weight of his rejection all too keenly.

Armene reached out to cup the side of my face with one of his hands.

He was a gorgeous creature, sprawled out before me with his full lips and dark olive skin. His hair had been swept back at some point into a long tail that dangled now over one shoulder, though some loose strands remained plastered by sweat to the sides of his face.

"Well first, because there's a limit to what I'll do while the enemy looks on," he said, one thumb running along the line of my cheekbone.

Color surged in my cheeks as I glanced over his shoulder at the fae still pinned to the wall behind him. I'd entirely forgotten about the scout. Already, his own wounds had healed to the point he no longer bled. He just stared at us with an unfettered hatred, the thoughts turning over in his mind surely not the kind that would allow him to forget either me or Armene for a second.

Let alone what he'd witnessed us do while he looked on in agony.

"And second, because my conscience won't allow it."

His hand dropped down to his lap, where it remained, the void tangible where he'd touched me only moments before.

"Lovemaking in my court is a sacred bond," he said, the words coming out strained as he formed them, as if he was trying hard not to offend me. "It wouldn't be right for me to take you into my bed knowing the future I've condemned you to."

It wasn't until he looked away and his hands curled up at his side, that I realized I'd read him wrong.

His hands didn't simply curl up, they'd turned white. His breaths were shallow and measured, as if he was carefully timing each one. More telling, still, was the way he tilted his body away from mine, one leg coming up to cross over the other in an attempt to hide the throbbing need between them.

He wasn't trying not to offend me.

He was trying to restrain himself.

Across the cave, the scout made his first sound in hours. Armene ignored him, but still started to get to his feet, the spell of our night spent together broken as his hand reached for the blade he'd only recently removed from my thigh. His fingers fumbled for a moment to reattach it in its holster at my side before he reached for the torch to once again light it.

"Now we really should be going. If you can walk, all things considered …" he said, with one last hint of a wicked smile flashed in my direction, "Caldamir and the others are probably wandering the canyons looking for our remains. We shouldn't keep them waiting any longer."

His hand had not so much as grazed the torch, however, before the scout made another desperately strangled sound and this time we both turned to face him. Only for it not to be his face peering back.

It was something else.

Something huge emerging from the depths of the cavern.

And that something lashed out and struck Armene before he could so much as reach for a weapon.

He flew back, head cracking against the wall before he crumpled to the ground in a heap. Still, it wasn't this sight that made my blood turn to ice. It was the way he lay still, unmoving afterwards, without so much as a breath to make his shoulders rise and fall.

I didn't have time to reach for him, not when the creature that had attacked him was moving close enough for me to finally see what it was. A fiend. Not a bat, as great and terrible as those creatures outside the cave were in the blinding moment they attacked. No. This was a great fiend.

Just what I'd been warned of.

As soon as I knew it, as soon as I saw the great armored flanks of its sides, the long whip-like tail ending in a wicked spur and the eyes that gleamed with intelligence, it struck again. This time, however, it aimed for the helpless fae now thrashing against the wall he was pinned to.

Until Tallulah and Armene had told me otherwise, I'd always been under the impression that fae were immortal, that their ability to heal made them essentially impervious to attack. Even when I witness Armene snap the fae's neck earlier, the true weight of what I'd witnessed hadn't dawned on me.

But then here, this time, I saw the light leave the scout's eyes —and it shattered me.

I'd never seen a human die before, but somehow, I didn't

think it would amount to this. This wasn't the cutting short of a life. This was the ending of an eternity.

It was more like watching a star die, the light in his eyes burning so fiercely for that final moment as the huge piercing end of the fiend's tail sliced straight through his body as if it were nothing more than smoke that I thought I might be blinded by it. I saw something in there, an anguish so cutting I felt it in my own soul. It didn't matter that this fae had been all too eager to murder me only hours before, I felt his death as if it was my own.

Just as quickly as that light sparked in his eyes, it turned black. The color in his body drained as every inch of him went limp. He collapsed onto the tail of the fiend, still stuck through as if on a pike.

It wasn't until only his body remained that I felt fear for my own.

In one smooth motion, the fiend ripped the fae off the sword and flung the scout's body out of the mouth of the cave like he was nothing more than an insignificant rag doll. He disappeared into the darkness as the fiend rose up to size me up next. Here, in the dim light of the cave, I was just barely able to make out the actual creature that would make me meet my end.

The closest thing I'd seen to it was from drawings in the books at Lord Otto's estate, long before he betrayed me to the fae —however unwittingly. It was scorpion-like, with huge, segmented parts of its body leading to an immense curled tail. I followed the line of its body, half-clinging to the back wall of the cave, until I saw where straw and bones were littered at the many feet clicking against the stone.

It had been hiding there all along, camouflaged into the stone until it saw its chance to strike. We were fools not to see it before.

We were too preoccupied with our own fight to see the true one right in front of us. Until, of course, it was too late.

Though this was a beast, the look in its eyes was far from dumb. It regarded me in the moment before it struck again, finding me—rightly—an unworthy opponent.

The fiend wound back its tail like a great, deadly snake, and then struck. The blow landed squarely against my ribs, but it didn't pierce through me as it did the scout. It flung me backward, a sharp pain erupting across my quickly bruising body.

I hit the wall with enough force to knock the breath out of me, landing in a heap on top of Armene. The fiend let out a howl and coiled back, drawing its body another segment up onto the wall. It drew its sharp tail back to examine it, surprise flickering across the uncannily human features of its face.

Beneath me, Armene remained so still that I daren't look closer to see if he, like the scout, had already died. Besides, I didn't dare look away from the fiend.

Not when it was already coiling back to strike again.

This time I met it standing, one hand reaching toward the knife that I realized had blocked the first blow—a knife that had now nearly killed me and saved me again in the span of a few hours—but I was too slow to draw it from its sheath. I would've, *should've* been killed by the fiend's next blow, but the tail struck lower this time, aiming for the wide target that was my ruined skirts—an object the creature, as intelligent as it appeared, seemed unfamiliar with.

The blade of its tail sliced through the fabric, tearing through easily until it reached the armored trunk of its appendage, where it snagged and grew tangled. The fiend let out a second confused, frustrated roar, and made the unfortunate decision to try and drag its tail back to its side—taking me with it.

It was all I could do to protect my skull from the sharp rocks on the floor and walls of the cave as the creature whipped me back and forth. Eventually, it did manage to tear its tail from my skirts, but by then the screeches issuing from its throat were far more than frustrated.

There was rage in its eyes.

The next time it struck, it didn't pierce my side. Its tail wrapped around my torso, drew me the rest of the way back up to my feet, and started to squeeze. The air rushed out of my body without my bidding, my lungs too compressed to draw in more. It crushed and crushed until I felt the blood start to pool in my face and the strain on my ribs great enough to crack bone.

My head swam, my heart raced, my pulse pounded so fiercely that I was sure the blood vessels in my temples were going to explode.

But then it stopped. The great thing loosened its hold just a bit and pulled me closer to it, drawing me near enough that I could feel the prickle of the short hairs growing from between the plates of its armor. Plates that, upon closer inspection, seemed to almost *breathe*.

"It can't be …" it said, speaking for the first time with sudden disgust. The tail that had only moments before attempted to first stab and then crush me, loosened so quickly that I fell gasping and scraping to the cavern floor. "You don't look like fae."

My breath rushed back into me so quickly that it left me spluttering, barely able to keep track of the creature circling back a bit to give me my own once-over out of the corner of my eye.

The fact that it could speak didn't surprise me. At this point, I would've been more surprised if it *couldn't*. But the way it looked at me, the way it paced the short length of its own cavern snorting and hissing … *that* surprised me.

It stopped suddenly, glaring at me as those little holes on its body once again pulsated. *It was breathing,* I realized. Taking in the scent of me.

The scent it found made the great creature's head lower as it examined me, differently, this time.

"Why, if you aren't fae, do you still reek of one?"

It took me a moment to realize the creature was actually waiting for an answer. It took a moment more for my voice, hoarse and spluttering, to be found.

"I—I've been traveling with them for days."

"No." It pulled back the front of its jaw to expose two long, pincer-like teeth in the front of its mouth. "You don't reek of *them.*"

Its tail pointed at Armene, still crumpled on the floor.

"You reek of the real fae."

I sat in dumbfounded silence until the creature, with another frustrated growl, bared its pincers a second time.

"Are they back then? Are you their herald?"

"I really don't know—"

The fiend silenced me with another roar, its tail pulling back to point at Armene on the floor. "I *knew* I smelled royal blood on him. I'd heard rumors the princes were gathering."

"Rumors?"

"Don't play dumb with me," the creature hissed, its voice giving way to angry splutters punctuated with more clicking of its pincers. "I know what you are. I know what you're trying to do."

This time, when the fiend reared back, the determination on its face was far more terrifying than its rage.

"Starlight Fae or not … it can't be allowed."

It didn't reach for me, however. It reached for Armene, still splayed out on the floor.

That was its mistake.

It wasn't a hidden blade stuffed inside Armene's garments that saved him. It was, instead, the outstretched hand of Waylan. The demon appeared calmly, as if stepping effortlessly between two pages of a book, and caught the fiend's massive tail between two fingers.

The pointed end glinted inches away from Waylan's brow.

"Waylan!" I gasped out his name. "Where have you been all this time?"

"Waiting until the prince needed me, of course," Waylan replied, keeping his gaze fixed forward. He examined the appendage clamped between his fingers coolly, turning it over in his hand as the fiend's eyes grew wide. Its attempts to draw it back were unsuccessful. The creature slipped from the wall as its many legs scrabbled against the floor. It moved with increasing urgency even as Waylan continued to look disinterested.

"What is this?" the fiend cried, its body struggling not to slip out from beneath it just as I struggled to keep from being impaled by one of the massive and abundant legs that kept stabbing into the cave floor dangerously close to me.

"This," Waylan said, his voice as emotionless as the rest of him, "is what happens when you attempt harm on the Prince of Sands."

With that, Wayland closed the two fingers that held the trunk of the fiend's tail, crushing it as easily as if it were one of Nyx's gnats.

The scream that issued from the creature's mouth was earsplitting. Blood spurted from the crushed and mangled tail, the scent of it foul as it filled the cave. It hadn't hit the ground before Waylan appeared at the monster's side, once again moving with speed that its body—and mind—couldn't register.

He stood beneath the creature, reached up with the same

indifference with which he'd crushed its tail, and plucked the creature's heart from inside its armored torso.

By the time the rest of the dying fiend had collapsed, Waylan was kneeling over Armene's body, taking it up in his arms with a gentleness that made my head spin—given the violence of a moment before.

"Such a silly boy," Waylan said, shaking his head as he lifted Armene's limp form from the ground.

The fiend writhed and twisted against the opposite wall, and it was all I could do to crawl away before it crushed me in the process of expiring.

"Is he …"

"Alive, of course," Waylan said, looking at me for the first time. "As unfortunate as that is for me."

I blinked up at him in surprise, but he offered nothing in the way of explanation.

"I'll be back for you," Waylan said. "So, unless you'd like to be picked apart by another one of these … things … I suggest you stay put."

I opened my mouth to respond, but he was already gone.

I was left alone with the dead fiend.

Or I thought it was dead, right up until it spoke once more. Its voice was strained, barely recognizable as words. Each syllable took effort, drained another drop of the remaining lifeblood of its body.

"The high king can't be allowed to return. You must stop them. Kill them, if you have to."

A dark shadow settled over me. Stay alive … that was a task I could do.

But kill a fae? Once, not so long ago, I wouldn't have blinked twice at the thought.

But now …

"I can't. I might have fae blood in me, but I'm only human still. At least, in every way that matters."

Every way but one.

"Even a human can kill a fae. They just need the right tools. As you've seen, small one, even the immortals have their weaknesses."

With immense effort, a great shudder wracked its body. The end of the shriveled, broken tail snaked closer to me, releasing the pointed spur with a soft click to the ground. I reached for it hesitantly, unsure whether or not to touch it.

"Take it as a gift from all the creatures of this world," the fiend hissed. "On this side and the next."

I didn't have the heart to tell it that no blade would make me strong or skilled enough to kill a fae the way Armene had, the way it had. Fiend or not, I didn't want to let it know its dying gift was all but useless in my hands.

The fiend wasn't finished, however. Its voice issued a final, spitting warning.

"Unless you wish to see the end of your kind, you won't let the princes succeed."

"What?" I scooted closer to the fiend, as close as I could without muddling the foul dark blood. "What do you mean by that? The end of my kind?"

Anything else the fiend might have said was ended when Waylan reappeared, this time, right in the middle of the creature. More blood and entrails spurted from the fiend's carcass as the demon looked down in disgust, his nose wrinkling up as he reached for a handkerchief to dab at the splatters that had appeared on his jacket.

"What a waste of a good suit," he muttered, before suddenly looking at me with a sharpness that made me shrink back. "Did it say anything to you before it died?"

I glanced back at the crumpled form of the beast, one hand tentatively reaching toward the form of the tail-blade hidden beneath my tattered gown. I'd grabbed it the moment Waylan appeared, when he was too preoccupied with the blood to pay attention to the human sliding something up beneath her bodice. I forced my hand to still, to drop back down to my side before I revealed my secret.

I wasn't sure what prompted me to take it.

Even less sure what prompted me to lie.

"No," I said, the back of my throat feeling thick with the feel of it. "It didn't."

CHAPTER TWENTY-EIGHT

I DIDN'T EXACTLY MAKE IT OUT OF MY ENCOUNTER WITH THE FIEND unscathed.

It wasn't until Waylan had scooped me up into his arms and the adrenaline was wearing off that I realized it. To him, I was as light as a feather—but to me, I was as heavy as the stones that made the canyons themselves.

Though Armene had healed my wound, my body had still lost a lot of blood before being whipped around like a rag doll— to say nothing of the toll Avarath itself had been taking on my body over the days since I arrived. It turned out that it would take more than a good night's rest for me to recover.

More than a couple.

By the time Waylan had pulled me through the veil alongside him, I was barely conscious of the shift at all.

All I saw was dark stone. Silk sheets. Concerned faces shadowed in the doorway.

The last thing I saw before my eyelids were dragged closed with this immense, invisible weight, was the form of a body tucked beneath the sheets in the bed beside me.

Armene.

He still didn't move, and despite Waylan's promises that he was alive, it was fear for him that consumed me as I fell into a deep sleep. It was a sleep plagued with nightmares of burning forests, ice-cold pools, and canyon walls so dry that simply breathing beside them dragged knives down my throat.

Between the fits of nightmares, I was vaguely aware of brief moments of waking. I saw faces hovering over me, some familiar, some strange—more strange than familiar as the nights wore on. The strange faces blurred together into these nightmares, joined the fae scouts and the humans who'd wanted me dead for the blood that ran through my veins. They sneered down at me with hatred. With pity.

By the end of it, I wasn't sure which was worse.

Between all the dreams was the voice of the fae in the pool. The voice in the puddle, in the darkness. It was always faceless. Always watching. Always saying the same thing. Telling me to stay alive.

As if I had any say in the matter.

Those dreams should have been the most exhausting, but they were nothing compared to the dreams I had of Armene.

We'd survived our night in the caves, but we'd carried something with us when we left, Armene more than me. Though my body was the one that lay broken long after his appeared standing at my bedside, he was the one who was the most changed.

He was the one, that even in my dreams, could no longer bear to look at me.

The prince of the Sand Court in my dreams was not the prince that saved me in that cave. This prince was broken. This prince was afraid. This prince was ashamed.

I didn't understand it.

But it was only a dream.

Only a dream … unless it wasn't.

Finally waking was like emerging from the dark water of the pool that first time. The film of sleep remained over my head, the sheets like water trying to drag me back down as I fought to sit up in bed. Sleep pulled at my eyelids, hot and sticky, even as my body shivered in a cold sweat.

I would've let it drag me back down if it weren't for the sight of the bed beside mine. In all my half-waking states before, the shape of Armene's body had been there.

Now, it was empty.

Something about the pristine way the sheets had been pulled up and tucked neatly underneath the down mattress made my stomach turn. In my mind, it could only mean one thing.

I struggled to swing my legs over the edge of the bed, pausing to pull the long rope of my hair away from where it clung to my shoulder. My hair had been plaited at some point, but it now stuck in curled tendrils to the back of my neck. My bare skin glistened in the flickering light of a fire beneath an enormous mantle.

Bare skin.

Someone had undressed me.

The realization shocked any lingering sleep from my body. Ice ran down my rigid spine as the color—or what remained of it—drained from my skin. I started frantically searching the blankets piled up around me with an ever-increasing sensation of dread.

"Looking for this?"

Shame burned hot on my skin as Waylan, appearing as only he could from thin air, procured the curved end of the fiend's tail from his pocket.

The demon stared unblinkingly down at me over the length of his long, pencil-thin nose.

I wet my cracked lips, wondering if he could hear the way my pulse had begun to race unchecked beneath my skin. "I … I found it in the cave when you were gone."

A solitary eyebrow arched up Waylan's forehead. "Is that so?"

I started to nod, but one look up at the demon, and I knew any deceit was useless. My shoulders slumped as I tugged the soaked sheets back up to cover my shivering shoulders. It was cold despite the fire and the late summer weather. Too cold.

And I was too tired for any more lies.

"No," I said, staring straight ahead at the way the oranges and yellows of the fire fought for oxygen in the grate. "The fiend gave it to me."

I expected Waylan to be angry with me. He had every right to be. He'd saved me, and in return, I'd lied to him.

That was why what he said next shocked me.

"I don't blame you for lying to me. This is a dangerous weapon in the wrong hands."

Waylan turned the blade-like appendage over in his hands, then made a short, tutting sound with his mouth when the dull end of it still caught his finger. It left the tiniest prick, not enough to draw blood, but enough to make him screw up his face and hold it out at arm's length.

"Much too easy to hurt yourself with. That would have sliced off the end of your finger."

"But—"

"We'll just have to do something about that."

Before the end of my protestation could fall from my lips, Waylan had set the blade back down on the end of my bed. He pulled a familiar blade—the one given to me by Tallulah—from pockets that shouldn't be able to hold one let alone *two* blades, and laid it beside the fiend's tail.

I looked on as he hovered both his hands over the knife first. The gnarled, bony fingers made strange, methodical patterns in the air above it until, like the peel of a fruit, the handle pulled back and the blade could be plucked out and tossed aside as easily as a useless piece of scrap metal.

Which in my hands, it really was.

Waylan took the peeled handle and slid it into place over the fiend's tail. He waved his hands once more and the handle reformed and hardened across the new blade. When Waylan once again plucked it from the bed, I saw that the spike had changed shape slightly, becoming flatter and shinier so that only the most trained eye would realize it was not, in fact, the same blade I'd once been gifted.

Still, Waylan knew, and so when he handed me the knife, he instructed me to take great care with it.

I turned the new blade over in my hands, and though I was grateful for Waylan's forgiveness, I couldn't help but feel how pointless the gesture ultimately was.

Astute as ever, the demon cocked his head at me and asked, "What is it? Aren't you pleased?"

"I am!" I said, hastily, though I couldn't stop my face from falling when I turned the new blade over in my hand. "It's just … it doesn't change anything, does it? Even if it's sharper than the last one, I'd still not be able to do any real harm."

"Oh, I wouldn't be so sure of that," he said, his voice deliberate. "You should be especially careful with this one. Not even the fae's healing powers will work on a wound made from that fiend's blade."

I stared down at the new knife in my hands, and for the first time in a long time, I felt that dangerous spark of hope as I realized what he meant. This is what the fiend had tried to tell me. This was the tool that even a human could use to kill a fae.

To kill a fae.

Is that something I'd be able to do, even if the time came?

I'd never have doubted it before that night in the cave. But after seeing the light die in a fae's eye for myself, after feeling what it meant for them, I wasn't so sure anymore.

Still, when I glanced up at Waylan again, this time, it was with true gratitude. I'd started to wonder if I might have more allies than I thought.

It wasn't just the Starlight Fae who didn't want the old king awakened, even in exchange for the glamour. It was the fae of Avarath, those with no allegiance to the courts. It was the very fiends that crawled its surface.

It was the demons enslaved by their princes.

If I could keep most of them from killing me themselves the first chance they got, then maybe I would live long enough to see the new moon set. It couldn't be too much longer now.

I should have showered Waylan with thanks, with my eternal gratitude, but instead when I looked up at him, I ended up blurting out, "How is it that you have magic still?"

It was a question that'd bothered me ever since I met the demon. The fae kept going on about how magic was gone, how its fading was closer to ending their world with each passing moment. And then there was Waylan, who dripped magic with every movement.

Waylan pursed his lips, but I was sure it was to keep from revealing a smile. "Like you, I don't come from this realm. My magic isn't bound by the same deals of the glamour."

I looked over Waylan again, in his simple servant's jacket that did nothing to conceal the magnificent power possessed beneath, and I once again wasn't able to stop myself.

"Then … then why are you here?"

"You mean, why do I serve my prince?"

My eyes flickered over to the empty bed again, as much as I hated it, I couldn't stop my heart from skipping a beat.

A grimace tugged down the corners of Waylan's mouth. "Humans aren't the only race the fae have found a way to enslave. I've served Armene's family for millennia."

"Armene … he's alright, then?"

Waylan looked at me all-too-knowingly before he answered, this time bringing color to my cheeks for an altogether more embarrassing reason. "Of course, he is. A little shaken … but alright."

I sat back in my bed, and for one moment, I allowed myself a small sigh of relief. "Could I see him?"

"Strange you're so concerned with the fae's wellbeing," Waylan said, but something about his answer made me pause.

"What is it?" I asked.

"Armene has specifically requested to be left alone."

"Are you saying he's asked not to see me?" I asked, heart sinking.

Maybe the Armene I saw in my dreams wasn't in my dreams at all. Maybe the Armene I saw was in those brief moment of waking.

Waylan looked unsure for a moment. "Armene was once a powerful fae, Delph. I don't think he ever truly realized how much he'd lost until that night, with you. The Armene I once served never would have been knocked unconscious by a fiend —great or otherwise—to speak nothing of being kidnapped in the first place."

The look on my face made him clear his throat. "I think he needs some time to come to terms with the inevitable now that it's finally arrived."

The tone of his voice made me sit up again. "What are you saying, Waylan?"

The demon stepped aside to reveal a mirror set at the far wall that I hadn't noticed before. It was too dim to make out my reflection, so the demon waved a hand to make the heavy drapes draw back of their own accord.

I threw up a hand to shield my eyes, only to pause. Even in the stark transition between dark and light, I saw immediately what Waylan meant.

More importantly still, I knew what he meant by it.

The black marks around my eyes had vanished.

That wasn't the only thing that had changed. I barely recognized the face that looked back at me.

Sure, it was me. I had the same dark eyes, the same stark white hair … but I'd transformed.

I was human, still.

But I was also fae.

My face had barely had the chance to begin to pale at this realization when Waylan suddenly cocked his head to the side. It took me a moment longer to realize why that was.

Footsteps. At least half a dozen pairs of them were fast approaching down the hall, headed directly toward us.

"Ah, yes, my message must have reached Caldamir," Waylan said, with a single, curt nod. "Armene told me to notify him as soon as you woke."

Armene. Hearing what he'd told Waylan felt like a knife to the gut.

"I should be going," Waylan said. "Unless you'd like to meet the whole of the court in your natural state, I recommend dressing."

He waved one hand, and a new gown appeared on the bed

before he turned to go—this time, heading toward the door instead of simply disappearing.

"Wait!"

I ignored the gown and crawled forward on my hands and knees to call after him before he could leave.

"The fiend," I said, breathless. "Would you like to know what it said to me?"

The phrase had its intended effect. Waylan paused, his back going rigid for a moment.

"It gave me a warning."

He still didn't move.

"It said something about awakening the king … that it would be the end of my kind. Do you have any idea what it meant by that?"

"Armene was very particular in my instructions this time," Waylan said, carefully. "On what I can tell you."

The footsteps outside the door had grown louder. I'd be lucky to have time to pull the gown over my head before they burst in. Waylan still didn't turn to face me. His voice, strained, seemed to wrestle with itself as he forced the next words out of his mouth.

"Be careful of who you trust here, little one. The dangers outside these courts are nothing compared to what you'll find within. You've done the easy part. You've survived Avarath itself. Now begins the more difficult part."

That part he didn't need to articulate.

We both knew what he meant.

I was alive, a miracle in and of itself. The more difficult part was, of course, *staying* alive.

CHAPTER TWENTY-NINE

CALDAMIR ARRIVED WITH A STORM OF FAE FLANKING HIM. NYX AND Tethys were at his side, making Armene's absence all the more notable.

Half of the Mountain Court must have come along as well, the sea of curious fae faces spilling out into the hallway behind the princes. Most of them looked on with the same expressions I remembered from my fever dreams, faces half curious and half disgusted—come to gawk at the same creature that barely had the time to pull on a chemise over her naked, recently recovered form, before they'd burst in without so much as a knock.

I'd forgotten, up until the moment I saw Caldamir's golden curls framing those features as stony as the court he heralded, how much I *hated* him. One look, however, and I was quickly reminded.

"Ah good, so you didn't die."

Caldamir's comment earned him a half jab from Tethys, but I couldn't help but see how Nyx stood noticeably still at his side. His face was downturned, the spark in his eye not returned since he first laid eyes on his ruined forest.

The fae closest to Caldamir and the other princes were by far the oldest, their faerie faces still far fairer than any human ones in comparison, but with a certain dignity in their eyes and the way they carried themselves that only came with age. In this case millennia instead of decades. Caldamir's court was markedly more sober than Nyx's. Everything from the expressions on their faces to the colors of their clothes—all shades of gray and slate like the mountains surrounding us—was almost grim.

It was one of these older fae that reached out to touch Caldamir's arm, the touch close to fatherly.

"It's just as the demon told us," he said, eyes widening as he leaned in closer to peer at me as if I was an exhibit in a cage. "If I may, my prince," he turned to Caldamir, hands clasping in front of him. "I'd like to examine her. Take a look—"

"No, Navi. Not this one."

The answer was firm, though from the way Caldamir was looking at me himself, I was surprised he cared at all what happened to me next. The rest of the fae might be looking at me like a pet, but he was looking at me like a meal.

A means to an end.

A sacrifice, little more than flesh and bone for one singular purpose.

That purpose, of course, being to die.

A slight murmur broke out among the eldest of the fae behind Caldamir, and from the glances they exchanged amongst one another, I guessed they weren't used to having their requests denied quite so easily. *His advisors, probably.*

"There's no need," Caldamir continued, his voice steady though I noted the way his feet shuffled slightly beneath him, as if he too wasn't used to having to deny the council outright. "It's clear she's fae of some kind. If not completely, then enough."

Enough.

He didn't elaborate.

He didn't have to.

I realized, from the way the faces peered at me, from the way hands clasped in anticipation or wrung out of anxiousness, that there was no longer any secret surrounding why I'd been brought here. After all, if what Caldamir and the others had said was true, it'd been decades since the fae dared venture into the human realm.

Longer still since they brought one back with them—let alone for one to survive long enough to set foot in his court.

I'd have been a curiosity either way.

"Is it really going to be enough?" the advisor, Navi, asked, fighting against the instincts that made his hand twitch to reach out and touch me.

"It's going to have to be."

A hum of energy hung in the air around the fae, more than the whispered words shared between them.

"How disappointing," one female fae said, just loud enough to be overheard from over Caldamir's shoulder. "I was certain she'd have horns."

"Humans usually do," the male at her side said. "I guess that's the fae in her."

The fae in her.

More footsteps shuffled and necks craned to get a better look at me. I wanted to shrink back, to climb under the covers and hide from them, no matter how sodden they were with my own sick sweat.

"I don't care how she looks, so long as it means we get the glamour back," another fae said, not even trying to keep her voice low. "What's the point in waiting, Caldamir? Why not do it now and have it over with?"

I froze, my heartbeat quickening until I could hear my blood rushing in my ears. It was a fair question, one I'd been wondering myself.

More mutters broke out, but from the sound of it, not everyone agreed.

Most surprisingly of all, was Tallulah.

The prince's guard pushed her way to the front of the crowd, making more than a few of Caldamir's advisors grumble loudly. She ignored them, instead choosing to set her jaw still tucked inside a metal helmet as always.

"Now that we know fae blood runs through her, then all the more reason to wait. It's one thing to sacrifice a human. Another entirely to sacrifice a fae, whatever the benefit," she said, shoulders squaring up as if daring anyone to challenge her. Even here, amongst all the other fae of Caldamir's court, she towered above the crowd. "She should at least be given a respectful death, one deserving of the sacrifice she's making for all of Avarath."

"I wholeheartedly agree," Tethys said, his voice practically singing. His eyes cut over to me for a minute, and in that instant, I thought I saw something like relief flicker there.

I only wished he'd been the one to speak up in the first place.

"There's no point in rushing things," he said, throwing one arm over Caldamir's shoulder, who immediately tried—unsuccessfully—to shrug it off. "Delph's here. She's safe. We should wait, at least until we've had time to make the proper ..." He trailed off a minute, his many-ringed fingers curling inward before he finished. "Preparations."

I couldn't help but glance over at Nyx at his side, expecting to see some sort of agreement there ... but found none. The forest fae was silent, his hands pulling and twisting at the ends of his loose locks of hair. Unless I was mistaken, he looked even more gaunt than I'd seen him last. It only could've been a couple days since I was rescued from the canyons by Waylan, but he looked haggard.

Well, almost. As haggard as he could while still somehow remaining to be the most gorgeous creature in the room.

His eyes had taken on a vacant expression. His lips parted, tongue moving behind them but his voice making no sound.

"Fine," Caldamir said, after a moment. "We'll wait. But not long."

That same, unsettled rustling broke out around him. I watched as advisors and courtiers alike exchanged a mix of glances, as many angry as there were relieved.

Caldamir felt their discord rather than saw it. Though his back was to them, I could see it in the way he kept shuffling his feet, shifting the weight from one to the other as if he shared their same indecision.

"It's settled," he said, finally. "Tallulah, you'll stay with Delph. I don't want anyone here getting any ideas—one way or the other."

It was something of a task getting Tethys to leave and Tallulah to stay. One wanted nothing more than a few, private moments alone with me, while the other—the hulking brute of a woman now sulking by the window with a hand nervously itching at the hilt of her sword—wanted nothing to do with me.

Well, aside from being quite possibly the only reason I wasn't already laid out on some sacrificial pyre.

She'd escorted me out of what turned out to be the infirmary into an entirely new set of rooms in a part of the castle with so many winding corridors, I was surprised we didn't get lost along the way. I called the place a castle only for lack of a better

word. The rooms and corridors weren't made from hewn stone
and mortar, but rather tunneled straight out of the mountain
itself. All the rooms opened up with some kind of windows—
either looking out on the valley spread far below us, or a series
of inner courtyards filled with gardens of glowing mushrooms.

The room we found ourselves in now was one of the inner
rooms. Better, I supposed, to keep assassins from climbing in—or
me from diving out.

"Why'd you do it?" I asked, finally unable to stand the
endless silence stretching on between us. I was going to go crazy
from boredom soon, and it'd only been a couple of hours. I
waited until Tallulah looked up lazily from her perch, backlit by
a thousand glowing fungi in every color, before I added, "Why'd
you suggest Caldamir wait? Wouldn't it be better for you if I was
out of the picture already?"

Tallulah let out a sigh, and my heartbeat quickened just a
little.

"Do you still have the knife I gave you?"

"What?"

For a moment, something like sadness flickered across her
face. I couldn't be sure, not with the way her face was cast in
shadow, but I swore for that single moment, she carried the
weight of all of Avarath on her face.

"The knife I gave you before, in the forest. Did you lose it?"

I blinked at her a few times before carefully, ever so carefully,
pulling out just enough of the hilt from where I'd tucked it
beneath my new set of skirts that she could see it.

She nodded once, then went back to looking out into the
cavernous inside garden.

"There's more to this life than magic," she said, head tilted
back as if bathing in some warmth emanating from the
mushrooms.

Before I had the chance to respond, to press her further for more answers that might lead me closer to the truth, another voice answered for me. Another voice I recognized all too well from the way it made my heart pound in my chest.

"Indeed, there is."

It was Tethys.

I'd recognize that voice anywhere. The mischief in it was unmistakable.

The one thing I couldn't recognize, and neither it seemed could Tallulah, was where it came from. Tallulah stood at the ready, two steps away from the window, hand on her sword.

"You heard Caldamir's orders," she barked, head swiveling back and forth. "No one is to step foot in these rooms."

Tethys' tongue tutted, this time the sound coming from another corner of the room. I tried to follow it, but by the time Tallulah and I had turned to that corner, Tethys' voice was already coming from somewhere up above us in the rafters.

"What are you doing with that sword, Tally? Are you really going to run a prince through with it?"

"Tally?"

It was all I could do to stifle a giggle as the guardswoman's face turned a shade of maroon I never thought possible.

"I wasn't so sure about that before, but I'm starting to think I might enjoy that."

"Well then," Tethys' voice responded, this time so close to my ear that it made a small shiver run down my spine. "Why don't I give you a good reason to do it?"

I whirled on my heel a moment before Tallulah did, but this time, I didn't find empty shadows. I found my prince.

And in that moment, he gathered me up in his arms, pressed his lips to my ear, and whispered, "Do you want to stay here, cramped in this room?"

I was so close to Tethys that I could feel every shape of his body. He towered over me, all muscle and sinew and excitement. I could feel his blood racing from beneath his skin, feel the press of his own excitement standing so close to me again.

All it took was a shake of my head, and suddenly, I was Tethys' captive. His arms grabbed me roughly, spun me around, and pulled my back up against his chest—knife to throat.

"Careful now, Tallulah, or I'll slit your precious charge's throat."

"You. Wouldn't. Dare."

Tethys paused, the knife pressing dangerously close to my skin until I let out a small gasp at its prick. A single, hot bead of blood dribbled down the length of my neck.

Tallulah froze, eyes widening with panic. "Tethys, what are you doing?"

"Just giving the lady what she asked for," he said. In the moment that Tallulah let down her guard, Tethys dropped his knife, grabbed me by the waist, and plunged us both out the window.

CHAPTER THIRTY

It seemed Caldamir was worried about the wrong kind of kidnappers—and more wrong still about the inner gardens somehow protecting me from them. The glowing gardens provided a far better mode of escape than the sheer cliff walls on the outside. Pathways and rooms honeycombed out from between the iridescent fungi, each one leading to more and more of those same winding passageways. Tethys never once let go of my hand, even long after our footsteps had slowed from their original skittering sprint.

By the time we stopped, backs pressed to a thick wooden door in some other part of Caldamir's castle, I was the only one who's chest was heaving from lack of air.

Tethys' was heaving too, but for an entirely different reason.

My back might've been pressed to the door, but it was Tethys' front pressed to me. One of his hands was still clasped with mine, his fingers tightening their hold when I finally realized how close we were standing and slowly, ever so slowly, lifted my face to look up into his.

His golden eyes were hooded, but their gold still somehow glinted with that mischief of his that never seemed to fade.

Standing here, in front of him, it was like the rest of Avarath began to peel away at the edges. The world beneath was gilded, like him.

His eyebrows arched up as he searched my face in a way that made my pulse race. He towered over me so close, not that he didn't usually, just that he was so near to me that I was all too aware of how small every part of me was compared to him. His hand clasped in mine. His waist against my chest. His excitement, so unmistakably growing even more now that we were alone.

I should have been leaning away, should have felt my instincts telling me to run rather than draw closer to him—but that's exactly what I did. I found myself rising up on the tips of my toes, the inches bringing me only minutely closer to him, but enough to make my breaths hitch a second time.

This time, for the same reason his still did.

"I've missed the feel of you in my arms," Tethys whispered. He leaned his salty lips toward mine so I could taste the sea on his breath again.

"You say that like it's been an eternity since that night."

"An eternity sounds about right. Though if we're being exact … thirteen days."

I leaned back from Tethys then, to see the look on his face. "You kept track?"

Thirteen days. That meant the new moon was nearly upon us. The idea made a second kind of excitement blossom in my chest, made the heart inside me race more than it already was. It was so close that I was almost sorry. Here, in Tethys' arms, it was easy to forget for a moment why I was in such a rush to leave the realm that held him in it.

If only for a moment.

"I thought I'd lost you back there, in the canyons," he said. "You can't know how afraid I was that I'd never get to see you again. Never feel the warmth of your hand or the …"

"Stop, Tethys. Stop right now."

I tried to draw back again at his words, but Tethys only held me tighter.

"What is it?" he asked, voice low and thick as the honey that once sparkled on Nyx's lips. *Another pair of lips I'd almost forgotten the taste of.* "What's wrong?"

That mischievous sparkle in his eyes dimmed for something more like concern. I missed that mischief the moment it was gone.

"Is it something I did?"

His questions had served to bring everything rushing back.

Too much had changed from the night I lie with Tethys beneath the stars. I'd come to know Avarath, I'd come to know the princes. More than that, they'd come to know me.

That was the part that left my mouth dry and my stomach turning sour.

I dropped Tethys' hand and—finding the press of the door still against my back—shoved him away from me. Only, he didn't budge. I shoved him again and this time he obliged me, stumbling back a step of his own accord.

I'd been so consumed with escaping Tallulah and my quarters that I'd never paid attention to where Tethys actually brought me.

I'd expected the prince to try and take me to some secluded place—his bedroom or a largish broom closet or something of the like—but instead, we'd found ourselves in an abandoned corridor. The windows here looked out on that valley below, the lines of the plains and rivers so far below us that they looked like a patchwork of colors.

Even more windows came into view, a row so long that I could almost make out the whole line of the horizon behind him.

"What are you doing here?" I asked, sharply, if only to mask my own breaths I struggled to force back into line. "What did you bring me here for?"

"I just thought you might want to get away from that old windbag."

"She's hardly a—" I cut myself off, shaking my head free of the words before I could be distracted. "That's not what I meant, and you know that," I said, glaring up at him. "How can you say you were worried about me when you know … when you know what you have planned for me?"

Tethys started to take a step toward me once more, but he forced himself to stop. "You think I wanted this?" His chest was heaving again, his voice growing louder. "I didn't ask for this. For you. It's not my fault that you consume my every thought. Night or day. Waking or sleeping. You're there. You're always there."

"What are you saying?"

"I'm saying …"

He moved forward, taking me up in his arms before I had the chance to decide whether or not I wanted him to. "I'm saying that I think I'm falling in love with you, Delphine."

His golden eyes flickered between mine. His face was alight with a barely refined passion—a passion that I matched, but with violent fury.

I tore my hands from him and jutted my chin forward in anger.

"You don't get to say that. How long do I have, until tonight? Tomorrow? Next week?"

Tethys' lips curled up. "I don't know what Caldamir has planned."

"That doesn't absolve you of your part in this," I spat back. "What's the point? Of … of this. Of us?"

Tethys' hands hard started twitching again, and it was clear he was struggling to control himself.

"Is there really anything wrong with savoring what's right before us, even if we know it has to end?"

"Yes!" I said, still glaring at him with all the despise I could muster. "It is when you could change it."

"Delph … if it was up to me …"

The tone in his voice reminded me of what Nyx had said before.

"Everyone keeps acting like this is out of their control, but it's not. At least Caldamir doesn't pretend otherwise. You have a say in this too, you know. Are you, or are you not, a prince of Avarath?"

"It's not so simple."

I took another step away from him and looked him over again, bile rising in the back of my throat as I did. "That's your excuse? That it's not simple?"

"What's the point of all this, Delph?" Tethys hissed. "You've known this was coming from the beginning. None of us lied to you. None of us told you anything but the truth. No one's promised you anything different."

"So you think," I shot back. I should have been focused on keeping my head level, but every second I looked on as he struggled to answer me only made my temper burn hotter.

My response made Tethys pause, shock flickering across his face. He stilled, suddenly.

"What are you talking about?"

I'd been so careful to guard my secrets up until now. Now, I didn't know that I wanted to anymore.

When I didn't answer immediately, Tethys started to tug anxiously at his bound locks. "Was it Armene? I knew he was hiding for a reason. That bastard." His eyes took on a glazed expression as he paced the short length of the room. "It would be just like him to take the moral high ground at the last minute, try to make the rest of us look bad."

"No," I answered instinctively, protectively even. "Armene is … as set on this whole thing as you are."

As far as I knew.

"Who, then?"

The wild look in Tethys' eyes left me with no choice but to answer truthfully.

"My kind. My court is coming to get me."

"Oh, Delphine."

He finally stopped pacing. The pity on his face only made my rage burn brighter.

"Delphine … the Starlight Fae … they're gone. Really gone. They're not coming for you. Why would you think …" He trailed off, looking confused for a moment before a knowing look dawned on his face. "The pool," he said, suddenly shaking his head. "This is my fault. I should have seen it."

He reached out to take a hand that I jerked away from him. "Delphine, you've been tricked. The Starlight Fae aren't coming to get you. Any promise they've made to you is nothing more than a ruse." A slight tone colored his voice bitter. "That was always their specialty."

"No," I said, shaking my head so violently that the room became a blur. "That can't be true. I won't believe it."

"Whether you believe it or not doesn't decide the truth,

Delph," he said. He paused to drag one hand down the length of his face, his eyes shifting from side to side as he looked at something only he could see. "Better fae than you or I have gone mad from that pool."

My stomach turned. I couldn't believe him. *Wouldn't* believe him.

I had no reason not to trust the voice from the pool. No more reason than I had to believe *him*. Tethys could claim to not have lied about his intentions, but that was only true of his words. He and all the princes had played a dangerous game with me, a game played in stolen glances and soft kisses—or near kisses.

Or it had been a game until Tethys claimed to be falling for me. It wasn't a game anymore.

No matter what Tethys said, he was no longer a righteous player here. His words didn't make him a liar, but all the rest of his actions did.

"You're wrong," I snapped. "They're coming for me. Soon enough, you'll see."

I knew I sounded like a petulant child, but I didn't care. I was on the verge of something—a wild rage, tears, complete collapse —but whatever it was, I was saved from having to face it.

Tallulah had finally found us.

And a good thing too.

Any longer together, and I wasn't sure I wouldn't say something to Tethys that I'd regret. I'd already revealed too much. Whether or not Tethys believed the Starlight Fae were coming to my rescue, it'd be better if he didn't know how soon I expected them.

Nyx might have once rightly claimed that Caldamir was the only one of the princes worthy of my hate, but that wasn't the case anymore. It was one thing to wish a stranger dead, another entirely to claim to know me, to care for me even, and still be willing to spill my blood.

Tallulah swore when she rushed through the door and laid eyes on us, but still, the relief was painted plainly on her face.

"Really, Tethys, you brought her here? You couldn't come up with something more creative?"

I took one last look out the windows.

Avarath—the entirety of it spread out before me. It was breathtaking.

Even from here, at the peak of the mountains, the magic of it was unmistakable. The very air itself, once oppressive to me, had a spark of something to it. It had a sharpness, a bite. I could only imagine what it was like *before* whatever it was that had gone wrong.

I was grateful, in that moment, to see it at least once before I left.

Before the fae came and took me back to Alderia as they promised.

Tethys could claim all he wanted that it was all a ruse, but he hadn't been there. He hadn't made the deal.

I had.

And I chose to believe it.

It was all I could do to tear my eyes from the window to the predator that'd only moments before set my blood aboil.

"Still took you long enough to find her," he said.

Tallulah took a few, deep breaths. "And not a moment too soon. We've been summoned. Caldamir is holding a feast. To celebrate."

She turned to me, next.

"So, are you going to come willingly, or am I going to have to force you?"

"No. We were finished here anyway," I said, turning a cold

shoulder to Tethys' frustrated one. "Might as well be tonight as any other."

"Oh, hell no. It isn't tonight," Tallulah said, taking hold of my arm with a vice-like grip that I knew would be impossible to shake. "It's tomorrow. But trust me, it's going to take at least that long before we make you presentable."

CHAPTER THIRTY-ONE

WHEN I CLOSED MY EYES, I COULD STILL FEEL TETHYS.

I could feel his rough hands where I didn't let him touch me.

I could taste his saltiness in the kiss I didn't steal.

I could hear the gravel and honey of the words I didn't let him speak.

Each of these things made the anger boil inside me again. I was a fool to look for allies in the princes, even for a second. Caldamir's opinion was as unchanging as ever, much like the stones of his court. Nyx was desperate to prevent more of the destruction of his forest. Armene felt powerless, the magic stripped from him leaving him naked and ashamed in his own eyes.

And then there was Tethys—the prince who had the audacity to tell me to my face that nothing we'd endured together actually meant anything to him.

Now that the end drew so near, now that the new moon already peered down at me from its perch in the daylight sky, I shouldn't have felt as devastated as I did.

Try as I might not to let Tethys' words get to me, each hour that passed before Caldamir's dinner seemed to drag out in increasing agony. I tried more than once to peer into a dark cup of wine, a bowl of water, a bath of milk and try to summon the fae that had promised to take me away from here in mere hours … but I received nothing more than a lungful of liquid in response.

In the end, I had the same choice to make that I'd been making all along.

Trust in the fae.

Trust in the fae that had promised to murder me, or trust in the fae who'd promised to rescue me. It wasn't a hard choice in the end, because it wasn't really a choice at all.

I didn't know what Caldamir had planned for me at the dinner. I didn't care. I just had to make it to the end of it, until the new moon set beneath the horizon of Avarath, and I was to be taken away from here.

Unless, of course, Tethys was right.

My attempted kidnapping had affected Tallulah in two very particular ways. She'd fallen into a silence stonier than before, if that was even possible. From the moment she'd practically dragged me—entirely unnecessarily—into a new set of rooms, she'd set her jaw and refused to say a single word to me. That, and between the many series of baths I was subjected to, by the time I'd been corseted up into a traditional Mountain Court gown, she'd gotten all too familiar with each and every nook and cranny of me.

It was these two things that I blamed for my particular edginess when Caldamir finally came to collect me.

It certainly had nothing to do with the way he looked in his royal regalia—a tailored jacket with a high neck that looked like it had been carved from the same stone crown that encircled his forehead, sitting just above his brow. It was all hard lines and sharp edges, accentuating the tallest of the fae princes so that he looked like a stone pillar himself.

My foul mood had even less to do with the way he looked at *me*.

It wasn't the first time he'd seen me since the fae blood in me had settled, but Tallulah in her angry silence must have worked some kind of further magic. When I looked at myself in the mirror, I still saw nothing that compared to the full blooded fae.

But Caldamir stood in the doorway, staring at me seemingly incapable of speech. His jaw, usually set with the same anger that'd been radiating off his guard for the last day, had gone slack, softening the features that otherwise might have looked lifelessly chiseled by a sculptor.

His stare wasn't what made me purple with rage, however. It was my own feelings, the same betraying ones that had risen up in me when he first dragged me into Avarath, that made me spit my next words with venom. I'd let myself get carried away with Tethys, with Nyx, with Armene. I couldn't let that happen again.

Not when I was so close now to making it back to Alderia.

Still, I may have grown a little *too* bold in the hours leading up to dinner.

"Do you always look at your dinner like you want to fuck it, or is that something you've specially reserved for me?"

Caldamir balked in the most satisfying way, but it didn't last long. Tallulah was still gaping at the both of us, one hand hovering near her sword as if she wasn't sure whether or not she should run me through with it when he finally responded.

"Dinner? Do you really think we're going to eat you?"

"I don't know what the fae do with their sacrifices," I spat back. "I don't know anything about the fae. I've been cooped up in here, without answers, ever since I arrived."

Something sparkled in Caldamir's eye that was usually reserved for Tethys.

"No, Delph, I'm not going to eat you, not after a greeting like that. Not unless you beg me to. Though …" Here his eyes became hooded, his chin lifting up as he peered down at me from above, "I do like the thought of what it'd be like to see you on your knees."

It was my turn to be speechless. In the open-mouthed silence that followed, with only Tallulah's choking noises to fill the space between us, Caldamir grabbed me roughly by the arm and pulled me straight to his side.

"Now, unless you have more outrageous claims to make, we'd best be off. Better not to keep fae waiting. I have no doubt that if any of them decided to make a dinner of you, it'd be far less *pleasurable* than what I have in mind."

CALDAMIR'S HAND didn't leave my upper arm until he'd practically thrown me into the seat at his side in the great hall. There was no formal introduction of the fae prince, nor one for me either.

Not that it was needed.

Not when Caldamir's advisor, Navi, the same fae who'd asked for permission to poke and prod at me like some kind of science experiment when I first woke up here, took that upon himself.

"Ah yes," he said, standing the moment Caldamir had settled down beside me. "Here we are, our guest of honor."

He lifted up a cup that shook in his hand as if it'd already been filled several times already and called for a toast. "For the sacrifice that will return Avarath to her former glory. Let us all hope it's worth it."

The silence that fell for a moment was as telling as any words in response. The fae of Caldamir's court drank to his toast, though some less enthusiastically than others.

Caldamir grabbed a jug of wine and filled first his own cup to the brim, and then with only a moment's hesitation, did the same to mine. "I have a feeling we're both going to need this."

Unlike Nyx's table in the Woodland Court, Caldamir's head table was round. It was scattered with faces I recognized, advisors and princes alike, with one noticeable absence.

I scanned the length of the two long tables that ran along either wall leading up the great hall, and though every face I searched look back at me, I saw no sight of the one I sought out. Armene was still nowhere to be seen.

Perhaps even more noticeable, however, was how neither Tethys nor Nyx were seated beside me this time. That honor had been reserved for Navi who—from the way his hand kept trying to brush mine whenever he reached for his quickly dwindling cup of wine—had yet to give up on the idea of trying to get his hands on me.

Caldamir's arrival announced the start of dinner, with fae servants carrying out tray after tray of dishes they promptly began to serve. I instinctively tucked my hands under the sides of my thighs, ignoring the intoxicating scent of the food as I had at the last fae feast I'd attended. My head swiveled back and forth in search of the servant I was sure was already headed my way with some other variety of bland human food that had someone been preserved long enough not to poison me.

One of the female advisors, the same one who was complaining that I didn't have horns the first time she spotted me, leaned forward across the table until she caught my eye. "You know, it's rude not to eat at a fae's table."

She spoke loud enough that more eyes turned our way. Beside me, Caldamir stiffened a little, but I answered for myself before he could try to do it for me.

"Humans can't eat the food of the fae."

She let out a laugh that made me shrink back a little in my seat.

"What do you think you've been eating the last two days?" she asked, sitting back in her own seat with a smirk on her face. "Stop acting so provincial. You're embarrassing yourself. You're fae now, might as well start acting like it."

My eyes slid down to the gilded plate in front of me, at the food that smelled bewitching enough to cast a spell without so much as tasting it. I supposed she was right. I hadn't paid much attention to the change since I'd awoken in Caldamir's court.

Instead of reaching for my fork, however, I reached for the glass of wine Caldamir had poured me earlier. He'd been right. I was going to need it.

"Lilliope, no need to torture the girl."

I wished it was Caldamir's voice that chided her, but instead, it was Navi at my other side.

"I'm just saying, why waste empathy on a creature that's basically already dead?"

"Careful now ..." the advisor said, hand tightening a bit on his cup. "Caldamir hasn't set an official date. For all we know, she could be a guest here a while yet."

Lilliope eyed the advisor's shaking hand a little too closely as he re-poured his glass before lifting her own to her puckered lips. "Whatever you say, Navi. We all know you're just not looking forward to picking up the sword again. You always did say the human realm didn't agree with you."

The walls of the castle for a moment, seemed to be crashing down around me.

"Sorry," I said, leaning forward. "What are you talking about?"

"The Great Enslavement, of course," Lilliope said, batting her eyelashes at me in false surprise when she saw the way my face paled. "Or hasn't anyone told you?"

"Lilliope …" Caldamir's voice carried a warning. It was a warning that Lilliope immediately heeded, but Navi, at my other side, was far too drunk to.

"Once the king's great deal is fulfilled, we won't need him anymore," he said, patting my arm. "It shouldn't take long to take over the human kingdom, and then the high king can be put to rest for good this time—glamour intact."

I couldn't tell if I was going to vomit or faint.

"Such a shame about the humans though," he continued. "I'd always hoped to study them in their natural habitat. That'll be quite difficult to do afterwards."

"That's enough, Navi," Caldamir growled at my side. He fixed the advisor with a look that even in his drunken state, he managed to understand enough to fall back into his chair, lips sealed this time in terrified silence.

I whirled on the prince.

"What is he talking about?"

Caldamir kept his face pointed stiffly forward, refusing to look at me as he lifted his wine glass to his lips. "It's nothing for you to be concerned about."

"It sure as hell sounds like I should be concerned about it," I hissed back. "The *Great Enslavement*? Taking up the sword? What's really going on?"

"Now is not the time," Caldamir said, carefully.

"Now is the *only* time," I shot back. "Tell me now."

"Or what?" Caldamir was finally looking at me. "Tell you now, or you'll do what?"

I felt my hand twitch toward the fiend dagger concealed beneath my bodice.

Though she was the one to stir the unrest to begin with, Lilliope suddenly shifted uncomfortably in her chair. It must have been something about the anger in Caldamir's eyes, or maybe the murder in mine, but she suddenly leaned forward and loudly gave an excited squeal.

"I, for one," she said, "can't stop thinking about the glamour. Oh, how good it will be to *feel* fae again."

Her interruption, however planted, had its desired result.

Caldamir's chest rose with the breath he'd been holding and I moved my hand back to the table, away from my knife.

Titters broke out all around us, with conversations quickly turning to nearly breathless recounts of what each fae would do once magic was once again at their fingertips. Even Tethys was among those who couldn't help from drumming his fingertips excitedly across the curve of his cup, his eyes taking on that bright, excited look that had alit on so many of the other faces around him.

In fact, the only fae at the table who didn't look drunk at the thought of magic's return was Caldamir.

"I expected you to be more excited than most," I said, finally picking up my fork to aggressively stab it into the closest thing on my plate. I still couldn't bring myself to eat it. The scent of it had quickly turned from intoxicating to rancid. "I thought you were the one who wanted magic back more than the rest of them."

Caldamir kept looking ahead. "Excited wouldn't be the word I'd use for it," he said, after a moment. He too scanned his subjects and peers, a strange look on his face—something closer to disgust than anything else. "I'll have magic back. But not for the petty reasons the rest of them would."

"What reason then?" I asked. I leaned closer to him in his throne-like seat beside mine, my voice growing bolder from the single sip of wine. "What could possibly be so important that you'd be willing to—what is it—enslave the whole human race?"

"Only Alderia," he shot back, before stopping to mull over the bad taste in his mouth. "My reasons—"

I never did hear Caldamir's excuse.

The doors at the end of the hall burst open and a figure strode in, a familiar dark cloak streaming over his shoulders. I didn't have to see the symbol embroidered across the back to know what it was—or who it was that wore it.

It was the scout, the only remaining one of the three that had escaped the canyons alive.

And he bore, in each of his hands, the heads of his two slaughtered companions.

Guards streamed in after him, catching up to him only when he'd already reached the middle of the hall. They caught him with rough hands, dragging him back so he stumbled as he struggled to shake their grip from his shoulders.

Not before his voice rose up into the rafters.

"Prince Caldamir!" his voice boomed out, catching in the high vaulted ceilings so that it echoed with dangerous intensity. "I've come to claim retribution. I demand to see the fae responsible for committing the highest of fae crimes. I demand to see Prince Armene."

He held the heads up for all to see before letting them drop with two sickening thuds to the ground. Feet lifted up with soft shrieks as they rolled close to the fae seated closest to him.

"Silence!"

I thought the scout's voice sounded dangerous, but it was nothing compared to the sound of Caldamir's voice when he stood.

"There will be no trial for the prince. He did what was necessary to secure our freedom—the freedom of all of Avarath."

Caldamir looked down at me then, chest heaving.

"As we will all do."

The entire court looked on in breathless silence. Faces paled. Hands clenched at dinner knives. Glasses of wine stood untouched.

Caldamir nodded once to a guard at the back of the hall, and suddenly more guards filed in and began to line the outer corners of the room. The Mountain prince kept looking forward, but his hand clamped onto my shoulder.

"A new era is dawning in Avarath," he continued, head lifting once more to face his court. "The greater courts have deserted us. We can no longer live as if still bound by their rules. We have no jury. No judge. No executioner. We only have ourselves."

Behind us, the late afternoon sun illuminated him in a golden orange glow.

Soon the new moon would be setting with it, but maybe not soon enough. The moment I'd dreaded had arrived.

"We've watched as our world drew to the brink of destruction too long already. Delphine, the last of the Starlight Fae, will die tonight—for all of us. For the glamour. For Avarath."

Despite Caldamir's impassioned words, it wasn't met with unanimous enthusiasm.

In fact, the moment his words finished settling over his court, the entire hall around us erupted into violence. Tables turned over. Swords flashed. Bows appeared from where they'd been hidden under skirts.

The guard made a hard wall between the head table and the rest of the hall, but still that didn't stop an arrow whizzing dangerously past the side of my head. It seemed I had more allies than I imagined, not that it mattered. Those allies were still the kind willing to see me dead so long as it wasn't in the name of their old king's resurrection.

"I had a feeling this would happen," Caldamir said, turning to Tallulah. "Fetch Armene. I'd hoped it wouldn't come to this tonight, but I've been left with no choice. We're not waiting any longer, and I need every prince of Avarath standing together in this."

Only then did he pause to look at me.

"I'm not your friend, Delphine."

Any hope that Caldamir's resolve might fade disappeared with his final words before he dragged me, surrounded by guards pouring in at all sides, to my feet and toward the door at the back.

"I'm your enemy. I think it's time both of us remembered that."

CHAPTER THIRTY-TWO

THAT WAS THE PROBLEM WITH CALDAMIR.

He assumed I'd forgotten.

Of all the fae I'd remembered to hate, he was at the top of my list. No royal regalia or chiseled jawline could make me forget that *he* was the fae who came into my world to take me away. He was the fae willing to watch me die in Avalath as a human based on nothing more than a hunch.

He was the fae that, despite the misgivings of his own court, his advisors and friends, insisted on going through with my murder. They could call it a sacrifice all they wanted, but that's what it really was.

Murder.

And it was finally upon us.

I paid no attention to the twisting path of tunnels that plunged us further and further down into Caldamir's maze of a palace. All I looked for was the brief glimpses out the windows toward the coloring sky.

I'd made it this close.

So close.

I just had to make it a little bit longer.

We were soon plunging so deep into the mountain that the temperature began to steeply drop. I shivered in my gown, each breath bringing with it a cloud that steamed out from between my lips.

We didn't stop until we came to a massive stone door. More guards stood at its entrance, though they parted at the sight of Caldamir.

Armene waited there for us too.

It was the first time I'd laid waking eyes on the Prince of Sands since we were in the cave together—and I almost wished I hadn't.

Much like Nyx, something had changed in him in the last days. A shadow had taken over him, a fear that wasn't becoming. It kept his eyes from meeting mine, kept his lips from parting to offer so much as a single word in my defense.

He just stepped aside with the guard, moving back to join my other betrayers.

Nyx. Tethys. Armene. Caldamir.

For that was what they were. It didn't matter that this is what they brought me here for. That fact didn't absolve them of the guilt of what they were about to do—no matter what any of them thought.

Caldamir moved to press his hands to the doors. The massive blocks of stone swung forward at the barest of his touches as the sound of voices and clashing swords echoed down the tunnels behind us, growing closer by the second.

He ushered me in alongside Nyx, Tethys, and Armene. Half the guard came in after us while the other half remained on the other side to secure the door. Tallulah led those that came with us, moving in a small semi-circle around the outside of the doors, their arms lifted up to light a trough of oil branching out into the far reaches of the darkness.

The flames raced along the outer walls and into gutters carved into the ground, stretching further and further out as the light it brought followed a moment later.

I'd expected us to find some kind of prison, but instead, we'd found a tomb. A massive one.

It wasn't just the fae king that had been sealed away beneath the mountain—it was an entire other court. Glass coffins lined the massive room like a grave, stretching out beyond where the fire's light could reach them.

Tethys was the first one to let out a breath. "I'd forgotten how many fae were in Avarath before the war."

At his side, Armene nodded solemnly.

Nyx just stared into one of the coffins closest to him, his face growing pale before he hurried to rejoin the other princes at my side.

The closer we got to the dais, the more my heart raced.

This was it.

There, at the top of the steps, was the only casket not made of glass. It was huge, easily twice the size of its companions, the stone sides carved with intricate designs.

The sight of it made me dig my heels into the ground, but it did nothing to so much as slow Caldamir down. He continued to drag me up the dais, step by step, with his face fixed ever forward.

"You told me when you kidnapped me from my home that I was saving my village from enslavement," I said, panting. "You lied to me."

Behind me, I saw Armene hesitate for a second. "Is that true, Caldamir?"

Caldamir suddenly stopped, only a few steps remaining until

we reached the top. "When did we all forget who we are?" he asked, turning to glare at all three of the fae princes down below him. "We fae have always used humans."

"That was usually the high king's doing, as I recall," Tethys said, settling his weight on one of his hips. His many rings glittered in the light of the flames. "The Sea Court has never had much use for humans."

"The Sand Court, either," Armene agreed with a grumble.

Nyx fixed me with a stare of his own. "I always though humans were pretty, sort of like dolls," he said. "I was always excited when a fae brought one to my court."

He looked away then, brow furrowing. "It was always so disappointing when they died."

"All humans die," Caldamir growled, his grip on my arm tightening. He tugged me forward a little, to the edge of the step between him and the other princes. "Delph will die. Whether or not we're the ones to spill her blood, she's going to die—probably sooner rather than later."

He finally cast his gaze back over to the casket behind us. "We've all been so determined for her to be fae, we've forgotten that in the end, she's only human."

Human, like the race they plan to enslave as soon as they've gotten their magic back.

I suppose the truth-bringers of Alderia were right after all. A great fae war was coming. The one good thing that might come out of dying was I'd never have to see the smug looks on their faces when they saw it for themselves.

Across the cavern, bodies started throwing themselves against the doors. The guards' shouts on the other side grew louder. Tallulah, standing at the foot of the dais, looked uncertainly between us and the doors. Her hand had long since drawn the sword at her side.

Caldamir swore.

He pulled me up the last few steps and pushed me up to the edge of the casket—as much like a sacrificial pyre as anything else I'd imagined.

"I knew we should've done this sooner," Caldamir muttered, drawing a knife from his belt. "No more fae blood needed to be shed."

"Except for mine. Tell yourselves I'm only human now that it suits you, but you spent an awful long time trying to convince me I'm fae."

Caldamir did pause then. For the briefest of moments, a terrible sadness settled over him. But it was brief—all too soon replaced with that stony hardness that only he could muster.

"There's no other way," he said. "We must stop Avarath from dying."

Just as I needed to stop Alderia from meeting the same fate.

Nyx, Tethys, and Armene all came to stand along the outer corners of the casket. None of them looked at me. They all stared at the shape of the fae king carved into the top of the stone slab.

Then, in turn, each one of them took a knife from his belt as well.

It was impossible here to see if the new moon had fully set, though in my heart, I knew it already had.

Tethys had been right. No one was coming to save me.

I'd been tricked, but that didn't mean I was powerless. I too, like the princes, had a blade. I felt the weight of it still tucked into its hilt beneath my skirts.

If the princes here weren't willing to stop this madness, then I had to.

It'd been so long since I thought about my curse.

I thought my curse was being brought here to Avarath, but I was wrong. I wasn't cursed. I *was* the curse.

In trying to save my village, I'd damned the whole kingdom —the whole world, for how likely were the fae to stop at the borders of Alderia? If I had to die, it wouldn't be to save Avarath, not when it meant destroying my own realm.

If I had to die, then it would be by my own hand.

Before Caldamir could force me up onto the tomb for whatever frightful ritual he'd prepared, I ducked beneath his arm and ran to the edge of the stairs. The four of them froze, not daring to come after me, because I'd already pressed the point of the dagger to the middle of my chest.

"I won't let you do this," I said, my voice choking. I looked to each one of them in turn, wanting to gaze one last time into their eyes. "I came to Avarath expecting to die to keep those I loved from being enslaved, so that's just what I'm going to do. And there's nothing you can do to stop me."

I half expected them to try, and they might have, if it weren't for the appearance of a second blade—this one far longer than mine—between us.

It was Tallulah.

"I'm sorry, my liege," she said, head bowing slightly as Caldamir froze in surprise. "I vowed to protect you all your life. Now, I protect you from yourself. I can't let you do this."

Across the cavern, the doors finally burst open. The fight spilled into the tomb, the flickering light of the fire catching on the metal of swords and glass coffins.

"We don't have *time* for this," Caldamir said, stepping forward. The other princes mirrored him, but Tallulah only raised her sword.

Caldamir was right. There was no more time.

I had to do this now.

I'd never see my world again, I'd never see my brother, Sol, but at least they'd be safe. At least I'd die knowing I'd done what I came here to do in the first place.

I pushed on the hilt of the blade until it started to pierce through my gown, prepared to plunge it into my own heart—when it was stayed.

Not by any hand, mine or another, but by the earth-shattering rumble of the world itself splitting open.

I knew, even before the back of the cave exploded in light, what it was.

Who it was.

A fae emerged from that blinding light, hair spun from sun-bleached bones and eyes so dark they looked like two pools of blackness.

He held out a hand to me and I took it.

The Starlight Fae had come at last.

As promised.

For me.

A NOTE FROM THE AUTHOR

I can't thank you enough for reading the first part of Delphine's story in A Veil of Truth and Trickery. I've been honestly over-whelmed by the support for this series, and I am so, so grateful for it! I hope you enjoyed reading it as much as I've enjoyed being the one able to bring it to life.

The Veiled Realm will continue with book two in the series, A Veil of Stardust and Savagery.

With Love,

Made in the USA
Las Vegas, NV
17 August 2021